THE DOLL WITH THE SAD FACE

The Adventures of a Family Man Private Detective

May 16, 2022

To Jane:

Enjoy the adventure!

THE DOLL WITH THE SAD FACE

The Adventures of a Family Man Private Detective

JOHN RICE

For my dad, Ed Rice, who made all of this possible.

CHAPTER 1

Fighting for breath, Mike Sullivan lay on his back on the frozen lawn. Twenty years as a private detective and no one had worked him over as brutally as his rear stairs. His lungs burned with every gasp. It had seemed a simple task to carry the garbage out to the alley but the loose tread at the top had sent him tumbling.

He couldn't muster enough volume for a good cry for help. Besides, Ann and the kids weren't home and there wasn't a Good Samaritan in sight. He rose on his left elbow. Something warm was running down his face from above his right eye. It hurt. But that didn't compare to the stinging in his left shoulder and right knee.

He got to his feet and stepped carefully over the rotten step lying at the foot of the stairs, nails pointing up. He grabbed both banisters and hoisted his way to the top. He shut the door and locked it.

Flicking on the vanity light, he looked at the gusher above his right eyebrow. He grabbed a thick bath towel, soaked it in warm water and pressed it tightly. It would take him twenty minutes to stanch the bleeding. While he patted the wound, he reflected on the circumstances that had resulted in a mid-morning exercise in trash removal.

Back when his agency was busy, Sullivan wasn't home much morning or evening. He was receiving at least fifteen new assignments a month and billing out a hundred hours. He also had a big account that paid him steady for investigating mishaps at a hospital. He didn't do any marketing – the calls and e-mails flowed in – the invoices flowed out.

1

Alternating the wet towel with a dry one, Sullivan finally controlled the cut. He looked at it closely in the mirror. It was ragged and deep. He hoped it wouldn't need a stitch. Health insurance was but a warm memory.

Sullivan studied his reflection in the mirror. He had his father's strong features but lacked his "black Irish" looks. Frank Sullivan looked positively swarthy in the summer. His second son, though, had inherited the fair skin of his mother. He also had her light brown hair. Now that he had entered his 40s, gray was creeping in. The lines on his broad forehead had deepened. Like his dad, though, he had a broad smile that could win over strangers.

He had nothing to smile about, as he fished through the medicine cabinet and found some Band-Aids. He put a big square one above his right brow; it stuck painfully to the hairs. He put two more on his shoulder and knee. He was almost ready to report the injury to Ann.

First, he sat down and finished the last cup of coffee. It was as warm as dishwater. He was alone. Sullivan had long feared working alone – especially after his dad died. He had dreaded going to the empty office, where they had bantered about the Bulls and White Sox, played chess, gin rummy and bridge. Even with the golf course on speed dial; they solved seventy-percent of their cases.

His father was still reporting to the office four days a week when he succumbed to a stroke at 72. Sullivan's mother, Beatrice, had died from breast cancer two years before. She had also worked at the company as their bookkeeper. She wasn't content to just pay the bills, she inserted herself into every aspect of the business. She disapproved of the investigators playing cards, while they waited to go out on their assignments. She never understood that detective work lent itself to working late afternoons and early evenings. These were the times to to find people home.

Sullivan seethed, while Beatrice criticized. On more than one occasion, he exploded in anger at her, in front of the other employees. He would be instantly embarrassed, while she acted hurt, silently gathering her bookkeeping records to take home. Sullivan would apologize but the damage was done. Beatrice may have been critical of their work habits but she had a grudging respect for the difficult work they did.

After his parents were gone, Sullivan hired the first investigator he could find. The fact he was an antagonist from his grade school days – he didn't care. Like many investigators, Carl had an unsteady personal life and sporadic work schedule. But he had an unparalleled talent for getting drivers to sign statements they were drunk at the time of the accident. Even the States Attorney couldn't get that. It was unfortunate that "abnormal" people like him were the ones drawn to detective work – if they were normal they wouldn't be any good.

Sullivan decided the throbbing had subsided enough that he could speak in regular sentences. He punched in Ann's work place on his cell phone. She did the bookkeeping at a small firm that made the eye charts for optometrists. Someone has to make them.

"VisionClear," Ann answered.

"Hi," his voice was strained.

"What's wrong?"

Before he could answer, "Wait a second – I've got another call."

He listened to smooth jazz relying on a tenor sax dangerous to diabetics.

Ann sounded concerned when she reconnected, "What happened to you?"

"I was taking the garbage out – you know that step"-

"You fell?" she asked in distress.

"All the way down – ended up halfway to the garage."

"I don't understand."

"That stair – you know, – the one I said I was going to fix - down I went. Luckily, the bag didn't break."

"I'll drive you to Stewart – to the ER."

"It's not that bad – besides, – remember it was five hundred bucks last time," – Sullivan was referring to a false alarm involving chest pains.

Turned out to be severe heartburn. "I'll be fine. I'm just kind of in shock. I think I'll lie down for a while."

Sullivan climbed the stairs to their four-poster and grabbed a book off the nightstand. He was re-reading a collection of Irish short stories. He sank onto the mattress and propped up some pillows. It was 11:15 AM on a Tuesday and he was opening a book in bed. Sullivan felt like the world had passed him by. Someone told Sullivan he was the last guy still knocking on doors. The milkmen, the peddlers, the friendly neighbors, the days of suprise visitors were over. Sullivan alone persisted in getting strangers to answer the door.

People had been more receptive back when he first took over the business. But finding someone to work with him had proved problematic. After he fired the grade school acquaintance for prolonged absenteeism, Sullivan searched for a replacement. He hired an ex-IRS agent, who, in a civil servant sort of way, knocked on doors during the middle of the day, never found anyone home and charged hours Sullivan couldn't pass on to clients. After he let him go, Sullivan was out of ideas. He went to play golf.

At his favorite nine-hole dog track, set in the middle of the city's West Side, he was paired with a sophomore from the University of Illinois. He was a criminal justice major looking for an internship. By the third hole, Sullivan had offered him a position at Sullivan Investigations. He became the first of many.

Year after year, semester after semester, students worked for cash and course credit. Sullivan was energized by their youthfulness. He taught them the basics of locating hard-to-find witnesses and how to interview them. He taught them how to best serve papers. For example, if they were serving subpoenas with small witness fee checks attached, he would have them fold the papers so only the check was showing. For serving Summonses, Sullivan emphasized the element of surprise.

These interns, though, had their limitations. Not one of them understood the difference between a Subpoena and a Summons, no matter how many times Sullivan explained it. Subpoenas were for witnesses.

Summonses were for defendants. Subpoenas had to be personally served on the witness, while Summonses could be handed to any family member over the age of 13.

None of them had the ability to take a signed statement from a witness. It was a highly-developed skill that challenged Sullivan every time. It was the only time he purposely made mistakes with his writing. He would deliberately write the wrong word, so he could cross it out and have the witness initial the mistake. This way, they couldn't claim they had signed the statement, without reading it.

Sullivan enjoyed teaching the interns and watching how they overcame their fear of strangers. Some liked the job so much, they wanted to stay on after their internship. Sullivan didn't think that was wise. He could never afford to pay them a living wage. He sent them on their way to find their own future in investigation.

Some started brilliant careers with the FBI or big city police departments. Sullivan was envious. He felt like George Bailey, stuck in a shabby office, while these Harry Baileys went onto high-flying careers.

He could hear Ann downstairs. She had stopped home for lunch. She gave a little gasp when she saw his eye. "Don't you think it needs stitches?" she asked peeking under the Band-Aid.

Ann was bent over him. She had long legs and was an inch or two taller than Sullivan. She had chestnut hair and fine features, with brown eyes filled with concern over his injuries.

"It's not that noticeable," Sullivan insisted, "It's mostly in the eyebrow."

She had brought him a container of chicken soup. She sat on the bed and spooned it. Sullivan liked the attention. His mother had always been nicest to him when he was sick or injured. Chicken soup could soothe any pain, even external ones. After finishing the soup, he told Ann he was taking a bath. Steaming water was another cure-all.

Sinking into hot water he could barely stand, Sullivan felt his bruised muscles relax. His mind went back to the interns. Most of them were good.

Some came up with fresh approaches to the work that hadn't occurred to Sullivan. Others were clueless. No matter – there was another voice besides his in the office and car.

Five years before, he finally settled on a full-time employee – Charly. He still took on interns but she was a constant. She didn't talk sports, play chess or cards but they shared some passions that Ann considered nerdy. They talked about foreign films, exotic novels and New Yorker cartoons. Charly was usually guarded but she could be luminous when she was comfortable. He recalled how she attracted a circle at a law office Christmas party.

They proved to be a good team. Charly was a whiz with electronics, while Sullivan had a phobia about the latest contraptions. Sullivan was scatter-brained. Charly was organized. She trailed behind, picking up his phone, keys and reading glasses. He also left behind crucial items – like the file! He was providing a comfortable living for his wife and kids, while Charly could support herself as a single woman in the city.

Sullivan had been raised to be a good provider. He made enough for Ann to stay home and care for Tara and Flynn, when they were young. They took family vacations and ate out regularly. When they reached school age, Sullivan could afford to pay private tuition. They were never rich but middle-class comfortable.

All was well until the worldwide economic collapse suddenly struck. The steady work dried up. Checks stopped coming regularly. Sullivan wined and dined clients, brought free lunches to law firms. He spread his business card at parties. Nothing worked.

Sullivan lost his role as provider. Ann became the breadwinner. Financial uncertainty crept into the lives of his kids, just as it had clouded his own childhood. Joining a sports team, taking a music lesson, or buying a new outfit – these all depended on whether a check came. There were no more vacations to Florida.

Dining out was a rare luxury. In fact, Sullivan stopped going out in general. In the evenings he used to take brisk walks to his neighborhood tavern, McGaffer's. It was a down-home joint that smelled like stale beer. Union electricians, iron workers and liquor salesmen occupied the stools. Softball teams would descend on the place to celebrate their games, whether they won or not.

Sullivan's buddies would stop by to grab a Guinness. Now, instead of hanging out with his friends, he isolated himself in his basement. He felt he could no longer afford fun. He had been broke before but never for such an extended period. He had a couple of pet sayings when he was broke: "I'm wearing a cardboard belt!" from "The Producers" and "Money thinks I'm dead," from "The Treasure of the Sierra Madre." Neither seemed funny anymore.

Sullivan was filled with anger at his fate. He didn't cause the economic downturn and didn't deserve to suffer because of it. Still, he was mad at himself that his business was on life-support. Sullivan had been stuffing his anger, resentment and sorrow his whole life. He had not been allowed to express anger when he was young – his parents had exclusive rights to that – and now he wallowed in it.

When he had become a parent, he continued to hold his anger inside. This only worked for so long. A minor setback could set off an explosion. Tara and Flynn were wide-eyed, when he screamed over lost car keys, or a broken appliance. When he took out his frustration on them, he instantly regretted it. As his father did before him, he would trudge up to their rooms to apologize.

His anger was impotent. He was losing a thriving business that he loved. They were even losing their house and the fear of eviction overshadowed their daily lives. Sullivan faced this future by sipping beer in the evenings, while he lost himself in watching basketball.

For the first time in his life, his days were empty. There were no daytime assignments to gather records - no need to drive around bothering strangers in the evening. Sullivan slept late and busied himself with domestic chores: Dishes, laundry, meals and, of course, garbage.

CHAPTER 2

Sullivan had met Charly five years before. He was working for a plaintiff's lawyer, suing the city bus company. Sullivan got the assignment within days of the accident. When he took pictures, there were still specks of blood on the pavement. The police report listed only one witness. For the race and gender they had marked "unknown." It was the first time Sullivan had seen both these boxes X'd on an accident report.

The witness lived only a half block from where Sullivan was photographing. He decided to leave his car and walk. A slender figure with short dark hair was puffing on a cigarette, reclining on the front stairs of a three-flat. Sullivan looked at the police report for the tenth time trying to get a handle on the name.

"Hi, I'm looking for – Charlevoix Rydzinski." It was a mouthful and he stumbled over both names. The figure didn't answer but continued smoking and looking straight ahead. "Do you know if . . ." he didn't know whether to say she or he, "They live here?"

Getting no reply, he continued up the steps. He was reaching for the bell marked "Rydzinski" for the second floor apartment, when he heard a voice behind him. It was lower register but unmistakably feminine. "Don't. My dad's still sleeping." Sullivan stepped down and sat beside her on the steps.

Her complexion was a light shade of golden jade and she had an odd assortment of features that blended into a subtle loveliness. There was nothing lovely about her sullen voice and impassive look. "I'm here about the accident at the bus shelter," Sullivan explained, "I'm working for the lawyer" –

"I already talked to the police," she said curtly, "I'm done talking about it." She looked to be in her early-20's. She was wearing a grey and white checkered flannel shirt, shapeless jeans and tan work boots. Her fingers shivered, as she hoisted the remains of her last cigarette to light a new one.

Sullivan glanced at the accident report, "The police put you down as a witness but all they wrote was your name, age and address."

"That's not my problem," She didn't move her eyes from the cars, cabs and busses parading past her building.

"They didn't write down your race or sex."

"I wear men's clothes in this neighborhood. Nobody bothers me."

"We want to help this man's family," Sullivan told her, "He had a wife and four kids. The oldest is ten." She scraped her cigarette on the step and didn't light another. She stood up and turned to face the front door. Sullivan rose with her. "I don't want to disturb your father - could we talk inside?"

She looked at Sullivan – like she was noticing him for the first time. "I've got to fix his dinner. He starts work at three."

"Maybe I can help?" Sullivan said lightly. She didn't change her expression but dug a key out of her jeans and unlocked the street door. The floor of the tiny lobby was littered with fliers, red final notices from utilities and letters addressed "Dear Resident." There was a hand-written sign above the radiator warning tenants to "Keep the Front Door Locked At All Times." It was signed "The Mgmt."

He followed her up a flight. She knocked and called something in Polish through the door. A man 50-ish, wearing a sleeveless white t-shirt and gray uniform pants, yanked a little too high, opened it and resumed drying his hands on a pink bath towel. He had a semicircle of sparse hair clinging to his scalp, a less than inviting stare and a large frame, the powerful shoulders and arms starting to sag. He glanced dismissively toward Sullivan, as his daughter explained his presence. The man shrugged and returned to the bathroom. Sullivan followed her into the kitchen.

When she offered, Sullivan said water would be fine. She filled a jam jar with lukewarm water from the faucet and handed it to him. Then she got about her business, taking a cooked sausage and a baggie of sauerkraut from the refrigerator and placing them into a plastic container. Sullivan surveyed the cluttered kitchen – she really did need help.

The father emerged from the bathroom, wearing a blue uniform shirt, advertising his first name as Jerzy. After inspecting the container, he gave a few gruff orders to his daughter. She dropped a mango, a slice of rye bread and a plastic bottle of cranberry juice into the bag. He shrugged into his leather jacket and added a leather cap - suddenly a character from Krakow. As he opened the front door, he asked her another question in Polish. The only word Sullivan recognized was "policja." Her reply was brief but satisfactory.

After Sullivan heard his steps retreating down the stairs, she said, "I told him you weren't the police but wanted to talk to me about the accident." Sullivan detected the slightest Polish accent as she shifted to English, "Would you like more water?"

He handed her the empty jar, "I hate to bring this accident up," he said raising his voice above the faucet, "The man who was killed – he was working two jobs. His family – they don't know what they're going to do. We just wanted to see if there was some way to get them some money."

"You mean, get *you* some money," She snapped, turning with lifeless eyes.

"Sure, I want money," Sullivan said taking the jar, "But I get paid the same, win or lose."

She picked up some cups from the counter and placed them in the sink. Sullivan grabbed a plate with fragments of fried egg and walked it to the counter.

"I have to do everything now," she said in exasperation, "My mom went back to Manila. She couldn't – she never liked it here. My dad doesn't do a thing. I'm like – I do all the shopping, cook and clean up the dishes, wash his shorts."

Sullivan grabbed a wet cloth from the sink and squeezed it to wipe the table. "Are your parents divorced?"

"Not officially – she had a nursing degree but never learned the language, so she couldn't get a hospital job. She took care of old people for cash. That's how they met. She was there for his mother all the way through – but. She never got used to the winters and wasn't getting along with" – she stopped, with her back to the running faucet, her striking features animated for the first time.

Drying the table and using the dampened towel to sweep the counter, Sullivan said he hadn't meant to offend her with personal questions.

"It's OK," she shrugged, "I just hate living with my father. He wants me home all the time. We don't have a car. He's too cheap to get a phone and I can't afford one. I was calling my boyfriend from a pay phone, when" – she turned to shut-off the water.

"Were you using the phone at the bus shelter?" Sullivan waited for an answer.

"Yeah, but what I saw – I didn't know it was a person at first. I thought it was a bundle of clothes under the bus. I really don't want to talk about it."

"I know," Sullivan said, searching for something else to help her with. He spotted a pile of jeans, and uniform shirts on the living room floor. "Hey, there's a bundle. Do you need help carrying it down?"

She poked a finger into her cigarette pack, before crushing it and dropping it on the sideboard.

"Are you in school?"

She was a sophomore at a community college and – she liked her art class and no hadn't decided on a major. After a long stillness, Sullivan offered.

"You know if you don't want to tell me what you remember – maybe you could draw it?"

He tore a fresh sheet off his pad and laid it on the table with a pen beside it. She sat down and sketched left-handed. Sullivan didn't look, until she slid it toward him. It was a very detailed overview of the corner. She had lined the sidewalk, put in some bushes and included the aluminum bench of the bus shelter. There was a small square designating the pay phone.

All the drawing lacked was the bus and the pedestrian. He had her sign and date it anyway and placed it in his file. The buzzer rang. "It's just my boyfriend," she said, rising slowly, "He said he was coming by."

Sullivan heard hard shoes on bare wood and a quick rap on the door. When she opened it, the boyfriend's eyes instantly fixed on the stranger at the kitchen table. Sullivan looked him over – he may have been a friend but he certainly wasn't a boy. His thin brown hair was gelled far back on his forehead, his lined face looked at least thirty. He was wearing an iridescent dark suit and an overstated tie, which hung loosely around an open collar.

"Ted, this is – I'm sorry I'm terrible with names."

Sullivan scraped back his chair and walked halfway to the door. Ted had a salesman's handshake and an over-friendly smile that failed to hide suspicion. After introductions, he sat opposite Sullivan, while – he still didn't know what to call her - Ms. Rydzinski seemed a bit much – stood by the sink. Ted called her Charly when he requested coffee. She brought him a cup of instant.

Ted had stumbled on three paragraphs about the bus accident in the Metro section and peppered Sullivan with questions. Charly scrubbed the last breakfast pan, her irritation growing. Sullivan confirmed the newspaper facts, before switching to Ted's job, which seemed to involve an internet pyramid scheme selling cleaning products. Ted started pitching Sullivan on buying a franchise. Sullivan sensed Charly wanted Ted to leave, but was pretty sure Ted wanted him to go first.

"So, if you're done, Mr. Sullivan," he grabbed her gently around the waist, "Charly and I are going out for some Thai."

She pulled away. "You didn't say anything about dinner. He brought fish home this morning. It has to be cooked today."

"I'm just saying" – "Is there anything else you need, Mr. Sullivan?"

"We haven't even gotten started. Charly hasn't told me a thing about the accident."

"Charly," he said with too much syrup, "Was that the time you were on the phone with me?"

"I need cigarettes," she said coldly. Before Ted could respond, Sullivan sprang up.

Charly handed him a twenty for two packs of Marlboro Lights. Ted wore a bewildered look as Sullivan quickly exited the apartment. Just as Sullivan reached the sidewalk, his cell phone rang. He saw it was his wife.

"Are you coming home for dinner?"

"What are we having?"

"Pizza casserole – what are you doing?"

"I'm buying cigarettes –for a witness."

"Oh - well everything's ready." He could hear the commotion of dishes and Flynn's high-pitched voice. "Well, save me a plate." Pizza casserole was his favorite gooey dish.

"I might be having fish."

"Since when – where are you?"

"I'm going for the cigarettes. Her boyfriend is over. I might be joining them for dinner. I'll be home by 8:30."

With faint uncertainty, "OK – I'll save you some."

Sullivan heard the street door behind him. Ted came down the front steps wearing the same bewildered look. "Charly" he said resignedly – "We're supposed to take her dad out for his birthday tomorrow night – she wants me to get him a bottle of – do you know anything about vodka?"

"No, but I'm heading to the liquor store."

Ted fell in beside him. "So, you were on the phone," Sullivan began, "Did she say anything about the accident?"

"We were talking about – actually she was just ready to say goodbye. All of a sudden, she's screaming, "Stop." I had to hold the phone away.

"She said it again – I could hear pounding – she got completely hysterical. I told her to wait till I got there. I only live ten minutes away."

"When I tried to get down the street - police cars were all over – there was a big crowd. She was standing with two cops. They were asking her about it – she just stood there. She was wearing a big coat–an old one that I gave her and my Cubs cap pulled low. The officers told me to get her out of there. She was shaking."

"Did she say how it happened?"

"Not a word – of course I didn't ask her then. I tried the next morning." Ted stopped in front of the store and faced Sullivan. "I really wish you'd stop bothering her about it."

A gallery of patrons lounged by the entrance to the liquor store, which was decorated in garish yellow paint. Sullivan brushed by one of them on the way in and asked the Middle-Eastern clerk behind bullet-proof glass for the cigarettes. When Sullivan caught up to Ted, he was hoisting a fifth from the shelf. "That's Russian," Sullivan said, "He might prefer Polish." Ted put it back and took a bottle that promised it was made from potatoes grown in Poland.

As they came out, they were looked-over by a group of young men holding brown bags. One of them asked Sullivan, "How you doin'?" He was about to answer, when his phone buzzed again. He told Ted to go ahead.

It was a retired Chicago cop on the phone. After he left the force, he had set up shop as a private detective. He was a big ruddy-faced Irishman with an irrepressible personality. He pitched Sullivan his prices for rap sheets, autopsies, unpublished phone numbers and running license plates. Sullivan already had someone in place for all these services. "You're charging ten per plate," Sullivan interrupted, "My guy does it for five." The conversation switched to the White Sox.

Charly buzzed him back into the apartment. He could smell and hear northern pike – sizzling in the pan. A lonely bottle of vodka stood on the counter.

"Where's Ted?"

"Oh, he left. We're going out tomorrow night."

"Yeah, I know – how old's your dad?"

"He's turning 57. Do you like wine?"

"I like red."

"That's all we have," she said, filling two jelly jars half full. She had set the table: potato salad, red Jell-O and applesauce. She placed a filet on his plate. It was white and flaky. He grabbed his wine – "Well, here's to" – he stopped.

"To the chef, of course," she said clinking his jar, "I hope you like it" –

"Oh, fish – I wish we had it more often."

He devoured the potatoes, avoided the Jell-O and picked at the filet. After a last sour swallow, he shrouded the remains with his napkin. While he helped her clear up, he asked for a re-fill. She emptied a trickle from the bottle and tossed it into the trash.

"How did you get into this job, Mr. Sullivan?" She was washing, he was drying.

"It's a family business."

She handed him a fistful of dripping silverware – "I mean how do you become a private detective?"

"Oh," he said off-handedly, "Either become a police officer" reciting the official code, "and attain the rank of sergeant. Or, you work under someone else's license for three years. Either way you have to pass the Private Detective exam."

"Is it hard?"

"No, it's impossible. All the questions – none have anything to do with the job. You have to memorize. I spent $500 on a seminar so I could pass it on my second try."

The dishes were stacked in the strainer and she swung the spout to rinse out the sink. "Give me a question?"

"OK, what's the most important trait of a detective: ability to reason, powers of observation or persistence?"

Charly had a far-off look as she took a seat at the table. "Ability to reason," she repeated.

"Well," Sullivan said, "You could be reasoning on the wrong set of facts."

"Persistence!" she blurted out triumphantly.

Sullivan said nothing.

"Well, I guess it has to be powers of observation."

"Didn't you read any Sherlock Holmes when you were a kid?"

She looked at him blankly.

"Holmes said that most people see but don't observe," Sullivan said. "How many front steps does this building have?"

She hesitated – "Five?" she offered weakly.

"It's seven – but I don't expect you to notice. I am expecting you to notice a man being run over by a bus." He glanced at his phone. It was 8:17. "Do you want to talk about it now?"

Her face froze. "Because, if you don't want to talk about it, someone else – another stranger is going to come here. He'll have a subpoena. It's going to say that you have to come downtown on a certain day and time. If you don't go, he's going to come back with an order that says you're in contempt of court. If you try to ignore that – the sheriff" –

"Stop," she demanded.

"I'm sorry," Sullivan intoned, "This isn't going away. Your name is on the report." Sullivan swallowed the last of his wine. "I can get between you and the next stranger" –

"I was on the phone," she said returning to the trance where he had first met her. "I was looking through the plastic, when a man walked up. He was short – looked like a Mexican. He was holding two grocery bags – one in each hand. He waited for a bus to pull in."

Sullivan reached for his long-neglected briefcase and took out his pad. Her eyes searched as she continued.

"– It must have been five minutes – a bus pulls in. It's a lady driver. She gets out – there's a Porta-Potty there. The man waits until she gets back. She opens the front door and I watch him – he climbs the stairs and puts something in the fare box. He walks to the back and sits down."

Charly is swallowing hard. Her breath comes fast. She repeatedly smacks a fresh pack on the table but doesn't open it.

"The lady driver gets out of her seat- she's about halfway down the aisle – and she starts yelling at the man. I can't hear what she's saying."

Charly rips open the pack but just stares at it. "He gets up. He's yelling something back at her. She goes to the front and grabs the radio. After she says something into it, she walks back."

She pushed a cigarette halfway out – "The man was sitting down again but – the driver's pointing at the rear door. He gets up and" – she pushed both hands back through her hair – her voice choking.

Sullivan kept his head down, waiting for her to continue.

"She's got her arm straight out toward the door– he heads for it. I can tell he's mad. She goes back to her seat. He pushed open the doors. He came out sideways, with one bag first. The other bag" – Her body shook.

Sullivan grabbed the pack, tapped out a cigarette and handed it toward her. She gazed vacantly, stood up, turned around to hang a dish towel from the oven handle.

He stopped writing. "I know this is hard."

She turned to face him. She was crying like the first time he'd seen his dad cry – the morning Beatrice died. Her face scrunched up like his. She sobbed like a lost child.

"She shut the door – she started to pull out. He was trying to – his arm with the bag was stuck. I saw him – he was pounding on the bus with his other hand."

Charly went to the sideboard and rested her face on her hands as she shook, "I was screaming – I started hitting the plastic" she pounded the counter – "She couldn't hear. She just kept driving. He ran along next to the bus a few steps and" –

Her shoulders heaved. Sullivan got up and walked to her. She turned into his arms and hugged him tightly. He was just someone to hold onto.

17

He could hear her words over his shoulder. "I don't know – all of a sudden" –

"Was he caught by the wheels?"

Charly released him and stood straight. "Yeah," she said, grabbing the towel to dab her eyes, "He couldn't get away" her voice rose to its loudest – "I was screaming stop and she kept going! She turned onto Chicago Avenue and – I told you – it looked like a bundle of clothes."

CHAPTER 3

Three weeks after he met Charly, Major Accident came out with their fifteen-page reconstruction report on the accident It featured graphic accounts, grisly photos and scale drawings. There were now ten witnesses listed, in addition to Charlevoix Rydzinski. They claimed various west side addresses Sullivan wasn't keen on visiting. The bystanders had one thing in common: they were lounging in front of the yellow liquor store when it happened.

Sullivan skimmed their accounts. They all said the same thing. They claimed the victim dove in front of the bus, as it made its turn onto Chicago Avenue. They described it as suicide, though the Coroner had ruled the death an accident. Prior to that hearing, an investigator from the bus company, interpreter in tow, visited the family of the late Hector Cortez to inquire if he had been depressed.

Adding the report to his thickening folder, Sullivan wondered how these statements had been obtained. They completely contradicted Charly's account but weren't inconsistent with the blood stains and other physical evidence. Naturally, the driver agreed with the liquor store crowd, claiming she had no chance to apply her brakes. Sullivan was filled by a sinking feeling on two counts. The report refuted all the allegations in the lawsuit his client had hurriedly filed. It also necessitated another interview with Charly. To get her handwritten statement that night, he had promised to never ring her doorbell again.

Sullivan didn't want to surprise her but there was no way to phone

19

ahead. He pulled up in front of the three-flat and got no answer from the Rydzinski apartment. He slipped a card through the narrow slot of their mailbox and heard it hit bottom. It bore a blue inked message asking Charly to please call.

Several days of no response went by, before he went back. This time Charly's father buzzed him into the building. Jerzy Rydzinski was standing in the doorway, wearing a suspicious stare. Sullivan tried one of the few Polish greetings he knew. "Dzien dobry", which translated to "day good." The man asked him what he wanted in halting English. He frowned, when Sullivan explained he had to speak with his daughter again about the accident. It was a bit tortuous but Sullivan finally gathered that Charly was working at a suburban library.

Sullivan parked across the street from a four-story gleaming glass and steel box. He didn't ask for Charly but started in the children's department and worked his way up to adult fiction. He found her shelving books from a cart. She was wearing headphones, staring down at titles. She didn't notice him standing a few authors' ahead. He reached and lightly tapped her arm.

Charly looked up startled. Annoyance spread from her eyes to her firmly set mouth. "I'm working," she said impatiently, "We're not allowed" –

"Do you have a break coming up?" Sullivan asked, as she lowered the headphones, "There's – I could buy you a cup of coffee downstairs."

"I don't drink coffee," Charly said curtly "And – didn't you – you said that if I gave you the statement – you wouldn't" –

"I said I wouldn't come to your apartment."

Charly glowered and asked Sullivan his least-favorite question, "How did you find me - did you follow me?

"Following people only works in movies, your dad told me."

A thirty-ish honey-haired woman, wearing a rather daring blouse (or she had missed a button) radiated disapproval from the reference desk. "I can't explain it right now," Sullivan hushed his voice, "But something's come up" –

The librarian was walking toward them. Charly had resumed shelving selections into the mystery section. The woman with the gaping white shirt and tight mouth addressed Sullivan. "Excuse me, but Ms. Rydzinksi is busy– you're going to have to talk to her outside of work."

"Oh, what time does she get off?" Sullivan asked offhandedly.

"I can't tell you that but the library closes at 9:00. Now, if you have a card" –

"No, I have plenty to read," Sullivan said, waving goodbye to Charly. She gave him a look like she was gazing through plastic.

Sullivan headed home, intending to go out that evening. Ann walked in, surprised to find him catching the Cubs in the early innings. Her face was bright red and he rose to receive a damp embrace. She had been jogging in a never-ending battle to recover her pre-baby physique. Sullivan appreciated the effort and the results.

At the end of the game, Sullivan, a White Sox fan, took a perverse pleasure in seeing the L flag hoisted at Wrigley. Tara was surprised to find him in the kitchen boiling pasta, chopping vegetables, shaping meatballs and placing them on a cookie sheet. She had come from an after school babysitting gig that paid her cash.

"What's all this?"

Sullivan told her it was his world-famous mostaccioli rigati. She wrinkled her nose – "I don't want any meatballs." "But that's the best part," Sullivan called, as she retreated to the back stairs to field a phone call.

Flynn sauntered in. He kept his backpack on as he perused the refrigerator. "You can have a snack," Sullivan said to his backpack, "But this will be ready in about a half hour." He slid the cookie sheet into the oven and started setting the table. Flynn slung his bag down on a chair and unscrewed a sports drink.

Sullivan wanted to break the silence with something besides, "How's school?" but nothing came.

"How was school?"

"OK," Flynn said noncommittally. "We had fun in gym. They're teaching us golf."

"Really," Sullivan said, spreading garlic butter on some stale bread that otherwise would have been tossed to the birds. "Are you swinging left-handed?"

Flynn frowned, "All they had were right-handed clubs but I was hitting it pretty good – you know plastic balls."

"I'll take you on a real course." Sullivan offered. Flynn's summer vacation was starting in a week and Sullivan vowed to take time off – maybe Friday afternoons -to stroll down fairways. "But first we'll have to hit the driving range."

As the four sat at dinner, Tara described another unforgettable day with her babysitting kids. The boy was six and the girl had just turned three. They were playing Frisbee at the park. It had rained hard the night before and Micah was mucking his way across a quicksand infield toward the Frisbee. It was perched on the pitcher's mound and Micah got stuck at shortstop. Tara took off her low-heeled shoes and went for him. When the mud threatened her Capris, she retreated. She thought Micah was going to freak, waiting for – the guys driving around in golf carts - but he was laughing. Aurora was worried in the stroller, murmuring "My-My is stuck."

One of the golf cart guys finally stopped. Like a swimmer testing the waters at Oak Street Beach, he took a few steps with his work boots. Then motored back to the garage for firemen boots. They were almost sucked off before he got to Micah. During the rescue, which involved Micah being yanked out of shoes, socks and pants, the Frisbee was trampled. The park guys promised to return it when it surfaced. There was one bright spot: Micah was thrilled riding home in a golf cart, splashing puddles all the way.

Tara was paid well for these calamities but admitted she felt a little scared by house noises.

Ann complained about organizing quarterly financial statements for the company accountant. She didn't get the salary she deserved but her health insurance covered Sullivan and the kids. Sullivan made a hasty promise to take her on a real date that Saturday.

"That means you have to actually plan something," Ann said, "That Cuban restaurant – didn't you say your stomach lining was gone by the time they served us."

"They dropped our plates. We got it on the house," Sullivan parried – I'll make reservations – Flynn, do you feel like cleaning up?"

"No," he said slinking from the table, "I've got a book report – I have to finish reading it first."

Tara said she would help and the two of them tackled the mess. "I hate this house," Tara sighed, "I mean, it's nothing against – it's just that – there's so much to do at my friends'. Eliza just got a home theater – you should see Tanya's – they have their own gym. We don't even have a dishwasher."

Sullivan offered to take her for ice cream. She looked at him like it was the lamest idea ever.

"There's a new place on Lake Street – you can pick out all these toppings."

"But – don't you hate ice cream - you wouldn't even eat a brownie at my birthday?

"I can tolerate a kiddie-cone," Sullivan assured her. Tara said she might be able to go after her show ended at 8:00.

They were sitting outside at a little round wrought iron table, perched on wire-backed chairs. Sullivan was losing a battle with an enormous scoop of coffee ice cream, while Tara dug into a sundae swimming with Swedish Fish. They were almost directly across from the library.

"Next time, I'm getting sprinkles," Tara said excitedly, "They're made from cookie crumbs. Dad" – she scolded – extracting a napkin from the holder and thrusting it at him. He dabbed at some wetness on the left side of his mouth. The cone was dripping like an icicle and his hands were bathed in stickiness. He didn't dare touch his phone.

"What time do you got?" he mumbled, maneuvering his tongue around a cold lump. She glanced at her phone, "8:47." He always got the precise time from the digital generation.

"I was wondering if you could – I need an extra set of eyes."

Tara faced him excitedly. "Are we working on a case?" Sullivan had brought her along on many assignments. They had staked out a pay phone on an "L" platform for three hours on a raw winter night, hoping to spot a teenage runaway, who had used it the night before. They didn't have any luck but Sullivan persuaded a police commander to station an officer on the platform. The girl was apprehended the next night and the cops returned her to her group home.

Tara loved accompanying him to fire stations. The firemen always made a fuss and let her sound the horn during their run for Italian ice. Back at the station, she climbed on the apparatus, while Sullivan paced, waiting for the ambulance to return. Once, when they both tired of this game, they scouted nearby emergency rooms, until they spotted Ambulance 39 backed into a bay at St. Anthony's. Even when they didn't have actual assignments, they pretended to be following the car ahead – cupping their mouths to garble imaginary calls.

"Who are we looking for?"

Sullivan got up. "I want to catch somebody getting off work at the library. There's two exits, so we'll have to split up. You'll call me if you see her." Sullivan gave a description of Charly and what she was wearing. After sitting Tara on a park bench near the west entrance, he took the east side of the building.

He watched the last patrons filing out of the east exit. The lights blinked off on the upper floors. At the employees' exit, a security guard held the door saying goodnight to the workers. Sullivan's phone vibrated. "Dad," came Tara's hushed tone, "I think I've got her. Hurry, she's walking real fast."

Sullivan striding quickly, kept her on the phone. "Where is she now?" Tara told him she was walking down Lake Street. "Which direction?"

"I don't know – to the right." Sullivan guessed she was heading west. As he dodged pedestrians, bikers and strollers, he caught sight of Tara's blond ponytail bobbing ahead. He broke into a jog. Tara heard pounding and looked back. "Is that her?" she asked when he was huffing alongside.

Charly was smoking as furiously as she walked. Headphones were on and she seemed like she was trying to get someplace fast, or get away from something or maybe this was just her natural prickly state.

They saw her duck into a coffee shop. Sullivan remembered her aversion to coffee, as he and Tara crossed the street. They watched her ordering at the counter. She was alone. When he walked in with Tara, Sullivan didn't pretend it was by chance. She turned away from the cashier with a tall iced tea, almost spilling it on Sullivan. She gave him an exasperated stare.

"I'm calling the police, if you don't leave me alone." Tara looked up at her stunned. She had seen her father get a poor reception before – but – the cops right away?

"That's OK with me," Sullivan replied calmly, "They usually take my side. I just wanted to tell you that there are at least ten people calling you a liar."

Charly stormed out the door and sat down on a concrete planter. "This is my daughter, Tara," Sullivan said, as they walked up.

"Hi," Tara said extending her hand expectantly.

"You drag your kids into this," Charly said contemptuously, "*They're* your little spies."

"Oh, she likes it – besides she got ice cream."

Tara grabbed his arm, "Dad, I've got an algebra test tomorrow."

"Charly, you know I wouldn't be going to all this trouble, if I didn't need your help."

"Who are these – who said I lied?" Charly's dark eyes shone – she looked like a cornered animal.–

Sullivan sighed. "There are ten witnesses that say Hector jumped in front of the bus."

Charly gave a snort. "That's crazy – how can they – that doesn't make any sense."

"Well, you never know – maybe they got paid off – I don't know. Maybe you just imagined" –

Charly stood up – "I know what I saw. Those people – who are they anyway?"

Sullivan explained that they been standing in front of the liquor store and had a view of the accident. "They couldn't see him." Charly retorted, "He was on *my* side of the bus."

"Dad – it's 9:30," Tara moaned.

"Charly, I don't have time right now – didn't you say you were interested in detective work?"

She looked at him coldly, then shrugged. "I liked – the first time you came, I felt better afterwards. I thought – maybe I could get paid for helping people, people like me - besides"-

"I already know you like disguises," Sullivan said softly. A ghost of a grin curled the corners of Charly's mouth.

"I was going to say – I've always been good at sneaking into places. My friends and I used to climb the fence at Clemens Pool" –

Tara, unfolded her arms at the mention of her neighborhood pool. "Really – weren't you scared?"

"Of heights – my foot got stuck near the top. But I was already on the other side – so there was no choice. I don't know why I tried it in sandals."

Sullivan asked Charly what time she started work and she agreed to come to his office beforehand. "I'd like to try something – I mean before you have to testify." Charly gave her patented sour look but, as they parted, she answered Tara's question about the safest spot to sneak into the pool.

At 10:30 AM, the following day, Sullivan tried to concentrate on a hospital chart while he scrawled notes. He was rankled that Charly was an hour late. He felt pinned down. He wanted to go to the Chinese joint down the street for a Thai iced tea. Sullivan finally slapped a note on the door. He was walking back toward the office, sipping and chewing on ice cubes, when he saw Charly enter the front door of his building.

He climbed the threadbare stairs and found her sitting facing his door. She was wearing a light gray cotton skirt and a short-sleeved charcoal blouse. Her black shoes had delicate straps. She looked positively professional. Charly stood up quickly, apologizing for her lateness, as she smoothed her skirt. "I had to take my dad for his physical this morning. It took longer than we thought."

"It always does," Sullivan said, as he turned the key. The air conditioner was still working hard as he motioned Charly to sit down at an adjoining desk. Looking around at the spartan surroundings, Charly asked, "Who else works here?"

"No one, at the moment; my spring intern finished his semester last week and – I don't know if I'm getting a summer one yet." She stared at his magnifying glass standing on its tripod. "You use this?"

"It comes in handy when I'm looking at doctor's notes or forged signatures. So, you start work at 1:00?"

"Actually, I'm off today – I forgot it was Wednesday. Am I really going to have to go to court?" Sullivan didn't answer. Her hands twisted, "What was your idea?"

"Well, let's say you give your deposition – it's still your word against ten. I just thought there might be another way to handle this. Have you ever been to the courthouse downtown?"

Charly shook her head. "That's a good sign," Sullivan said, "So, you've never been in trouble?"

She clasped her hands – fighting the urge to smoke. "I was caught for curfew when I was 16," Charly confessed, "The judge yelled at me more than the people who got DUI's. I guess he was trying to scare me."

Sullivan got up and stared at an "L" lurching out of the station for its long journey to the south side. "I could use your help at the courthouse."

"You mean, right now?" Charly asked.

"Sure, "Sullivan said, turning, "We're both dressed for it. If we get hungry, I'll buy you lunch at Porterfields."

"I've heard of that – is it vegetarian?"

Sullivan smiled, "It's a steakhouse but I'm sure they have salad. They're famous for their turtle soup."

"That's disgusting. Sure - Are we taking the "L"?

They spun through the revolving doors of the courthouse and passed through the metal detector. On the 9th Floor, they found a public access terminal that was free and Sullivan pulled the Major Accident report and a pad from his briefcase. "Let's run them for traffic first – then criminal," Sullivan said.

He let Charly operate the keyboard and gave her the codes and passwords. The Major Accident report furnished names, addresses and dates of birth. The first name they put in – Keyshaun Andrews – there were two pages of traffic cases – thirty in all. They were mostly minor offenses: tinted windows, no seat belt, improper lane usage.

"OK, let's run him for criminal," Sullivan instructed her.

Andrews had twelve arrests, enough to earn him his own FBI fingerprint number. Sullivan had her check by the number. This brought up cases where he had used an alias. Now, there were fifteen more file numbers on the screen. He had given cops names like Andrew Johnson.

"This is fun," Charly said, "I didn't know you could check people's criminal records. Could we run some of my friends?"

Sullivan shifted her focus back to business. "We're trying to see if they have any convictions for crimes of dishonesty," Sullivan explained. "In civil cases it's better to have a murder rap than shoplifting. A witness convicted of a deceitful crime – their testimony can be automatically impeached."

Sullivan had no idea whether Charly would work out. He didn't know if she'd have staying power but that trip to the courthouse marked the beginning of a long and pleasant partnership.

CHAPTER 4

L ong after Charly came on board, Sullivan found himself at an office supply store. He needed paper clips, copy paper and ink cartridges. He was eyeing a brown briefcase, when Sullivan's cell phone danced on his hip. It never failed to startle him.

"Is this" – the voice cut out and he strode toward a floor-to-ceiling window looking for better reception. "Hello, is this Mike Sullivan?" Before Sullivan could answer, the phone went dead. Fishing a pencil from his pocket, Sullivan copied the number from the caller ID onto the back of a crumpled bank receipt. He stopped at the sliding glass entrance and punched in the number but couldn't get a connection.

Walking out to his car, he got in, lowered the windows for some air and dialed.

"Capitol Insurance, Rafael speaking," the voice answered mechanically.

"Yeah, this is Mike Sullivan, were you trying to get a hold of me?"

"Hey, Mike, I don't think I've dealt with you before but Dan Parini in claims gave me your name. We have an accident with three fatalities. We need you to interview the owner of the car. She's the mother of one of the victims. I don't know how long she'll be willing to talk, so you need to get over there right away. I'll fax you the police report. By the way," a motorcycle thundered past Sullivan's driver's window. He put a finger in his ear.

"So, good luck."

"I'm sorry," Sullivan said, "What was that?"

"The neighborhood she lives in – it's really rough."

Sullivan drove to his office to pick up the accident report. Seeing the fax had used his last sheet of copy paper, he regretted the shopping cart of supplies he had left in the aisle. He reached in a drawer and grabbed a legal pad that still held a few pages and hurried out the rear exit down the fire escape to the parking lot.

As he banged down the iron stairs, he skimmed the report: three teenage girls – two were sixteen; one was eighteen. There was so much carnage; the police couldn't tell who was driving.

Tossing the report into his briefcase on the passenger seat, he punched the radio to sports talk and pulled out into traffic. Half-listening to the strained banter between callers and host, he thought of what he would say to the mother. But the image of his 14 year-old crowded in. He considered calling Tara right then – she'd be at her babysitting job - didn't want to distract her.

On his way to the mother's house, he stopped at the accident site and saw the tree. The giant elm stood on the parkway of a busy street. A swath of bark was missing about three feet above the ground, exposing a band of bare wood. Scrape marks on the curb and parallel ruts in the grass marked the path of the convertible.

Piled at the base of the tree were stuffed animals, wilted flowers and rain-smudged signs. One of these bore a photograph of a smiling girl in cornrows. Sullivan squatted down to read the simple message, "Tamika, We Miss You."

Back in his car, the picture of the smiling girl haunted him. He dreaded talking to the dead girl's mother but knew many questions had to be answered. How did the girls get the car? Who was driving? Where were they going?

Driving past dilapidated houses and vacant lots, scanning house numbers, he failed to see the pothole. It swallowed his right front wheel. Jolted back, he hoped the rim wasn't bent.

On several street corners, young salesmen offered him his drug of choice. He didn't look at them. Only a half block south of one of these bazaars, he found the house. It was a brown frame, with the requisite peeling front porch. Standing in the doorway was a woman arguing with a man.

After edging to the curb, Sullivan grabbed his weathered black briefcase with the broken strap. He stepped carefully across the garbage-strewn parkway, avoiding unpleasant piles. As he approached the porch, he could hear the woman. There was iron in her voice as she told the man, "I'm under a lot of stress right now – I don't have time for this." She looked to be in her early 40's, neatly dressed. She gripped a phone in one hand, the front door knob in the other.

"C'mon big sister, you gotta help me out," the man implored. His eyes were glassy and his skin pockmarked. He looked like he might be a regular at the corner bazaar – or bar. Sullivan looked up at them from the bottom of the stairs.

"Can I help you?" the woman asked in an exasperated voice. "I'm sorry to bother you Ms. Dobbins," Sullivan said haltingly, "It's about the accident. The insurance company sent me."

The woman's eyes narrowed, "Life insurance?"

"Hey, sister, just a little something," the man interjected, swaying slightly as he spoke.

She turned to face him. "I've got business now, so you got to leave. You're not getting my last twenty."

Sullivan fingered three singles in his pocket. Stepping onto the porch, he extended the bills, "Here, Ms. Dobbins, if this will help any."

"Thank you," she said snatching the bills from his hand and thrusting them toward the drunk, "Now, leave me alone!"

"Thank you sister," the man muttered, "Thank you big sister," as he shambled down the stairs.

"I'm sorry about that," she said to Sullivan, her face and voice softening, "What did you say your name was?"

"I'm Mike Sullivan. I'm very sorry to bother you, it's about the accident."

"O.K., well, c'mon in."

As soon as the door closed behind them, the phone went off in her hand. She excused herself. Alone in the living room, Sullivan walked to the photographs displayed on a set of metal shelves. The muffled voice of the victim's mother came from the next room, as he peered at a picture of a smiling girl — the same girl whose photo had been propped against the tree. She wore a scarlet graduation gown, offset by a golden tassel. Three shelves held pictures of her at various ages, from tiny sundresses to an elegant prom gown. In some frames, a large man with hard eyes held her hand. In another, she sat on a gray haired woman's lap. She was smiling in every shot — not just with her mouth but with playful brown eyes.

There was a lone figure on the bottom shelf. Sullivan squatted down to look at a cloth doll. It looked like a Raggedy Ann doll but Sullivan was disturbed by her downturned mouth. He didn't know that a doll could have a sad face.

Across the room from the photographs, he saw a hand-carved wooden lamp. The name "Tamika" was engraved in the base. Next to the lamp was a framed certificate stating that Tamika Dobbins had completed a course in carpentry. He could hear the woman's voice slightly raised, as she ended her call. Sullivan strolled to the center of the room.

"I'm sorry about all this commotion," the woman said as she reentered, "The phone hasn't stopped ringing since," her voice trailed off. "So you're here about Tamika's accident."

"Yes," Sullivan said, swallowing, "I feel terrible bothering you at a time like this. It's just that — the only thing the insurance company knows is they have three fatalities. And I was wondering if you knew anything about how the girls got the car and, well if you know anything about the accident."

"I don't know much, would you like to sit down?" She motioned toward a white couch protected by plastic. "Do you mind if we sit at the table instead?" Sullivan asked, "So I can write."

At the kitchen table, she put her face in her hands. "I'm sorry Mr. Sullivan – but I've been talking about this for four days now – I don't think I can take anymore."

Sullivan held up the one-page police report. "I know Ms. Dobbins but this is all we have until Major Accident finishes their investigation. And, it's just that the insurance company has so many questions."

"I don't know what I can tell you – my husband's been the one looking into it. He should be home soon."

Sullivan's spirits sagged. So many times an interview would go well until a husband came home and asked him to leave. He sipped ice water, while the phone consumed his host. Then he heard heavy slow steps on the stairs.

He knew Tamika's father would be startled to see him and started to stand. A tall, muscular man turned hard eyes at Sullivan. "Mr. Dobbins" – Sullivan began – but was cut off – "Clint, this Mr. – I forgot your name - he's from the car insurance."

The man spoke in a firm but not unfriendly tone, "My name is Lawrence, not Dobbins, who are you?" After Sullivan explained, he was invited to resume his seat and a glass of ice water was handed to Tamika's father.

"Mr. Lawrence, we're trying to find out how Tamika got the car and who was driving at the time of the accident?"

"Do you have any kids, Mr. Sullivan?"

"Yeah, in fact I have a daughter a few year's younger than Tamika. And - I just can't imagine what you and your wife are going through."

"Well, you know what it's like being a dad. You're Mr. Fix-it. Whenever something breaks around here, or with the car – you know what I mean."

Sullivan allowed a slight smile, "I don't know how to fix things. Whenever I try, I break them. But I know what you mean."

"OK – you have a teenage daughter. If she's anything like Tamika – my daughter was like a Third World country – the way she went through money."

"The day I had to pay for my daughter's dance class," Sullivan began –

"The night of the accident"– Lawrence continued, "We gave her my wife's car. It was about eight, Tamika was driving and her two girlfriends were with her. I knew Tamika wouldn't have gas money, so I slipped her a twenty without my wife knowing. I was always slipping her twenties."

"Do you know where they were heading?"

"There's a McDonald's on Madison, they were going there to hang out in the parking lot."

"Were they meeting someone?"

"Maybe Tamika's cousin, Marvin – Shorty, they call him, I don't know. The next thing – I get a call at three in the morning. And it's something I can't fix. Do you know what that feels like?"

Sullivan said nothing. Lawrence gave him the location of the McDonald's but had no idea where the girls had gone from there. How they hit the tree was also a mystery. Sullivan put the police report and pad back in his briefcase

Witnesses often gave him the most important information when he stopped writing. They gave him even more when he stood up. He got the best stuff when he was turning the doorknob.

Tamika's parents had nothing more to give. They chatted about their daughter, how she planned to go to beauty school. As he left, Sullivan admired the lamp again and asked for Shorty's number.

The tall man looked at him with hard sad eyes, took his business card and promised Shorty would call.

As he walked briskly back to his car, Sullivan turned on his phone. Chimes announced a voice mail. It was from Charly. He interrupted a long recitation from court files, to call her back.

"Charly, you still at the courthouse?"

"Can't talk right now," came a muffled whisper.

As he drove back to the office, he rolled past the bus shelter – the place where his professional relationship with Charly had been born. There were few Chicago intersections that didn't hold some memory.

She called back, asking if he had listened to her voice mail. "No, I saved it – Is the clerk's office still open?"

"Only until 4:30," Charly replied, "Sorry, I was in Judge Connolly's chambers. What do you have?"

"Marvin Frye, late teens, early 20's, I don't have a DOB."

"I better hurry. It's hard to get files after 4:00."

Sullivan could picture the faces of the clerks. He had watched them grow old from across the counter, bodies gone soft, hair grown sparse, or noticeably artificial. The women heavily made-up. Sullivan had aged with them and knew them well. This late in the day, they would have their purses on their desks.

His phone rang again. "Where are you?" his wife demanded, "We're all waiting." The Little League game – sullen 12 year-old boys slouching on an aluminum bench. "Shit, I have all the equipment – is Bob there yet?"

"Just hurry."

When he finally arrived with the bats, balls, shin guards and masks, he hurried the team onto the diamond to get in a few fielding drills. He knew they weren't necessary, because he was starting the only pitcher in the league who looked like he needed a shave. Andrew ploughed through the opposing lineup, coaxing weak come-backers and swinging strikeouts. When the Padres did put a pitch in play, Sullivan's fielders gave them a 50-50 chance of being safe.

With his team up 13-6, Little League rules against overwork forced Sullivan to take the ball from Andrew in the last inning. Enjoying a big lead, Sullivan, a former second string right fielder, concentrated more on getting his bench players into the game than winning it. His succession of soft-throwing right-handers were shelled. Meanwhile his only left-handed relief pitcher, his son, Flynn, squatted behind the plate in his catcher's gear.

When Sullivan's squad finally fell 14-13 in extra innings, the other team danced and hollered like they'd won the Little League World Series. Flynn fumed on the way home, wondering why he hadn't been sent to the mound. Sullivan thought of many answers but knew none that would cool Flynn's fire. "It was just regular season," he finally mustered. Silence.

The next morning, Charly walked through the glass door, fifteen minutes late as always, sipping tea heavily diluted with milk. After a perfunctory complaint about the summer heat, she pulled files out of her shoulder bag. "What was that last name you gave me, Frye. He's young, there wasn't very much." She gave him the date of birth, the same birthday as his daughter: Five traffic cases and two misdemeanors – for possession of cannabis.

"Who paid his bail?"

"Mabel Watkins – she gives the same address – 4410 Bristol – maybe his mother."

Charly typed up her notes from the courthouse, while Sullivan checked e-mail and returned calls. After performing Internet searches to find addresses of various deadbeats, criminals and nervous immigrants, he placed five files in his briefcase. He was heading to the northwest suburbs. Sullivan had learned early to group assignments geographically to keep gas costs down and profits up. He could charge five clients for the same Grand Tour, depending on the outcomes. It amused him that TV and movie private detectives worked one case at a time. No wonder their offices were shabby.

Before he left, he gave Charly a hospital chart to read and summarize. A woman in her 30's was suing one of his client hospitals for a burn she suffered during surgery. Sullivan had seen the photos her lawyer sent - a dime-sized scar on an oversized thigh. Not very impressive but worth something.

Back in his car, Sullivan thumbed through a street atlas. He kept it, despite calls from his kids to use GPS. He plotted a course to take him from one subdivision to the next. His first stop was to serve a summons and complaint on a couple. The credit card company had lost its patience.

Navigating down the gently curving lanes of Somerset Meadows, he spotted the house a half block away. The grass looked to be three feet higher than the neighbors. He saw a "For Sale" sign in front and newspapers strewn on the front sidewalk. Sullivan got out, gripping the summons.

He rang the doorbell but couldn't hear whether it worked. He pulled the screen door open and rapped on the inside door. Nothing. He walked around the house, until he found a bay window that allowed a view of the ground floor. The hardwood floors were bare of carpet and furniture. There was a hole in the dining room ceiling where a light fixture, or ceiling fan had been ripped out.

Sullivan stepped across to the house next door. A sprinkler swaying on the front lawn spattered his shirt. Refreshing. As he approached the glass front door, a Doberman rushed and pushed on it with his paws. Sullivan waited. A man in t-shirt and shorts shouted at the dog. Shutting the glass door behind him, the man lit a cigarette.

"Sorry to bother you, but I'm trying to reach . . ." Sullivan glanced at the summons, "Peter Chakiris?"

The man looked to be 40. He was balding and wore his blonde hair in a shaggy semi-circle. His beige sandals were frayed.

"So, you're looking for Pete." He took a long drag.

"When did he move?"

"Oh, he's been gone about four months now. The sheriff's been looking for him *and* his wife – "Hey, how's it goin?" the man shouted to a high-waisted old timer across the street who had turned off his trimmer to wave.

"Do you remember his wife's name?

"Sure, Cheryl – we used to party sometimes. They had a pool. Anyway, Pete got laid off from – I think he was a printer – at least a year ago. Cheryl was working daycare, making nothing. So, one night I'm parking my truck, they had one light on – I went over to see if Pete – I had tickets to a Sox game. They were gone, didn't tell anyone they were moving.

"Does anyone else on the block know them?

The man stamped out his cigarette. The butt joined companions squashed on the front stoop.

"My wife doesn't let me smoke in the house," he said drawing another. Sullivan was partial to smokers. Each time they lit up, they gave him ten more minutes.

"No, the people on the other side are new."

"Does he have any family in the area?"

Scraping a shred of tobacco off his tongue, the man said, "Pete's old man runs a restaurant. It's in Chicago. Let me think. Pete told me it was on Western, somewhere around 35th, I don't know the name. The four of us we're supposed to go there for dinner but Cheryl got sick."

Sullivan thanked the man and left for the post office. He wasn't surprised to find Pete and Cheryl Chakiris failed to leave a forwarding address. He called Charly and reached her voice mail.

"Charly, can you check the multiple listings on 11325 Hummingbird Lane, Rolling Meadows?"

Sullivan thumbed through his tattered atlas, looking for the best route to his next address. Milwaukee Avenue seemed the most direct way but when he turned onto it, he was caught in a conga line inching northwest. He endured the construction for twenty minutes, until he spotted the entrance to Kensington Condominiums.

He knew it well: cinder-block six-flats, with mansard roofs and locked street doors. If you could get in, the dim hallways smelled of spices mixed with squalor. Suburban subsistence had the same odor as the city version. He was pulling up to Building 6A, when Charly called back.

"It's a foreclosure, filed about six months ago," She began, "Owner was Chakiris. They tried a short sale first, then a sheriff's auction. I have the Realtor's name and number."

"I already got that off the "For Sale" sign. I don't suppose there's a lawyer listed for Chakiris?"

"No, just the lender's. If you want, I'll call the Realtor?"

"That would be great. I'm still in the area."

There were no names on the doorbells for Building 6A and the street door wouldn't budge. Sullivan peered through the glass, trying to make out the names scrawled on the mailboxes. He spotted the mail carrier's truck at the building next door.

She was in her 40's, brunette hair, too evenly dark to be natural, hung down shielding her face, as she slipped letters into the slots. Sullivan tapped on the lobby window. She had buds in her ears and took no notice. He read over the file as he waited for her to finish.

As she came out, Sullivan introduced himself as an insurance investigator, trying to contact an insured driver. He showed her the name.

"Yeah, he's still there, in 3C."

Sullivan walked alongside her, awkwardly commenting on the warm weather. She opened a small lock box and extracted the key to the front door. She held it for him. The mailbox for 3C had five names. Four were typed neatly on a white card. Another was scrawled boldly in black marker. "L. Kobiski."

"That's my guy," he said, before bounding up the staircase. It moved under him– plywood veiled by thin carpeting. He used the metal knocker on 3C and the sound echoed through the apartment. A tiny dog yipped. It scampered to claw the door. It barked excitedly but without much volume. Then he heard heavier slower steps and saw movement behind the peephole.

"Who's there?" asked a tired scratchy female voice.

Sullivan introduced himself and the woman told him from behind the closed door that "Larry" wasn't home. She said she didn't know when he'd be home, where he worked, or his phone number. Sullivan asked if he could leave a card and she told him to slip it under the door.

Sullivan left another card in the mailbox for 3C and went out the back door to see if he could leave one more on Larry's windshield. He was looking for an older model Chevy sedan. Walking down a row of cars, Sullivan found the rear plate he was looking for. The hood was up and a young man was working on the engine.

"Excuse me, I'm looking for Larry Kobiski," Sullivan said. The man wore faded jeans, a Harley-Davidson t-shirt and about three days of blonde stubble.

"I'm Larry." He looked for a rag to wipe his hands. Sullivan explained how the insurance company had hired a lawyer to defend him for his accident the previous July.

"That wasn't my fault," he said, giving up on the rag, wiping his palms on his jeans, "I was turning on yellow and that bitch – she never slowed down – hit me right on the driver's door. The cops gave me a ticket but I beat it in traffic court."

Sullivan had heard a thousand similar litanies and explained that the woman had sued him anyway and they needed his help to defend the case. Sullivan pulled a sheaf of court-ordered questions from his briefcase and asked if they could go inside to answer them.

"Let's do it right here," he insisted, slamming the hood. Sullivan led him through the questions: any drinking or drugs before the accident, license ever suspended . . . Kobiski gave short responses, with rising irritation.

"OK, one more, do you have any restrictions on your license?"

The man stared blankly.

"Do you wear glasses when you drive?"

"No," he growled.

"Alright, I just need you to sign here. I'll notarize it back at my office."

Before leaving, Sullivan handed Kobiski a card, reminding him to call if he ever escaped Kensington Condominiums.

As he walked away, Sullivan was feeling a bit queasy from the fumes that came from Kobiski's car and it occurred to him that the only thing he'd eaten that day was an apple. As he headed toward his next destination, Sullivan scanned both sides of the four lane street, trying to spot something edible amid the fast food wilderness.

Feeling he deserved an upgrade, after completing an assignment, he pulled into a casual dining restaurant that passed itself off as a neighborhood joint. Inside, he found the usual décor – imitation Irish pub – and was effusively welcomed by the hostess, Brandy, who led him to a table. Sullivan remembered he had nothing to read and wished he'd gone to a diner, where plenty of grease-stained Sun-Times would be stuffed under the counter.

The waitress took his drink order. Water was all he wanted. He ordered a BLT, convinced it was the one sandwich no restaurant could ruin. There were only a few scattered patrons, the lunch rush being long over. Most ate in silence, some studying their phones, oblivious to their company.

"I almost forgot," the waitress returned, interrupting his reverie, "You get soup with yours. Today it's baked potato." Sullivan didn't like the sound but said he'd have a cup. When she brought it, Sullivan inspected. It wasn't exactly liquid and it wasn't completely solid. He took a spoonful.

When she returned with the sandwich, Sullivan asked, "What is this? It's not soup and it's not a baked potato." She seemed flustered as she put down his plate. "If you don't like it, sir, I can substitute our macaroni and cheese?"

"No, as a matter of fact, bring me a box. I'm taking this to go."

Her hand trembled slightly as she lifted the plate. Tears made her eyes shine. "I'll bring your check," sniffing slightly.

"I'm sorry" – glancing at her nametag – "Morgan, I didn't mean to – it's just that I waited too long to eat."

In a wounded tone, she replied, "It's not you." She lowered her voice, "It's this place – I can't stand it. I just started two weeks ago and - everyone who works here is stuck" – she put the plate down and sank into the seat across from him – "and so mean." Sullivan gazed at his unexpected lunch companion.

She looked to be in her 20s. She had deep-set dark eyes and her rich brown hair was pulled back into a bun. She had a strong chin and cheekbones, offset by adorable dimples. Her complexion was olive and her wide mouth looked capable of a warm smile.

"If you've got a break, I'll be glad to talk but bring me a Coke first."

Morgan returned with a Coke and a cup of tea for herself.

"My manager said I could take 15 minutes," she said, attempting a smile.

"Let me guess," Sullivan said before taking his first bite, "You're an English major and this was the only job you could find?"

"Close – I got a degree in Archeology, a minor in Anthropology."

"Well, what better place to study Anthropology – isn't this a 'watering hole?'"

The strain started to leave her dark eyes, "I'd rather be doing archeology – that was my specialty." Sullivan started to ask another question but was too consumed with chewing. "I've been applying to some firms – they don't even answer my e-mails."

"Help yourself to some fries."

Again the hushed tone, "I don't eat *anything* here. What business are you in?"

Swallowing, "Private detective." Her eyes widened. "And, no I don't follow husbands – in case you have one worth following."

She flashed a mischievous smile before glancing over her shoulder to see if any customers had come in. "That sounds interesting."

"Yeah, I get some good stories but my wife's tired of hearing about it. Last week, I went to this two-flat. The people I want live upstairs. I can see them through the window but they won't answer the doorbell. Finally, a guy from next door comes over. He tells me they're deaf and shows me a switch in the lobby that makes a light blink in their apartment."

"Do you know how to sign?" Morgan interrupted, "We had to learn it in high school."

"No," Sullivan said slightly sore about the interruption, "So I blinked the lights. They came out. I wrote down my questions and they wrote their answers – they were witnesses to an arson on their block. Anyway, I'm telling my wife the story and her eyes are glazing over. I'm telling her," Sullivan cupped his hands into a megaphone, "They were deaf, Ann, deaf."

"I was going to tell her about the little girl with the sad doll" -

The manager walked up. "Was everything all right?"

"Have you ever seen a doll with a sad face?" Sullivan continued to Morgan, who was instantly uncomfortable again.

"No – my sister and I played Little House on the Prairie."

"If you're finished there, I can take it away" the manager offered. Sullivan pushed the plate toward him. He thought he detected a little extra clatter as the manager cleared the dishes. "Anyway," he extracted a card from his wallet, "If you ever need a new job – maybe I can help."

Morgan studied its slogan, "Specialized investigative services" engraved in cursive – "what does that mean?" Sullivan gave his usual answer, "I have no idea. My dad made it up."

CHAPTER 5

His father had been gone 10 years but, as Sullivan walked to his car, it was easy to imagine his dad walking beside him, settling into the passenger seat, stubbornly refusing his seatbelt and scolding him to "Turn the damn radio off."

Frank Sullivan used the radio silence of a car ride to picture every scenario, prepare for any shock. He trained his second son to do the same. Sullivan did this diligently at first: would it be a house, or an apartment building? Would the street door be locked? What if there was no one home? Would he get out of the car if there was a gauntlet of questionable characters between him and the front door? It didn't matter how many situations Sullivan could conjure, because he found circumstances he didn't expect and wasn't prepared for.

He pulled up to a former nurse's house on a hushed cul de sac. The screen door was swinging lightly in the breeze. The inside door was yawning open. A sprinkler lazily swept the front yard. Sullivan approached the doorway. He yelled, "Hello!" No one came out. He pushed the doorbell. The chimes were answered by silence. Sullivan hollered, "Anyone home?" He thought about going in, leaving a card and locking the door. He was considering whether to call the police, when a family of five glided up on bikes.

He recognized them, having scattered their outing on his winding drive into the subdivision. He had startled them coming out of a curve. They split apart to both sides of the empty street, straddling their bikes until he passed.

The mother braked closest. She had short blond hair, a narrow face and no-nonsense glasses. She eyed the open door and glanced at Sullivan standing beside it. She turned her head, "Hunter?" Feeling exposed by the opening, Sullivan descended the stairs and dodged the sprinkler to greet her.

"Hunter! "Weren't you the last one out?" A young boy with a sun bleached crew cut, emerged from the carrier hitched to the back of his dad's bike. Wearing a slight hangdog look, he ran to his mother and hugged her leg.

Sullivan grinned down at him and tried to keep a hint of that grin, when he faced her. "I'm Mike Sullivan," he put out his hand but she didn't take it. "I'm representing Stewart Memorial" - She finished his sentence, "Felipe Carrera." Sullivan glanced down at his script. "You were his mother's primary care nurse" – Her eyes welled up and were starting to spill. She bent down to peel Hunter's fingers from her legs.

"Obviously you remember this case," Sullivan began, "We need to speak with all the nurses" –

"He wanted to keep his C-Section's down," her chin trembled, "So his insurance premiums wouldn't - I need something to drink. Mr. Sullivan, would you like some ice tea?" She retreated to the house.

Her husband strode to the side of the house to turn off the hose, trailed by two daughters. The girls sent questioning glances Sullivan's way, while the husband ignored him. The nurse returned with two plastic tumblers and a glass pitcher of what she called sun tea. Sullivan took a sour sip.

She unfolded two green plastic lawn chairs and set them opposite, in front of her garden. As he eased into his chair, Sullivan discovered his zipper was wide open. He reddened, realizing a subtle tug wouldn't do.

"Is everything –are you alright, do you like the tea?" Sullivan clutched the file to his lap and admired the garden. She spoke of azaleas and zucchinis, while Sullivan weighed alternatives.

To close the white gap, Sullivan would have to stand up, turn keeping the file at waist-level, and show his back to her. There would still be an obvious yank.

Sullivan spread his file and pulled out a pad. He didn't have to ask his first question. "The baby was in a bad position. He was having decelerations." Her words came quickly. A tear crept into the corner of her right eye. Sullivan waited for the waterfall. It didn't come. "Did you call?" – "I called him four times in less than twenty minutes. I told him, 'We've got persistent decels – you've got to get here right now.'

"He came in a suit, smelling a little like red wine." Returning Sullivan's startled look, "He was OK," – She rubbed her right eye behind her glasses, but it only caused more tears to form, "He took charge."

"I'm sorry" – Sullivan intoned, as Janine Connor, RN slumped back in her chair. "This is what I do for a living. I bring up the worst moments in people's lives and ask them to describe them in slow motion. I serve them with divorce papers and foreclosures, sometimes at the same time." He leaned forward, "I wish I didn't have to do this to you."

There was a quaver in her tone when she started, "He reached in, to change the baby's position. Otherwise, he was coming feet first. The baby went into distress. The cord was compressed. We had the operating room ready but he" she sipped in silence. Her shoulders quivered.

"What was the delivery like?"

"He came down butt first but his shoulder got stuck. We were all screaming," She sat forward in the plastic chair, her right hand clenched, "Break it, break it, break his shoulder.' She broke into a soft sob. "He had to do it – he wasn't breathing. He came out – the first two APGAR scores were straight zeros, the third was a three. He was limp and blue. We suctioned him and rushed him to Neonatal ICU."

She inched closer, tipping the chair forward. "I quit nursing on the spot." As she said it, she thrust her right fist downward. She would later repeat this gesture from the witness stand. It was a pantomime of throwing her glove down on the floor of the birth center. The jury was moved to dismiss her and her fellow nurses from the lawsuit. But they brought in a big verdict against the obstetrician.

She slid back and the chair righted itself. "I moved to Arizona – my sister has a dress shop there and I got a job at a container store."

After a thoughtful silence, she continued, "But I missed my family and the seasons, so I came back here." She said this, on a summer evening as agreeable as a Chicago evening could be.

The glass door slammed, the inquisitive daughters could wait no longer. Hunter raced past them and tumbled back to his mom. He grabbed her right arm forcing her red-rimmed eyes to focus on the spot where he would show off somersaults and semi-cartwheels.

As the husband strode up, his girls trailing, Sullivan briefly turned his back, before extending his hand.

As Sullivan headed home, he became lost in a reverie about his parents. They had a mixed marriage in every respect. Beatrice had grown up in a lakefront mansion. She rode horses and got golf lessons from the Scottish pro at their country club. She was not only lace-curtain Irish, her family's roots were on the South Side. In Chicago, the West Side Irish and the South Side Irish were two distinct tribes.

Frank Sullivan's family were West Siders. They would have been considered shanty Irish in comparison to Beatrice's clan. Frank grew up in a ramshackle gray frame that had once been a stagecoach stop. His father, Cornelius, was in the beer delivery business and he put his sons, Frank and Jack, to work at an early age. Working on a beer truck led to Frank sampling suds when he was 11. He immediately liked it.

Frank met Beatrice on a blind date. They had been fixed up by friends. The sheltered girl from the North Shore liked the rough-and-tumble of Mike and his friends, who hung out at West Side bars. Frank was handsome and could charm any room he entered. The first time he kissed her, she blurted out that she loved him.

Beatrice was fun and carefree at first but she became distraught over Frank's drinking. He would stay drunk for days and miss work. He once told Mike that his goal was to stay drunk the rest of his life. However, no matter how long he drank, he eventually sobered up. He worked as an insurance investigator and told Mike of scary times on business trips. He would wake up in a hotel, in the *wrong* city with all of his money gone.

Beatrice finally had enough. She did a one-person intervention, confronting Frank at work and making his boss aware of the problem. The boss warned Frank that if he took another drink, he would be fired. He also told him his paycheck was going directly to Beatrice. Frank joined AA and never had another drink. He even helped his old drinking buddies recover, with varying results.

Of course, Frank didn't need alcohol to occasionally do crazy things but there was an armistice declared in their marriage. As peace reigned, they had three children, Patrick, Mike and Clare. Patrick was five years older than Mike but never assumed the mantle of big brother. He treated Mike with indifference. Mike literally had to fight to get his attention. His earliest childhood memory was punching his brother in the mouth.

This roused Patrick into one-sided fights that Mike always managed to lose. Patrick was tall and more athletic than Mike. He starred on his Little League team and was popular at school. Even at an early age, he held a mysterious attraction for girls. The brothers could never overcome their age difference and Patrick seldom tried.

Frank and Beatrice treated their oldest like a prince and Patrick felt a sense of entitlement. He was a bit arrogant but his friends forgave him, because no one made them laugh like Pat. Clare, on the other hand, was sweet and shy. She looked up to Mike. At first, he treated her, like he'd been treated, never giving her the attention she craved. They later became close.

Sullivan was learning multiplication tables, when his dad suddenly quit his insurance job to launch a detective agency. Up until then, Sullivan and his siblings had been having full plates at dinner. They would continue to have full plates but only after charging groceries under glaring eyes at the corner Certified.

One by one, as soon as they were old enough, the Sullivan kids were pressed into service at the agency. Dad would thump thick hospital charts down on Sullivan's desk with the task of numbering the pages. It numbed his mind and made his arm ache. Seven year-old Clare addressed the envelopes containing past-due invoices. Beatrice insisted she squiggle "please" on each one. They looked like letters to Santa.

The Sullivan children grew to resent the agency. The dips and turns of its finances filled their lives with uncertainty. It was far from poverty but it was uneasy: not knowing if they'd go on vacation, buy a new school uniform, or patch the old one, play Little League, or go on the school trip, if their father didn't come out of the post office with a check.

They were tormented by his smoky cluttered office, surrounded by battleship gray desks and towering gray file cabinets. Patrick resented the agency even more than his siblings. He was educated at elite Jesuit schools and looked down on detective work. But, during his brief tenure at the company, working summers during his college years, he taught Mike an invaluable lesson. Frank Sullivan had sent his two sons downtown to the courthouse to request some court records.

Patrick may have been arrogant at home but he practically prostrated himself before these public servants. They were the gatekeepers to the records and they knew it. They were experts at idling at their desks, avoiding eye contact with customers. Patrick's voice was almost a whisper, as he humbly requested the files. It worked. The clerks were able to lord it over the college kid, so they reluctantly responded to his requests. Mike Sullivan would use this servile persona to finesse bureaucrats in the future. He could get past their initial "no" and walk out with the records he needed.

During his senior year, Patrick dated a blue-blooded girl from the North Shore. After they graduated, he married her. Carolyn's parents bankrolled their new son-in-law into a seat at the Board of Trade. He traded pork bellies and other commodities. The job appealed to his gambling nature. He also liked the short hours. This allowed him plenty of time to carouse when he got off work. He was relieved he never had to work again at Sullivan Investigations.

For Clare, working there was not even an option. There were limitations on what a female could do in those days – detective work wasn't a possibility. Her parents later steered her into nursing: a steady profession that would be conducive to raising children. All through her school years and beyond, she remained close with Mike.

Like Patrick, Mike had vowed he'd never work at the family company. After high school, he worked mailrooms, landscaped trees and pushed cabs through the snowy streets of Chicago: Before reluctantly asking permission to come aboard the storm-tossed ship.

At first, Sullivan felt like a deckhand. His father gave him the most tedious duties. His first project was to compile a topical index of all their medical cases. It was as mind-numbing as numbering hospital charts. After summarizing hundreds of files, Sullivan's index showed that 90% were the fall-out-of-bed category. While his dad kept him from being underfoot with make-work projects. Sullivan hungered to get his own cases.

At the time, they had seven full-time investigators and two secretaries churning out reports. They all seemed much older than Sullivan. The few times he went to lunch with his dad and cronies the two topics were the Great Depression and World War II. Frank had a habit of hiring workers from his AA group. No matter how shaky their sobriety was, he would give them a chance. A few of them worked out. Some would disappear with the files, and Frank would have to track them down.

Every morning, Frank would arrive at the office in his three-piece suit. He would have his "shit-finder" turned up full blast. He'd seek the most unpleasant task they had to perform and tackle it right away. It would make the rest of work day relatively pleasant. Mike Sullivan copied this work model, when he took over.

Gradually, he was given more responsibility. He picked up new assignments at law offices – asking permission to review the attorney's file to make sure he had every bit of personal data, not leaving out tattoos and gang affiliations. He drove long distances to pick up police reports and medical records.

During these carefree journeys, Sullivan reveled in his new career. There was no pressure, no manual labor, no repetitive, soul-deadening routine. He gorged on music for hours, interrupted by a few minutes of concentration when he reached his destination. He got lost a few times. His father had no patience with that, "We can't *charge* for being lost."

Slowly he moved up to getting an insignificant piece of an assignment. His dad would give him multiple avenues to explore – they would all lead to dead-ends – and his father would try one thing and find the witness. It never failed. Once, when Sullivan had exhausted all his leads, his dad called a country club in Pennsylvania on a hunch. The witness was lunching in the clubhouse. It dawned on Sullivan that his dad was using him to build up the bill, while he grabbed the glory.

After two years, Sullivan's dad trusted him with his own assignments. They were routine matters mostly: Delivering a subpoena to Chicago Police headquarters, or serving summonses on businesses that failed to pay their bills.

Sullivan was 24. He tried to maintain a smooth manner but hid a volcanic temper he had inherited from his father – a man who boxed in high school and could dish it out at home. He chased Sullivan up the stairs with a fist one time but had enough composure to open his hand before delivering.

Sullivan had his share of scrapes in school. He often sought them out. He had so much anger boiling up from the chaos at home; he took it out on his grade school classmates. Though he always ranked smallest in the class – shorter than the shortest girl – Sullivan thought he could take anyone in an unfair fight.

He used a variety of choke-holds and headlocks to subdue bigger opponents. One time he was caught fighting on the playground by the bald fire-breathing gym teacher. He ordered the combatants into the gym and made them put on boxing gloves. His opponent was a kid Sullivan could easily defeat on the street. But with the gym teacher calling fouls, Sullivan was pummeled and lost on points.

In his early twenties, his temper was still drawing him into fights. He had the task to serve a summons on a company that had failed to pay their shipping bills. Sullivan picked up the summons from a firm that strictly dealt with maritime cases. Heavy-framed paintings of frigates slicing through waves covered their walls. The defendant company had been named Indian International but had recently changed it to International Export.

Sullivan pulled up to a characterless commercial building on Clark Street. The papers he carried bore the name of the old company. He was admitted into a warehouse and ushered to the boss' office. He waited. An Indian-American man, wearing a brown suit and built like a fire plug entered the office. Sullivan told him he had papers for Indian International.

The man said, "No, no, no – that company doesn't exist."

"I don't care about the name – aren't you Ramesh Bala?"

"Yes, but that is not my company any longer. My company is" –

"Yeah, I know" - Sullivan said, his voice rising – "But changing your name doesn't get you out of owing" –

"Please leave my office," the man commanded and he bumped Sullivan with his belly. Sullivan's anger simmered. He thrust the summons at the man. "This is for you." The man held his arms behind his back, so Sullivan shoved it into the pocket of his suit coat.

As he turned to leave, Sullivan was blindsided when Bala stuck them into *his* jacket. Sullivan hadn't played this game before, though he would learn it well. He pulled the papers from his pocket and tried to – the man bumped him again.

Standing belly-to-belly, Sullivan and Bala started pushing – Sullivan knew a fight would follow and thought he'd have no problem taking the fire plug. Suddenly, he was surrounded by ten or so employees who towered over him in a semi-circle.

"Are you messing with our boss?" The biggest one spat out.

"No," Sullivan said, backing away – "I'm just delivering some papers."

"Well, he doesn't want your papers," the tall man said tersely through clenched teeth, "Why don't you run along?"

His dad had taught him – no matter how threatening the situation – not to get back in the car with the papers.

"OK, OK – I'm leaving," Sullivan said as he headed toward the door. When he was a few feet from freedom, he flung the summons down on the cement floor. Bala and his employees lunged for him. One grabbed his right arm – tearing his sleeve and gouging nails into his skin. Sullivan used all the strength in his left arm to yank open the street door. Pulling his right arm loose, he staggered to the sidewalk. He was soon joined by the fireplug, also panting.

Sullivan cupped his hands and called out in a loud voice to no one in particular. "Can someone please call the police?" He repeated it three times. Bala was bent over huffing next to him, clenching the crumpled summons in his left hand. A 30'ish male, looked like a drifter, stopped to say, "I don't know what your problem is but the police are on their way." Another male stranger paused – eyed Bala holding the papers – "Man, you are served." Sullivan started to feel a little better – though blood was soaking his right sleeve.

A squad cruised slowly past – Sullivan lunged to wave it down – Bala pulled Sullivan's arm down with a surprisingly strong grip and the squad continued south. They were both breathing hard again and Sullivan – if only Bala didn't have that crew inside – His hands clenched anyway.

An unmarked car sped to a stop and parked the wrong way. A grizzled plainclothesman waved them over. "What's going on?" he asked laconically. Sullivan's indignation was overwhelming but he moderated his voice. "I'm a process server –I was delivering a summons – this guy won't let me go."

The detective looked Sullivan up and down, ripped shirt and all – he pointed a finger at him – "You – can go." His finger moved to Bala, "You - have to stay."

CHAPTER 6

The morning after interviewing Nurse Connor, Sullivan woke to bright sun assaulting his eyes. He had been dreaming of mopping an endless hospital hallway. He was swishing the mop across a red puddle that kept spreading. Startled awake – he heard only silence downstairs. Ann had left for work and Flynn must have caught the school bus. He stared at the digital clock – 9:17.

Sullivan threw off the sheet and navigated the stairs, unsteady with sleep. The coffee pot had gone cold. He flicked it on and started the shower. He was meeting Charly at the office at 10:15 to go over the Trident Chemical case.

He had long ago learned the detective business wasn't conducive to early rising but it seemed like, after his dad died, his starting time had gotten later.

On his way to his 500 square-foot world headquarters, Sullivan stopped at the post office. He turned his key and swung the metal door open but the box was empty. A prominent sign claimed that box mail was up by 10:00 AM. Sullivan never believed it.

When it was his turn at the window, he asked if the box mail had been sorted. The clerk with the white pancake make-up and smeared on eyebrows said she had only finished the flats. Before Sullivan could ask, she huffily closed her window and retreated to the rear. She returned extending a thin envelope that looked like it might contain a check. After he ripped it open, Sullivan saw that endorsing the $5,000 check would make him liable for a high interest loan. He decided to keep it.

He parked behind a tired building that faced the West Side "L." Every train that sparked by shook his office, rattling the windows. A number of small businesses clung to life inside its tiny offices. There was a life insurance salesman; a company that sold hotel furniture and – he wasn't sure what Philip Statebridge did, but just before he was evicted, Sullivan spotted him lugging a mattress into his office.

Just the other side of Sullivan's wall, an artist rented a small studio. Sullivan sometimes bumped into a kimono-clad model coming or going from the lady's room. There were afternoons when he and Charly heard audible proof there was more than brushwork going on.

The first floor was filled by a very upscale clothing shop, operated by an elegant couple that pulled up each morning in a Jaguar. Sullivan rarely saw a customer inside. The refined, well-tailored man who ran the place claimed they sold most of their clothes on-line.

After climbing the fire escape, Sullivan turned the key and almost bumped into the seller of nightstands topped by Formica masquerading as mahogany. He was heavy-set, had a white brush cut and moved stiffly. Sullivan had been saying good morning to him for three years now and all he got back was a cool stare over reading glasses.

Sullivan's office was stuffy with summer heat. He pressed the remote control for the window unit – got a kick out of it every time - and left the fluorescent fixture off. A two-car "L" clanked by. Sullivan thought he'd get used to it but the longer he stayed, the more he felt like he was working in a train yard.

He hit the button for the answering machine. Sullivan had kept the push button phones and the old-fashioned answering machine that had been cutting-edge when he bought it. A robotic woman's voice, "If this is accounts payable, we have an urgent message from Citicard. Our records" – Sullivan erased it. The second call was from a paralegal. He was being appointed by the court as a special process server and she needed his detective license number.

His license had cost him a good deal of money. He had paid a boyhood friend $10,000 just for the privilege of "working under" his license for three years. The only meetings they had were at weddings, wakes and birthday parties. He had spent another $500 on a seminar, after he narrowly missed passing the private detective test the first time. There was a hefty state fee and he was required to buy $1 million in insurance from the only company that offered it.

Sullivan had noticed the license application contained a box for child support. The State assumed that if you were a PD, you were at least separated. His fellow test-takers assembled at the ballroom of a suburban hotel. It looked like the racetrack crowd: Large bellies, advancing foreheads, baseball caps.

Sullivan considered himself an exception to these retired cops, along with his boyhood friend, Jake Houlihan, who sat beside him. He had worked under Jake's license and they took the seminar together. They quizzed each other on the drive to the ballroom. They knew that if they found an anonymous corpse in a forest, they should go with dental records over fingerprints. They memorized how many minutes they could carry a gun on an assignment. It was common sense that the lowest point of a fire was its origin. The two pals, who first met at four, playing running bases in the dusk of a backyard party, got 90% of the questions right.

After the test, they celebrated in a pub called Durty Nellie's. The seminar teacher had promised a $500 refund for graduates supplying Q&A. They wrote down all the questions – the right answers as well as the three wrong choices. They phoned them into the seminar teacher. He rejoiced at their recall but never did return their tuition.

A few days later, Sullivan had a large expanse of glass-sheathed desk between him and the only agent that handled PI insurance. He was large and gruff but immaculately dressed. "What are the other guys like?" Sullivan began. The agent looked at him gravely and said, "Most of my clients cannot complete the application."

After all that hassle, no one ever asked to see his license. Not one of the strangers he startled from sleep. He wasn't asked to show it when he was being deposed or cross-examined in front of a jury. It was just as well. The small blue square was about as impressive as the "birth certificates" that come with stuffed animals.

The third message – he had to listen to it twice. "Mr. Sullivan – this is Morgan – I met you at Delaney's – you said I should call – I'm trying to see if you can help – you said something about a new job." She left her number. It matched the one on his caller ID, " Manuel Medeiros."

At 10:30, he heard the fire escape door slam and hurried footsteps across the atrium. Charly banged the door open. She was texting on her phone, while sipping iced coffee. When she finally looked up, Sullivan asked her when she would be finished opening the Trident Chemical file. She had spent two weeks sorting a mammoth stack of reports and witness interviews into individual folders.

She set her shoulder bag down on the sleek second-hand wooden sectional Sullivan had gotten dirt cheap. He sat down behind his dad's desk built of indestructible gray metal. "I'm almost finished," she answered confidently– "I just have to make folders for the other – aren't we going to check newspapers and court files?"

"Yeah, we need to cover everything – water source, chemical releases, air quality reports. You know the drill."

Charly sighed – "No – we haven't done anything like this before."

"That's why we need it organized – it's like that case where we had the five hundred summonses for people who were stealing cable - remember the spreadsheet you set up?" Sullivan knew he had touched a special place in her heart. Charly had thrived on that project. Putting things in their proper place was her passion.

"I'm going to bill out the Kobiski case. What are you up to?"

"Marvin Frye is supposed to appear in Room 1005 at the Daley Center at one o'clock for his latest controlled substance case. I thought I'd take the "L" down and" –

"Oh, the Dobbins file." Sullivan got up and grabbed an outline of generic accident questions. He had composed similar protocols for finding witnesses, serving papers and reviewing court files – none of his investigators followed them as completely as Sullivan but Charly came closest.

"Here – I'll give you the accident report, too."

The landline rang again. He saw it was "Medeiros." "Sullivan speaking," he said mechanically, "Could you hold on a second?" After hitting the hold button, he asked Charly, "Could you run to the bakery and get me a cup of chicken soup and a Diet Coke?"

Charly was accustomed to late-morning requests for "emergency soup" on days when Sullivan missed breakfast. "What kind of bread do you want?"

"Cinnamon Paradise – but you can have it."

After she left with his ten spot, Sullivan reached to answer the call but the light had stopped blinking. He called back, a woman with a soft accent and elegant manners, said she would tell Morgan he was on the line.

"Mr. Sullivan," she began breathlessly, "Sorry, but my dog was barking and I had to let him out."

"That's OK. You didn't waste any time. That restaurant" –

"I don't work there anymore," she interjected.

"You quit a job in this economy?"

"No – I was fired. After you left, I had a customer order a patty melt, with no cheese or onions. I told the cook three times – but when I was walking it to the table, I could smell onions. The guy had a fit. I offered to scrape off the cheese and everything – he started yelling that I was a stupid" Morgan couldn't bring herself to say it, "C-word."

"Was it cheesehead, or something worse?"

There was a tremor in her throat – "I told him he couldn't talk like that to me. The manager came running over but before he got there" – she stopped.

"Don't tell me you threw water in his face?"

"Worse. He was shoving the patty melt at me and I knocked it out of his hand. It landed on his lap – he got up screaming like he'd been burned or something." There was silence. "I didn't work there long enough to collect unemployment. So, I thought about what you said."

"You know, Morgan. This might be your lucky day. You wouldn't happen to know anything about soil conservation, water reclamation - air quality tests?"

"I did an internship for Bureau County, in my junior year – it didn't have anything to do with air – I was taking soil core samples and, you know, plant samples – it was for an anti-erosion project."

"Well, me and Charly – she's my assistant – we've got a big pollution case. We could really use some help on the technical stuff. It might be just a one-shot deal for you – but" – Charly came through the door, bearing a brown bag and a glistening can of Coke.

"What's your schedule like today," Sullivan asked Morgan.

Charly eyed him strangely, as she set down the bag and pulled out the round white cardboard container of soup, "Who is it?" she whispered. As he pressed his hand over the phone, he couldn't hear Morgan's muffled reply. "Someone I met yesterday – she can help with the Trident case."

Sullivan got the fish-eye again.

"I'm sorry, Morgan, what was that?"

"Where's your office?" Sullivan told her and she said she'd be there in an hour. He hung up.

"Morgan?" Charly asked – "If this is another of your charity cases like – what was her name?"

"You mean, Isabel?"

"Yeah, you always had to buy her lunch – she never did give us our camera back."

Sullivan recalled the thin nervous blond, who gulped down food at every opportunity. Turned out to be a heroin addict.

"I just don't think we can afford" – Charly began, "I'm sorry, - maybe you should check with your wife - she's the bookkeeper."

"You're right," Sullivan said, removing the lid and dipping a white plastic spoon into the still-steaming broth, "We can't afford her unless she can really help us. She'll be here in an hour."

Sullivan spent the interval using two index fingers to type up the Kobiski report and invoice, while Charly wrangled sheaves of Trident material into folders. He had classic rock on the radio, which she drowned-out with techno from her ear buds.

Sullivan's reports were typically two to three pages, composed in the most stilted business-ese. They were full of "proceededs" and "obtaineds." When they were first married, he read one to Ann but never tried it again.

On the invoice, Sullivan charged a lump sum of 2 ½ hours and 48 miles for his encounter with Kobiski. He would prefer to itemize but that only gave adjusters an opening to nickel and dime.

The land-line rang again – "Mr. Sullivan – I'm sorry but did you say" –

"Where are you?"

"I just got off the "L" at Harlem."

"You know, Morgan, the first test is finding the office and you're not doing very well."

He gave her walking directions and she was knocking within five minutes. Charly kept her head down, while Sullivan let her in. Her brown hair was pulled back; she was wearing minimal make-up and a navy-blue pinstriped suit. It looked like something an MBA would wear for their first post-college interview. The material was anything but summery.

"We're very informal, here," Sullivan said, "You can take off your jacket, if you want."

"No, I'll" – She walked over to Charly with a big smile, "Hi, I'm Morgan." Sullivan grabbed a folding chair from the cramped closet and sat it facing his desk. Charly accepted her hand without warmth but couldn't help saying she liked her boots.

Morgan perched on the edge of the chair and glanced at the unpromising surroundings – the only decorations on the walls were a White Sox calendar and a tired watercolor of the brokerage floor at Lloyd's of London. There was also a lurching clock, the second hand powered by an AA battery.

Sullivan started to tell her about the case, while Charly excused herself for a cigarette. He told Morgan it was the biggest high-stakes investigation they had ever handled. They could prevent a potential billion dollar payout. It was an audition for future pollution cases. It was unknown territory but he was anxious to do it right.

His cell phone rang – "Mr. Sullivan, this is Crystal, Mr. Romano's paralegal – I called earlier – I need your license number."

"Sorry, I was just going," he stood up tugging his wallet from his back pocket, "To call you" he paused, – "It's 116-440148." She repeated it back.

"The summons will be ready this afternoon – you can pick it up, or I can messenger it – the statute is going to run and Mr. Romano needs it served as soon as possible."

"We'll pick it up."

"I have to get it stamped first. It'll be at the front desk at 2:00."

Charly came in slipping her cigarettes into her purse. Morgan sat in the folding chair, very eager.

It was almost noon but Sullivan was too satisfied from soup to consider lunch. "I've got an idea," he said and both women looked at him. "Morgan, why don't you drop off Charly at the courthouse and wait while she interviews Frye. Afterwards, the two of you can pick up the summons – Charly can run in."

The fresh acquaintances exchanged glances. "It'll be fine. Charly you can tell her about Trident in the car. I'll work on the file until you get back."

Charly seemed especially dissatisfied with the arrangement. "My car's a mess. There's no room for her to sit."

Sullivan tossed her his keys. "Take mine. It's in back."

He had often dealt with investigators looking for excuses not to leave. "Hey, if you're hungry," Sullivan offered, "Maybe you can eat Subway or something, on the way down."

Again, they locked eyes. "I always get the veggie," Morgan said with something approaching anticipation. "Subway's OK with me," Charly murmured.

After they left, Sullivan sat down with the Trident file for the first time. He had been shocked to get such a big case. It had started with an e-mail from a lawyer he knew, Janet Sterling.

She was a member of a defense team with a roster of eighteen top firms. The Dream Team was put together by a group of insurance companies, fighting a far-reaching lawsuit by a giant chemical company. Trident had acquired a firm called Universal Bauxite. It had working mines in the western US. It also had a small subsidiary in a Chicago suburb.

The cancer rate in the residential area surrounding the plant was four times the national average. The formerly rustic community of Maple Grove banded together to demand Trident clean up the plant. Instead of paying millions to have the waste removed by railroad, Trident filed a claim against it's insurers to fund the clean-up.

To defeat this lawsuit, the insurance companies had to prove that Trident and, by extension, Universal Bauxite, had knowledge of a pollution problem, prior to purchasing the insurance coverage. They had to show Trident was a company buying health insurance, without disclosing cancer.

Janet's e-mail indicated she had recommended Sullivan for the job, (He scribbled on a post-it to buy her theater tickets), and they were scheduled to have lunch with the head of the team – Evan Meriwether, of Meriwether, Price and Morningstar. Janet, apologizing for the short notice, said the lunch was scheduled for the next day at noon.

Before replying to the e-mail, Sullivan called Ann. "I've got a big meeting tomorrow, what should I wear?"

"What is it?"

"It's a huge pollution case – it could take months."

"Where's the meeting?"

"We're having lunch on the top floor of the Prudential Building. I'm meeting one of the biggest defense lawyers – this could lead to a lot of work."

"There's no way you can wear the brown suit," referring to Sullivan's earth tone uniform for wakes, funerals and weddings.

"I'll buy a new one."

"Where," she demanded, "You can't get a suit in one day."

"The shop downstairs." Sullivan was dedicated to stimulating the economy in his building. He bought whole life from the guy two doors down and an oversized dresser from buzz cut.

"That – are you kidding, they're so expensive."

After he assured he wouldn't spend more than three-hundred, he descended the stairs to the shop for the first time. The owners were surprised but pleased. They catered mostly to African-Americans. Sullivan said he didn't care about style, as long as he could get a suit quickly.

After measuring him as a 34, they showed him exactly three suits in his size. Sullivan had long lived with this lack of selection. One was white with tails, another had prominent black checks, the third was a navy blue double-breasted with gold buttons. He tried it on. The trousers weren't hemmed and impossibly long. The jacket needed to be taken-in at the shoulders, the sleeves covered his fingertips.

"We don't do alterations," the man explained, "But there's a shop – we have a special deal - it's only a block away."

"I'm going to need a shirt and tie,"

They showed him a dazzling rainbow of shirts that required cuff links, which Sullivan didn't own. "What about white?" he asked. They nodded enthusiastically and, with the French-cuffed shirt, sold him the cheapest pair of cuff links they carried. For the tie, they took him to the cotillion section. They recommended one with navy blue piano keys. Sullivan had never seen anything like it. Sliding the knot up, he felt like Duke Ellington.

He hurried to the tailor shop, with white wax marks on the pants and coat. He said he needed it by the next morning. The Ukrainian woman, speaking through straight pins, said it would be twenty dollars extra. Sullivan didn't argue. The whole thing came to $363.00, almost within his wife's budget.

The next morning, Sullivan picked up the suit from Olya's European Design, got dressed in his office and came down to the shop to show it off. The owners asked if he could wear a sandwich board advertising their store.

After feeling overdressed while riding the "L," Sullivan met Janet and Meriwether in the lounge. She was drinking Merlot and his glass looked and smelled like scotch and water. Sullivan ordered a Pabst Blue Ribbon. He had learned through extensive research that watered-down American beer was all he could handle.

When the hostess called, they carried their drinks to a linen-covered table. Meriwether was pink-complexioned, with a white crew cut. He had been an Air Force general and a commercial pilot, before turning his attention to law. He said he only had a few years left of litigation before becoming a bush pilot in Alaska.

After a miniscule appetizer of scallops that Sullivan consumed in two forkfuls, the main course was served. The plate was adorned with a swirl of au gratin potatoes, lightly browned, an asparagus stalk and a cross-hatched cube of filet mignon about four inches tall. Sullivan skipped the asparagus and found the center of the steak redder than he liked. He concentrated on the potatoes.

After each of them had three sets of dinnerware removed, the waiter rolled the dessert cart up to their table. Sullivan lifted a slice of cheesecake – Meriwether stopped him. "Those are just samples. Do you want cheesecake?"

"Yes," Sullivan said, attempting to recover, "But I like mine with raspberries. Do you have any?"

The waiter said he would try but would strawberries be alright? Sullivan nodded. Sullivan rarely drank coffee after breakfast but stopped him and extended his cup. The waiter dutifully tipped the silver pitcher.

Meriwether handed Sullivan a three-ring binder. "These are witness reports. We hired a big firm in California. They sent two people on every interview."

His voice rose like it was *his* money, "They charged a minimum $1,500 for each witness."

Sullivan flipped through the folder while he listened. "Every time I called this place," Meriwether hunched forward, flexing his shoulders, "There was a new person in charge of the investigation. It was like reinventing the wheel over and over" – the waiter returned with the desserts – "And I hate reinventing the wheel."

"I talked to the defense team. I said we should go with a small outfit, with one person doing all the work: one person to call. Janet recommended you. Do you see the problem with these interviews, Mr. Sullivan?"

Sullivan hadn't the slightest sense of what he had skimmed but felt empowered by caffeine. He held up the binder. "This has been a horizontal investigation," he said with a little too much passion, "They only skimmed the surface. They talked to the guy, who knew the farmer, whose cows ran away from the creek. They never talked to the farmer."

Sullivan laid the binder down. "I'm not going horizontal. I'm going vertical. If a witness tells me something – I'll dig down until I find – I'll talk to the guy who had black stuff coming up in his basement. I'll find the farmer –"

"It's more than just toxic, Mike," Meriwether said, "A plane from the superconductor lab – they were flying over Fermi Lab to measure for radiation. Their needles jumped when they flew over Maple Grove."

"Evan, I didn't hear." – Janet exclaimed.

"We didn't want to disturb you on your vacation. After they landed, they drove to the property with the highest readings. It was, excuse my French, Janet, ball-level radiation coming up from the front lawn."

Sullivan was staggered. He had never been hired to uncover toxic pollution, let alone radiation – he had no idea where to start.

"I'll contact the Nuclear Regulatory Commission," Sullivan improvised, "They're bound to have reports.'

Meriwether pushed back from the table. "Our subpoenas to the NRC are coming back empty but," he extended his hand, "We'll give you a try,

Sullivan – Janet will serve as liaison between you and the defense group. Send your bills to her – we approve them at our monthly meetings.'

Sullivan thanked him for the lunch. As Janet brushed past, she murmured, "Love your tie."

During his reverie at the office, Sullivan had been admiring Charly's handiwork in separating the investigation into its essential elements. Then he held up her bill. 52 hours to open the file! The most they had ever charged was 15. Charly knew he needed a steady framework for making vertical drops.

It was after 3:00, when Charly walked into the office. "Where's Morgan?" he asked. "She said she had to cook lamb, or something, I dropped her off at the Red Line. Here's the summons." She handed over a blank white envelope. She dug in her shoulder bag and gave him his keys.

Sullivan pulled the summons out to study the address: Crete, IL – a long haul south. "So, what do you think of her?"

"She's whiny," Charly said, "She complained about her car payment, her health insurance, student loans." She set her bag down with emphasis. "I mean, she's living at home with her parents."

"I understand – do you think" –

"Sure, she knows everything about soil and aquifers – rock formations– she's got a freaking acrheology degree."

OK," Sullivan said with some firmness, "We'll have her – she can start with water reclamation. You can do all the court records and newspapers. I have to do the interviews myself. I'd rather have you there" – Sullivan had often told her that her presence gave him instant credibility – "Meriwether" –

"Yeah, I know," she said weary of discussing the case they had dissected to death, "But after this – doesn't she have something better to do, in Egypt?

Sullivan smiled, "You really can't stand her. How did it go with Frye?"

"He never showed. I talked to the lawyer he paid with his bond receipt. They met for the first time in the hallway before his plea hearing. The cell phone number he gave the lawyer has a full mailbox.

CHAPTER 7

Sullivan suddenly had to shift his focus from Trident and his other cases to work on a rush investigation. He purposely kept himself available for such emergencies. Some were assignments he had to complete the same day he received them. Once, a lawyer needed him to find a key witness for a case that was already on trial. Another lawyer urgently needed him to find his client and immediately bring her to the courtroom. "I can't defend an empty chair," the lawyer whined.

Sullivan had more than a day for this new assignment, but the trial was only a week away. The lawyers represented a company that manufactured charcoal fluid. A man claimed he was grilling burgers, when the flame climbed the stream of charcoal fuel from his grill to the plastic container he was squeezing. He claimed the container exploded. He was suing the manufacturer for severe pain, disfigurement, and the loss of his wife's affections.

The defense attorneys didn't take the claim seriously at first. They thought they could settle it for a nominal amount. But, due to his client's severe injuries, the plaintiff's attorney refused to settle. In the weeks leading up to the trial, the judge tried to coax the parties to reach a settlement. Judges avoided trials if they could, which is why only five-percent of lawsuits went to court in Cook County.

The manufacturer of the charcoal fluid had never lost a case of this kind, so they fought it. A high-powered firm hired Sullivan to dig up the two-year-old reports and interview witnesses. They also retained a team of fire scientists to test the victim's claim.

Sullivan broke the news to Morgan that she would be on her own with the Trident investigation. He had no need to bother Charly, who was vacationing in Michigan's Upper Peninsula. Besides, the urgency of the matter, Sullivan had other reasons to give the case his personal attention. He didn't want to expose Morgan or Charly to the crime-ridden neighborhood where the fire took place. They also lacked the unique relationship Sullivan had with the Chicago Fire Department.

His Uncle Jack, Frank Sullivan's brother, had been a legendary firefighter on the West Side. He was stationed at a firehouse, where his crew was known for its fearlessness. They were the quickest to arrive at a fire and the last ones to leave. Their bravery was partly due to their reputation for being the hardest-drinking company in the department.

Drinking on duty was common in those days. Some firehouses had vending machines with a separate slot for beer. Jack Sullivan was a heavy drinker, with leather lungs. His exploits at some of Chicago's deadliest fires were still talked about in firehouses. His name was still magic within the department. Sullivan had no difficulty in getting copies of the reports he needed.

The next step was to recreate the incident as accurately as possible. Sullivan hunted for a homemade grill fashioned from a sawed-in-half 50-gallon drum. He spotted them for sale in a dusty West Side lot, where members of an informal club rested on a rain spotted sofa. Sullivan negotiated to buy a grill with a hinged cover, for fifty bucks.

He drove it to a fire lab at a local university and watched scholars in spacesuits fire up the grill in mad scientist chaos. They squirted the thickest streams of charcoal fluid from all different angles and distances. The flames danced higher and higher above their white-hooded heads but they couldn't coax the fire to rise to their containers.

The lawyers needed more. Sullivan had to check the seedy stores in the victim's neighborhood: the kind that sell single cigarettes for a dollar, to see if they stocked their product. He found three that carried the Keystone brand. One of the shops was an easy stroll from the burned man's home.

When Sullivan showed the shopkeepers a pre-fire photo of the victim, they denied knowing the man, or whether he bought charcoal fluid.

Most notably, the lawyers asked Sullivan to interview the paramedic who wrote the ambulance report. Sullivan found some difficulties with this mission. CFD ambulances were constantly in service and rarely returned to the firehouse. It took him months to hand them subpoenas. More than a few times he pulled up to a firehouse just as the ambulance and engine went screaming out.

If he managed to grab a moment with a paramedic, they would rarely remember the call but always stood by their report. Even after Sullivan showed a report about a subway accident to its author, the paramedic couldn't remember it. "I must be doing this too long," he confessed, "I can't remember a guy cut in two by an L."

Sullivan obtained the work schedule of Paramedic Carlos Reyes and headed to his firehouse hoping he would be in. When Sullivan arrived at Engine 83 and Ambulance 15's house, the red and green lights indicating whether they were home were dark. As he drove slowly past the firehouse, hunting for a parking space, he saw a thick crowd hovering around something on the driveway.

Sullivan parked, grabbed the paramedic report and a yellow pad and walked back. The jostling crowd spilled into the street. He slid his way to the front and saw a man lying motionless facedown; his arms splayed toward the station's overhead doors, a wooden-handled kitchen knife sticking straight up from his upper back.

Sullivan edged toward the firehouse and quietly entered the side door. The garage area was empty of ambulance and engine but filled by the scent of cooking. Sullivan strode to the kitchen and saw a sauce pan of green beans boiling furiously. There were other dishes bubbling on the stove. Just as he turned down the flames, he heard the echoing of footsteps and voices in the empty firehouse.

He walked back to the bay and saw that part of the crowd had followed him through the side door. The visitors, thinking he was with the department, begged him to call an ambulance. Sullivan assured them the ambulance was on its way but they needed to get out of the firehouse immediately. They muttered while they shuffled out.

Sullivan grabbed the joker phone. As soon as he lifted it, he was connected with Central Alarm. "Cosgrove," was the tired response. "This is Mike Sullivan – I'm at" – he glanced at the paramedic report, "Ambulance 15. There's a man down on the driveway, stabbing victim. Needs an ambulance."

"Who *is* this?" the man snarled. "I'm not a fireman, I'm an investigator," Sullivan stammered, "There's a big crowd out front. The guy needs help."

"OK," Cosgrove growled, "But you shouldn't be using this phone." As Sullivan returned to the kitchen to retrieve his briefcase, he heard a siren. It was Ambulance 15 responding to a call in their own driveway.

The stabbing victim never moved as they shifted him onto a stretcher and shut the doors. They wailed away toward Covenant Hospital. An hour later, Paramedic Reyes returned from rushing the victim to the ER - another DOA. He joined Sullivan for a cup of strong coffee in the kitchen. Sullivan handed him his report but Reyes waved it away. He said he could never forget a man who was too lazy to buy charcoal fluid, and used clear liquid from an unmarked jar in the basement. The man wound up rolling in the dirt of his backyard.

The attorneys for Keystone had assumed the paramedic's statement would be favorable and had provided Sullivan with a trial subpoena. Sullivan pulled the subpoena from his briefcase. A $25.00 check was stapled to it.

Reyes pointed to the check. "What's this for?"

"It's to pay for your trip to and from," Sullivan explained.

The courts had established long ago that witnesses must be paid their expenses for traveling to testify. Unfortunately, the amount of the witness fee check had been fixed long ago and hadn't kept pace with inflation. Twenty-five bucks wouldn't cover a downtown parking space.

"As least this will get me off the street for the day," Reyes said, as he scanned the subpoena.

He gave Sullivan his home address and phone number and Sullivan offered to drive him to and from the trial.

"Then what am I supposed to do with this?" Reyes asked, waving the check.

"Buy your family a pizza," Sullivan said as he left.

The morning came to pick up Reyes for the trial. Sullivan drove to his South Side two-flat, where he lived with his wife and three kids. During the slog downtown, Sullivan went over the statement Reyes had given him. Sullivan also explained what Reyes could expect. He would first be questioned by the defense attorney, who would lead him through his report.

After Reyes finished his direct testimony, the lawyer for the victim would cross-examine him. He wouldn't be quite as friendly but the Keystone lawyers would object to any improper questions. He warned Reyes sidebars and recesses would drag out the proceedings. It was nothing like TV. Sullivan had asked Morgan to come to the courtroom to observe the proceedings. He wanted her to see the exacting standards for getting exhibits and testimony into evidence.

As the court convened, Sullivan was the only person sitting in the spectator section. Reyes had to wait in the hallway. Witnesses were barred from observing the proceedings, before taking the stand.

Sullivan could only see the victim's back, as he sat with his attorney. Three lawyers for Keystone sat at the defense table. They were well-tailored and well-groomed. The judge was a tiny woman with short gray hair. The heavy-set bailiff called the court to order, before returning to his newspaper.

Morgan rushed in. It was the first time Sullivan had seen her in high heels and she seemed a bit unsteady. She caused quite a stir. The jurors all turned their heads, like they were at a tennis match. She was wearing her navy-blue suit. Her hair was down and she was wearing a bit of makeup. The jurors found her striking. Even the bored bailiff looked up.

Morgan whispered, "Did I miss anything?"

Sullivan didn't want to risk a single word with Morgan. He shook his head. He secretly wished she hadn't sat next to him. She would be branded as partisan.

The burn victim was the first to take the stand. Sullivan had stomached interviewing victims with ghastly injuries but he couldn't look at him. Morgan stared with a mixture of sympathy and disbelief. Sullivan suspected the victim was melting her heart.

The plaintiff's attorney wore a rumpled suit and his hair was tousled. He asked questions scribbled on a legal pad and gently led his client through his testimony.

As the victim spoke, Sullivan continued to stare at the floor. Gradually, though, the victim's humanity emerged through his words. After twenty minutes of testimony, Sullivan could look at him, undisturbed by his scars.

Then the Keystone lawyers had their turn. Most of their questions concerned when and where the victim had purchased their product. The man gave vague answers and couldn't pinpoint the place or date he bought the lighter fluid.

After he left the stand, the judge ordered a 15-minute recess. As they left the courtroom, Sullivan introduced Morgan to Carlos Reyes. He he was staring down at his phone. Reyes was shorter than Sullivan but in much better shape.

After a few pleasantries with Reyes, Morgan couldn't contain herself. "You should have seen – oh this man –his story," Morgan burst out.

Sullivan sharply hushed her. Morgan was stung by his harsh tone.

"If a juror hears one word from us about the trial," Sullivan hissed, "They could call for a mistrial. Carlos can't talk about it."

Morgan wore her hurt look. Sullivan attempted to cheer her up by suggesting a sweet roll and coffee. Morgan claimed she wasn't hungry.

After being chastised, Morgan recovered by striking up a lively conversation with Reyes about a high school serve project she had gone on in Mexico. Like many males she met, Carlos was captivated by Morgan. He also needed to get his mind off the grim case.

After the recess, one of the fire experts took the stand. His testimony was full of statistics about the ignition temperatures of flammable liquids. Under direct questioning, the expert insisted the accident couldn't have happened the way the man described.

The plaintiff's lawyer asked the scientist some perfunctory questions about his credentials. He didn't want the jury to hear any more about the experiment they had conducted.

The victim's doctor was supposed to testify next about his injuries but he had been called away for an emergency. Following a sidebar, it was agreed that testimony from the doctor's evidence deposition could be read into the record. The judge asked for a volunteer reader and Morgan's hand shot up.

The plaintiff's lawyer objected. "She's obviously an associate of the defense team," he stated flatly. When Morgan wasn't picked, the jurors looked deflated. The bailiff was chosen to drone on through the doctor's testimony. The judge ordered an hour lunch break. Sullivan, Morgan and Reyes spent it at a sandwich shop.

When they returned, Reyes took the stand. One of the Keystone lawyers asked him to verify his report so it could be entered into evidence. While Reyes calmly recounted the incident, the jurors were engrossed.

Closing arguments were brief. The plaintiff's attorney paged through a large volume of Bartlett's Familiar Quotations. After finally finding his place, he read a quote about sharks from the island of Fiji. The jurors stared at him quizzically.

While the jury deliberated, the entire defense crew repaired to a nearby restaurant. Sullivan was starving and Morgan was excited about a wrap she ordered. Reyes only wanted coffee. The dishes arrived and they were all set to eat when word came the jury was back. The Keystone lawyers abruptly stood up. Sullivan was reluctant to leave his untouched steak.

After they reassembled in the courtroom, the jury was ushered in. The victim was staring at them intently but they didn't make eye contact. After the foremen handed him a small sheet of paper, the bailiff announced that all counts had been dismissed against Keystone. Sullivan was pleased but Morgan seemed stunned. He invited her to come with when he drove Reyes home.

In the car, Reyes resumed staring at his phone. Sullivan hoped Morgan would continue her banter with Carlos but she remained uncharacteristically quiet. She did give him a cheerful goodbye when they dropped him off.

Finally free to speak, Morgan began, "I can't believe it. After all that, he didn't get a dime?"

"He didn't deserve a dime," Sullivan replied.

"What do you care?" Morgan countered angrily, "You couldn't even look at him."

Sullivan steeled himself. Twice before, he had endured angry outbursts from investigators. He fired them both as soon as it was practical. He tersely explained to Morgan that a plaintiff couldn't recover damages, if they were more than 50% at fault. As far as he was concerned, the plaintiff was 100% at fault.

She remained sullen. "Didn't you see the pain in his eyes? Sure he made a mistake but no one deserves that."

"OK," Sullivan said resignedly, "I feel bad for the guy but it doesn't mean he deserves money. You have to learn not to care. This is business – there's no room for feelings. If I thought about these terrible cases - I'd drive myself crazy."

"Well, maybe you can do that – but I can't," she said stubbornly – "How can I see someone like that and not care?"

Sullivan suddenly remembered his first big investigation and how overwhelmed he was with emotion.

"Morgan the first big case I handled was a car fire. These two guys and a young woman were driving on Route 12, when they got rear-ended. The gas tank exploded. She was sitting in the back seat and her – I can always picture her blond hair was on fire. The accident happened right in front of a McDonald's. A couple of the counter guys grabbed a fire extinguisher and ran out. The guys in the front seat got out – but her seat belt was jammed. They somehow pulled her out through a passenger window. She survived. The teenagers who saved her – there's still a plaque on the wall of that McDonald's – they were honored for their courage."

"Why are you telling me this – is it supposed to make me feel better – now *I* can't stop thinking about her hair."

"I'm only telling you how exciting it was for me. There was drama and danger. I felt like a hero just for doing the investigation. But that was 10,000 cases ago. Now, I don't feel anything – even when with it's with kids. Believe me, you'll get to be the same way."

"Why did you yell at me in front of Carlos?" Morgan interjected, "I was so humiliated."

Sullivan didn't like her question. Morgan had a habit of overstepping her bounds. He thought of how his dad would handle her and chose to be magnanimous.

"That was my fault, Morgan. I should have explained to you ahead of time that we couldn't discuss the case. I should have told you not to sit with me – just think you could have been a star at your first trial –"

"What reading all that medical stuff?"

"The jury would have been riveted. Believe me, Morgan, you have that effect on people."

She allowed a slight smile, "A star. You always exaggerate." Her tension was gone from her voice. Sullivan hoped Morgan would toughen up but knew she never would. The next day, they returned to their routine and were surprised Charly had beat them to the office. She was reading over the Trident file.

"Didn't you guys do any work while I was gone?"

CHAPTER 8

Sullivan met with Charly the next morning - Day One of the Trident Chemical investigation. After walking over with the stack of folders and positioning them on the center of his desk, she flopped into her chair. Sullivan gazed up at a mountain of reading.

Charly said she was going downtown to start checking the archives for lawsuits filed against Universal Bauxite. Few official documents in Chicago survived the Great Fire, and court files were among the casualties. Charly would search forward from 1871, hoping to find cases against the company.

Meanwhile, Sullivan would bill out the Chakiris case. Charly was walking out just as Morgan arrived. They had a quick chat about an awards show being broadcast that night. Morgan cheerfully wished her luck at the courthouse.

She was wearing khaki Capri's, a red short-sleeved shirt, and sandals. Sullivan had a tie on. He needed a veneer of decency to get citizens of Maple Grove to open their doors. Morgan pulled a plastic container from her bag and crossed the grey carpet to place it inside Sullivan's dorm-sized refrigerator.

"Morgan, do you know how to type?"

"I was one of the fastest in my class," she replied rapidly, "I'm kind of dyslexic when it comes to spelling but -"

"Well, I read somewhere that most office work is at the fourth grade level. Besides, if you use all ten fingers, you're way ahead of me. I'll dictate – you'll see how I want the report and bill done."

Sullivan's dad taught him to lead with the Holy Grail he was attaching with the report, be it an affidavit, report or some actual physical evidence. He followed with a summary of the information gathered, with a third section bragging about how brilliant they had been. This would justify the bill. Sullivan thought his dad's reports wordy until he recognized the slivers of meaning he was conveying. He had to admit they were entertaining. They made him feel *he* detected leaves rustling in the backyard, and took a statement from a sweating man resting on a rake.

Morgan's fingers fluttered as Sullivan paced up and down his "cage," scanning his handwritten notes and pausing to summon a fresh phrase now and then. Morgan wasn't just a typist. She was like human software – stopping Sullivan in mid-sentence to correct his grammar, or offer a less-clumsy construction. Sullivan appreciated the help but suffered a déjà vu of getting "D's" in English.

When it came to the invoice, Sullivan had a loose formula for charging clients, not always accurately reflecting time, effort, and mileage. His minimum was two hours, with a half hour added for the report and bill. This covered the simple assignments. For more involved cases, that required two trips, he'd bill 4 1/2. From there he went up to 6 ½ and 8 ½, depending on the degree of difficulty.

Her first day at the keyboard, Morgan tried to break the pattern. "4 ½ hours," she cried, "are you joking? You went all the way out to his house, interviewed a neighbor and checked the post office. Then you spent over an hour at his dad's restaurant."

Sullivan answered hesitantly, "I can't bill for all that – Charly and I were having dinner."

"You're not charging enough," Morgan said firmly, "It should at least be seven hours."

Unaccustomed to being criticized by a newcomer to his office, Sullivan couldn't deny Morgan was right. "How about 6 ¾?"

"7 ¼," she countered, "Didn't you say you had a goal of at least a hundred hours a month?"

"OK – 7 ¼ hours – 75, no make it 74 miles." Crooked numbers sounded more authentic than round ones.

"Morgan," he said, attempting an authoritative tone, "I want you to check with the EPA and the state environmental department to see if they have any reports on the plant." She was busy printing the Chakiris report on heavy linen paper, "The next time I'm heading to Maple Grove, I'll drop you at the Du Page courthouse to check for lawsuits." She was stapling the invoice to the front.

"I thought that was Charly's - she was going to" –

"Charly could be downtown for the next three weeks," Sullivan continued, recalling a case where they had searched back a century for lawsuits against a gas company, "She has to go through the index on microfilm" –

"They still use microfilm?" Morgan asked wide-eyed.

Sullivan wasn't sure, "I mean – last time – that's what we had to do. Anyway, after she finds a case, she has to order it from the warehouse. It's a long process." Sullivan had done the gas company investigation himself. One afternoon, he found himself with a roll of microfilm wrapped around his neck manually trying to re-spool it. When a fellow researcher asked if he knew how to use the machine, Sullivan had to laugh.

He told Morgan that when she found cases against Universal Bauxite or Trident Chemical she should write down the court numbers and request the files from storage. He remembered getting calls from the Cook County archives telling him another box was in.

The cartons were filled with yellowed, brittle files from the nineteenth and early twentieth century folded inside letter-sized packets, tied with red ribbon: the origin of the phrase "red tape." When he opened the packets, the paper threatened to tear along the folds. The pleadings appeared to be written in quill – the penmanship was like calligraphy compared to modern scrawl.

A large percentage of the cases were for gas explosions that shattered houses and businesses. Sullivan became familiar with the language, which never failed to mention timbers falling on plaintiffs. The gas company's lawyers successfully defended the great majority of these suits – but had to make small settlements on the indefensible ones, like when a gas truck ran over somebody.

What finally made the whole thing delicious for Sullivan was that his starched underwear grandfather had been a partner in the firm winning most of the lawsuits. He finally one-upped this grandfather, who had once struck with a fist. Sullivan unearthed a case that negated the gas company's coverage from 1954 forward.

He told Morgan what to expect, if she actually found any ancient cases. She nodded. In her classes, they had often discussed the handling of delicate documents.

As he busied himself for his trip to Maple Grove, Sullivan made sure he had pens, paper, reading glasses, phone, and car keys, He vowed he wouldn't be like his dad and make two or three cameos to retrieve essential items, like the *file*. There was no way he could forget the Trident file. He had carried it down to his car in a copy paper carton.

When he was ready to leave, Morgan was at the computer, darting from webpage to webpage, scribbling down contacts. Sullivan interrupted to tell her to lock the office when she left. He opened the door, "Here, you push this in." He fingered a small button on the inside of the door. He promised to get her a key.

It was about three-o'clock, a perfect time to hit the expressway, before the afternoon – well "rush" hardly described it. Besides getting a jump on the homebound hordes, it was infinitely easier to find addresses in daylight. Sullivan wasn't averse to arriving early at a destination. If no one was home, a mall, bowling alley, or driving range would do, depending on the season. He'd browse bookstores for hours, feeling guilty when he walked out empty handed.

He once told Flynn they'd have to kill time in the mall before they watched an action movie on the big screen. Flynn turned slowly with a horrified look. "Kill time," he repeated with disgust.

"Time is life!" he retorted with as much spirit a seven year old can summon. Sullivan didn't have much of an answer. "I'm a private detective," he huffed, "I'm an expert at killing time."

Sullivan didn't think he'd have to squander this afternoon. He was confident of finding his witness home. He was a retired foreman who'd spent his formative years handling stuff Sullivan wouldn't touch in a space suit.

When he exited the interstate, Sullivan sped north on a county highway into Maple Grove. As the limit dropped to 30, Sullivan slid past modest frames spaced close together, strip malls with Laundromats, convenience stores, and tanning salons, interrupted by rows of empty storefronts advertising "For Rent."

Following protocol, Sullivan headed to the plant (in auto cases it was the accident scene) before interviewing the witness. He parked in the deserted employee lot, close to a complex of low brick buildings that once served as the plant's headquarters. The sprawling facility was surrounded by a forbidding fence topped with razor wire. Signs warned trespassers.

There were other signs affixed to the fence he had never encountered before. They were yellow, with a red border. In the center were three slices of what looked like red pie surrounding a red circle. At the top were the words, "Radiation Area" and at the bottom they said, "Keep Out." The only activity on the vast expanse of brown land was a lonely bulldozer scooping and dumping dirt on a growing ridge of rock-strewn waste.

He could have walked to the foreman's house from the plant but needed his car for calling on other witnesses. He slid to the curb in front of a green ranch. Sullivan saw that the house and grounds received painstaking attention. The lawn had been freshly mowed and edged. The evergreens sculpted. A woman in her 60's wearing a duster with a flowery print answered the door. Her eyes looked a little spooked behind wire spectacles.

Sullivan introduced himself and asked for Tom Schauer. She opened the glass door a quarter-way, her right arm tensed behind it. "He's out in the garage," she said unaccustomed to visits from out-of-towners, "Is this about the plant?"

"I'm working on behalf of the insurance companies for the plant," Sullivan explained –

"Oh, you mean, you're on our side."

"I don't" – Sullivan was puzzled.

"Didn't you see the signs?" she continued.

"The signs at the plant?" Sullivan asked disconcertingly.

"No," she stamped her slippered foot, "The skull – you know like the pirate flag -"

Sullivan had passed three lawns displaying the skull and crossbones on his way to the plant. The banners were identical and prominently featured "Trident" in a red slashed circle. He had stopped to write down the house numbers.

"Oh, yeah" – he didn't know what else to say.

Peeking to see if any neighbors were out, she stepped onto the slab that served as their front porch. "You know," she lectured him, "The plant's been good to this town. Half the men around here – they wouldn't have had jobs – I used to work there myself."

"Really?" Sullivan asked, "What did you do?"

"I worked in the office with the other girls," she snapped, to what she considered a stupid question, "There was nothing wrong with that place I could see – that's how I met Tom." Her face brightened.

"You're kidding," Sullivan said sustaining surprise. She didn't need the encouragement.

"I was in accounts payable – I heard over the PA that someone in shipping had been hurt. I was 19 – I thought the men were all older – they were so dirty when they came in for their checks, you could hardly tell. So, when we heard the announcement, Doris said, "Good for the son-of-a-bitch." I don't talk that way, but I said, "Yeah, good for the s.o.b.""

"So Tom – I didn't know his name then – walked in – he was filthy. He was holding his right hand up - the nurse had wrapped a brown bandage around it to stop the bleeding."

Forgetting her attire, she stepped out to wave to a couple coasting by in their Cadillac. She retreated to the shelter of the doorway. "He just looked like a lost puppy – and he wasn't *that* much older than me. He didn't ask for anything – but I got him a cup of water from the fountain, while he waited for the ambulance." A question crept into her eyes, "We could never figure why that water didn't get cold."

"How bad was he hurt?"

"He's still got the scar on the back of his hand but he was back at work the next day. He asked me out to see – oh, it was something with Jimmy Stewart – he was a bandleader, well," she sighed, "We bought this place – raised three kids. They just threw us a big party for our fiftieth - rented the country club." Sullivan congratulated her – "And we've got seven grandchildren, with another – let's see Mariah is due in December."

Sullivan suddenly remembered an official disclaimer he was supposed to recite before interviewing any former employee. "Mrs. Schauer, I have to tell you – I'm working for the company's insurance company – but we're adverse to Trident in this case."

"What does that mean?" she asked spooked again.

"I'm saying that the information you give me" – Sullivan was interrupted by a tall rawboned man who slowly sidled up to his wife. He was wiping oiled hands on a gray rag and glowering at Sullivan.

"Mr. Schauer – I was just telling Mrs. Schauer that I'm an investigator for Trident's insurance company." The tall man waved him into the house. Sullivan wiped his shoes carefully on the bristled mat before stepping onto the beige carpeting that bore fresh lines from the vacuum.

Mrs. Schauer scurried after her husband. "Tom – I was telling him" – She stopped and faced Sullivan, "Did you say you're *against* Trident?"

"Yes," Sullivan admitted, "We're usually on their side but – in this case" –

Tom Schauer grabbed a can of cheap beer from the fridge and ripped it open.

"We're trying to defend a claim. So, anything you tell me could" Sullivan had no choice but to continue – "Jeopardize your pensions."

The day Meriweather handed Sullivan a copy of the disclaimer he had to recite. The one they had hammered out with Trident's lawyers, he doubted a single witness would talk to him.

Schauer looked to be a shade above six-feet. His weathered features wore a scowl that had worked itself deep. The beer can seemed tiny in his heavily veined hand. "So," he said, taking a sip, "Who else have you talked to?"

Sullivan gave him a nervous smile, "You're my first."

Mrs. Schauer said she needed to get something from her sewing room.

"What does this have to do with my pension?"

Sullivan had been searching for an answer. "Well, if Trident loses the lawsuit – because of – you know what we find out – it could bring unfavorable publicity – maybe hurt their stock price. So, I mean, there's no direct connection – I'm just required to" –

The man set the can down, his eyes narrowed, "Mr. Sullivan, – what could be worse than the PR they're getting now?"

Mrs. Schauer huffed back into the kitchen stripping a rubber band off a large black and white photograph. "Mr. Sullivan, I just wanted to" – she unrolled the photo on the dinette table –"You see, there I am." It was a group shot of the plant employees – the year was written in the top right margin – she pointed to a petite woman in her 20's, in the middle of the second row. She was wearing a sundress, smiling stiffly against a forested backdrop.

"This was taken at our company picnic at – have you been to our Waterfall Glen Park? – Sullivan shook his head – "Oh, you have to see it."

"Do you mind?" he turned the photo over – written in rows were names corresponding to each smiling face.

"A lot of them are gone," she said softly, "There's five of us office girls - we still get together on the third Tuesday at the Mill Run Restaurant."

"So, what did you do at the plant, Mr. Schauer?"

"Worked in the shipping department for thirty-two years – ran it the last fifteen," he said curtly. "We unloaded bags of radioactive sand from Brazil – low-grade stuff. We used to sit on those bags when we were eating lunch. We shipped out rare earth metals they were using in color TVs. Nothing wrong with that stuff, either."

"So, you're saying there were no problems" – Schauer grabbed another beer and sat down at the dinette, "No pollution problems, as far as you know?"

He tilted the can back, wiped his mouth with his hand, "Well, we had the occasional spill," he muttered, "We were working with some powerful acids."

"Mr. Sullivan, would you like a slice of pie, or something?" Mrs. Schauer interrupted. Sullivan hated sweets.

"That would be great," he answered heartily, "What kind?"

"I just made blueberry this morning," she said proudly, "It's still warm. Would you like ice cream with that?" Sullivan couldn't think of anything worse.

"Sure."

Looking a bit neglected, Schauer sulkily demanded his own slice.

"So, you were saying something about acid," Sullivan prompted, "Are those the spills" -

Mrs. Schauer rushed back to the table with the eagerness of a schoolgirl with her hand up, pausing to place pie alamode in front of their guest. "Mr. Sullivan – I was walking home for lunch – I heard the plant siren behind me. I looked back – there was a tanker truck on its side and this cloud –"

Schauer tapped the can on the table, "Oh, I'm sorry," she said, before returning with his piece. Sullivan couldn't figure him out, beer with pie.

"This gray cloud was coming toward me – I started running to get to the back door. Anyway" – She stopped with an intent look like it was happening right then. "It melted my stockings, Mr. Sullivan. My legs they started tingling and then I felt this burning. I ran into the bathroom and I got in the shower," she dropped her voice, –"With all my clothes on."

"I'm hearing sirens. I come out and I see – the Maple Grove fire truck heading toward the plant, my uncle Ned at the wheel. I rubbed some cream on my legs but they were still red."

She got up from the table and walked to the picture window. "Mr. Sullivan, I was standing watching the commotion when I noticed – come here?"

Sullivan slid back his chair to join her. "See this?" She put her finger on some deep droplets of white, "The acid etched our windows." She stopped, very pleased, and returned to the table. Schauer shifted in his chair, having heard the story too many times.

"I bought you new stockings," he rumbled, "And, I'm not," – glancing at Sullivan, "She wanted me to replace all the windows" – "She's the only one who notices those spots."

Sullivan turned another page on his pad, "Were there any other kinds of spills?"

Schauer crushed the can. "Well, if there was a heavy rain, some of the mud from the back acres – we'd have to clean up outside the fence – of course, that wasn't my job. I'm telling you Mr. Sullivan, there was nothing wrong with that sand. Mr. Lavelle – the boss – filled his kid's sandboxes with it - lots of those office guys did. The park used it. Heck, people all over town –who's going to turn down free landfill?"

Schauer started toward the refrigerator but his wife scolded him – "Tom, not another until dinner" – addressing Sullivan – "We're going for the early bird at the Golden Palace – it's all you can eat."

Sullivan stood to go – "I better not keep you. Mr. Schauer can you think of anyone else I should talk to?"

He stood, with his broad back against the fridge, looking down, with eyes skyward – he rattled off the names of four of his old work buddies that still lived in town. "We had some Mexicans, but they don't speak English." Sullivan took down their names anyway.

"Mrs. Schauer, do you mind if I borrow your picture – I'll get it back to you right away."

She looked at him doubtfully. "I'll – I'm coming back tomorrow – I'll return it then, if that's OK."

"Well, alright" she didn't sound completely sold.

As he rolled up the photo, Sullivan asked – "By the way, do you folks know a farmer named Paxson, supposed to have a place on – what's the name of the creek?"

"Sure, Buddy Paxson," Schauer said – you go south out of here on the highway – like you're heading out of town – and turn right on County J. His farm's about a mile, mile and a half."

"He's got a blue barn – can't miss it," Mrs. Schauer chimed in.

After Sullivan thanked her for the pie, he walked toward his car looking down at the missed calls on his phone. It had vibrated three times during the interview. Morgan's number appeared each time.

"Morgan?"

"Oh, Mr. Sullivan, I'm so sorry to bother you." Sullivan instantly guessed she had locked herself out of the office. "I went to use the bathroom," – she sounded flustered –"And I didn't think. I pushed in the button. I asked around at the offices but no one had a key."

"Morgan, it's no big deal." "The shop downstairs has keys to all the offices. Just go in there and" –

"I'm so embarrassed. The furniture guy had a slim jim in his car but" –

"He spoke to you?" Sullivan marveled, "A nice couple runs the shop – tell them you work for me, I'm one of their biggest customers."

"Thank you – thanks for being so understanding," Morgan said, "I need to get back in - to call the – I found out the name of enforcement officer for the EPA – the plant's in his territory –"

Sullivan looked at the clock in his car, "Don't bother – just shut everything off and lock up. You can call him first thing – Morgan, do you have any idea how many times I've locked myself out of the office?"

"No, but I was babysitting once, and locked myself – oh, it was so embarrassing – I couldn't get the – I was watching a three-year-old and I couldn't get him to open the door – So, I was going to call the couple – but a man next door had a ladder and I got back in through the window."

"Did the kid tell on you?"

"He wasn't supposed to have chocolate but - basically I bribed him."

"You're very resourceful, Morgan – I would have done the same thing. Anyway, I'll see you tomorrow morning."

"Right. I have – actually I found out a lot today. See you tomorrow," her voice sang as she hung up.

Sullivan paged through his atlas – he didn't completely trust verbal directions. Looking for County J, he saw Waterfall Glen Park was on the way. Liz Schauer said it was a must-see. After a short drive, Sullivan parked in a long narrow lot that held two other cars spaced far apart. As he walked toward an older model Buick, he thought he saw a person in the front seat. As he got closer, he saw it was two intertwined. Sullivan redirected his attention to the creek that flowed next to the hiking trail. The water looked clean enough, though the submerged rocks were veiled by some faint runoff.

He found a bench facing the "waterfall," a modest drop of five feet, and called home. Flynn answered. "Is your mother?" Sullivan started – "Mom, phone!" he shouted without shielding the receiver, Sullivan winced, "It's dad," he wailed.

Ann picked up; he could hear the washer rumbling in the background, "Hi Mike," she said sweetly, "I was just putting in a load." Sullivan remembered his one stab at doing the laundry. After cramming in the clothes, he couldn't find the newspaper he was going to read. After running to the store to get another, he returned to find newsprint on his dress pants and shirts. The memory of his peach slacks headlined from cuff to waist still pained him.

"I take it you won't be home for dinner," Ann said matter-of-factly.

"I'm sorry," he said soothingly, "But I'm going to miss a lot of dinners – I hope there's some decent places in Maple Grove. I already heard about – they've got a Chinese buffet."

There was no way Sullivan could do this work *after* family dinners. Prime time for finding people home was between 5 and 9 PM and Maple Grove was an hour drive.

"That's OK – but Flynn has a paper he wants you to help him on."

"What's the topic," Sullivan asked, hoping it was something familiar.

He could hear her muted voice calling up the stairs and a shouted answer down.

"He has to write a paper on "Our Town." Ann replied.

"Oh, that will be easy," Sullivan said. He had played the part of George Gibbs in a school production, "But tell him – shoot, I won't be home until ten. Tell him to write the rough draft and I'll fix it when I get home."

"Good, he was worried about it. See you then – that's not a bad neighborhood, is it?"

"Are you kidding, I'm looking at a waterfall and I'm visiting a farm next. Maybe we could grab dinner out here sometime."

"Oh, I'm sure we will," she said, hanging up.

Sullivan drove west on County J, the western sky was reddening, but there was still an hour of daylight left. He was reading the numbers off the rural route mailboxes when his gaze lifted to a blue barn looming on the right side. Sullivan turned into a long snaking driveway, sending up a shower of gravel dust. Two medium-sized farm dogs ran up and barked alongside.

They were mutts – one was black with odd splashes of white – the other looked part Golden Retriever. When he scrunched to a stop, the retriever calmly walked toward the house. The black and white, leapt and barked. Sullivan sat still while claws scratched his driver's door.

He heard a screen door snap and saw a man in overalls sauntering toward him. He looked to be in his 70's solidly built. Sullivan rolled down his window halfway – the dog's paws grabbed the top of the pane. He thrust his barking snout into the car. Sullivan retreated into the passenger seat.

"Can I help you?" the man asked in a faint twang.

"I'm Mike Sullivan," he shouted above the barking dog, "I'm an insurance investigator. I wanted to talk to you about Trident Chemical."

The man's laconic expression didn't change.

Sullivan grabbed the file – "Is it OK, if we talk inside?"

The man nodded and started walking toward the door. Sullivan called after him. "Is this dog alright?"

The thick man turned around, his hands jammed into his pockets. "What?"

"Is it OK" – Sullivan had two tiny scars from a neighbor's dog that had sunk its teeth into his right bicep two summers before.

The man stuck with the noncommittal look, "I don't know what to tell you, mister." He walked to the house and didn't care if Sullivan followed.

Sullivan opened the passenger door slowly and the dog rushed around to confront him. He eased out, fending the dog away with his briefcase. He started to relax. If the dog was going to bite, he would have already done it. That neighbor dog didn't make a sound before leaping at Sullivan when he had the impudence to jog past his house.

When he reached the screen door, the woofing suddenly stopped and the mutt curled up on the porch, panting. Sullivan knocked. The man called from his living room, "It's open"

He found the farmer watching an action movie on a big screen TV. The explosions were thunderous. Sullivan had talked over TV's countless times before – some never turned it off. Paxson motioned to a high backed chair. The farmer was sunk into a leather recliner, his right hand steadying the remote on the armrest.

"Mr. Paxson, I'm working on a claim involving the Trident plant" –

catching himself, he asked if he had ever worked there. Paxson shook his head slowly, "My family's been farming this land for 125 years. The agriculture department's sending me a plaque; I've got a good spot for it on the front gate."

"Wow, that's impressive," Sullivan said enthusiastically. The man shot him a look like he was selling life insurance.

"Anyway, I was wondering if you knew about any pollution problems – you know, we heard."

The TV snapped off. He stood up. "Come with me." They walked out the front. The dogs took no notice as they strode to a gate leading to a sweeping pasture. Cows were congregated at the west end under a shade tree. Sullivan scanned the grass in front of him for cow pies. When he lifted his gaze, he could see a thin ribbon of water glinting in the distance.

"Is that the creek," Sullivan asked, shading his eyes, "What's its name?"

"It was called Crooked Creek, when we first bought this parcel. Then—we had the same mayor for over forty years – Harold Carlson – so they named it after him about five years ago."

"When – were you here when the plant was built?"

"I remember its first day."

They had reached the bank of a quietly flowing creek that carved a five yard wide curve through the pasture. Sullivan could see it was well below high watermark, sliding slowly past at summer stage.

"I was back at the barn, filling a water trough," He stooped to snag a stalk of grass. Chewing on it, he was a profile from a pastoral painting. "My cows were running toward me– do you know anything about cows, Mr. Sullivan?"

Sullivan shrugged; He pictured the milking station at Lincoln Park's Farm in the Zoo. "They give milk?"

"They don't like to run," Paxson continued, tossing the worked-over stalk into the creek. "They ran right to the trough, pushing each other. I had to refill it three times. I walked out here to see – our cows always drank from the creek – that's the reason my grandfather bought this place. So, I'm standing about where you are and the creek – the water looked like milk. I went back to the house to get a plastic jug and I filled it."

Sullivan concentrated hard, no pen handy.

"So, I took the jug to – the county has a farm bureau office on the square – Sam sent it out to be tested. He called me the next morning and said the water had a very high ph – it was basically – remember when there was that talk about acid rain? It was something like that."

"No wonder the cows ran," Sullivan said, as they headed back toward the house. It was almost dusk. The herd was strung out in a line ambling toward the main gate.

"That's right," Paxson said an old regret surfacing, "And they haven't drunk out of it since. It's better since the plant shut down."

They returned to his living room and the TV flashed to life. A young woman was reciting a long list of medication side effects while a middle-aged couple paddled a canoe.

The key to the Trident case was whether anyone complained to the plant about contamination – was it written or verbal – was there a response?

Sullivan grabbed his pad and started writing down fragments from their conversation at the creek, while he asked Paxson if he had reported the problem with the water.

"Are you serious? "Why! If I complained to the village – they'd all stop talking to me – not that they say much anyway. I've known these people my whole life – what did they care about my cows – they care a lot more for that paycheck. Besides, – they had to put that stuff somewhere."

"Any chance, the farm bureau – what was his name, Sam," –

"Sam was married to one of the Lavelle girls," Schauer said with finality, referring to one of the plant manager's daughters.

Sullivan stopped writing. Paxson's attention was diverted by the hero dodging a villain wielding a flamethrower. He thanked Paxson and walked to the door. The farmer climbed out of his chair and followed him out into the darkness, leaving the TV blaring. The black and white dog nuzzled

Sullivan's leg, as they shook hands. "It's time to get these creatures back in the barn," Paxson said, walking heavily toward his herd.

CHAPTER 9

The next morning, Sullivan was walking down the corridor to his office. He could hear excited voices. He found Charly and Morgan – they were sipping pricey coffee and munching croissants. Charly was very animated for this early – it was probably the caffeine and sugar.

"Morgan stopped at the bakery," she said thickly her mouth full, "She got you something."

Sullivan saw a tall cardboard cup of burnt-smelling coffee and a croissant on his desk. "Wow, what a treat," he said, taking a sip and a bite. "That was very thoughtful." Unfortunately, Sullivan had been to France – what Americans called a croissant tasted like a Communion wafer.

"How'd you make out at the archives?" Sullivan asked.

Charly gave a little 'ta-da' as she displayed her outfit. "That's the last time I'm wearing anything civilized – it's jeans and t-shirts from now on – and guess what – they gave me my own desk."

Sullivan knew it wouldn't take her long to get in with the grey bureaucrats.

"There's this cute old guy – Chester – he fetches the rolls of Microfilm." Sullivan shot an I-told-you-so glance toward Morgan. She was too busy stabbing crumbs and licking her fingers.

"At lunch time, he eats a sandwich – then stretches out on the floor – flat on his back. So I told him he could use my knitting bag as a pillow."

Having already heard the story, Morgan busied herself highlighting e-mails she had printed.

"At first, he said he couldn't – and actually I wasn't sure I wanted – his hair – it's hard to tell if he ever washes it – but he took it and went right to sleep. After lunch, these two maintenance guys brought in a small desk for me. Chester is mine!"

"Did you find any cases?"

"There were plenty against Universal Bauxite," Charly continued, "One was filed by the City – I'm not going to know anything until I see the files. I ordered them – Chester said it normally takes three days to come from the warehouse – but since I remind him of his granddaughter, he's promising two."

"How long do you think it will take?" Sullivan asked, before popping in his last piece of pastry.

"At least two weeks to finish checking the index," Charly replied, "Then maybe two more to review the files."

"Well, make sure you charge all your time. We're billing them monthly. I'm going to have Morgan start on Du Page."

"That's OK with me," Charly said giving Morgan a conspiratorial smile.

After a pause, Morgan went first, "It's only that – Charly and I are practically related. I'm dating her cousin – he just got out of the Marines."

Morgan had chanced to meet one of Charley's more upstanding family members.

"Morgan, you're going out with – is his name really Stanley?"

"We call him Stan-The-Man," Charly said, "Doesn't he have the most perfect eyebrows?"

Morgan nodded. Changing the subject from male beauty, Sullivan asked Morgan if she had made any headway.

"I called the enforcement officer for Region 5 – I know you told me to wait until this morning – but I caught him just before five. He stayed on the phone – checking all their hotspots. He said the only ones he could find in Maple Grove were – a landfill where trucks have been dumping paint, two dry cleaners, a canning factory and, the village hall was built on a dump. He didn't have anything for Trident. He told me to check with the state EPA. I phoned there this morning – had to leave a voice mail."

Sullivan swept some crumbs off his desk into his cupped hand and deposited them in the wastebasket. "Maybe we'll get lucky with the state."

Charly was loading up her shoulder bag – "I'm bringing a kiwi for Chester," holding one aloft in its brown wrinkled glory. "He said he's never had one," she sang over her shoulder, as she left for the "L".

After the door closed, Sullivan asked, "How'd you meet Stanley – excuse me Stan-the?" -

"I go to this trivia night," Morgan said excitedly, "It's at a bar – it's kind of a hole in the wall called the Workingman's Palace. The happy hour is from 7 to 9. AM! Can you imagine? A lot of Polish guys go there – Stan told me it was just so they could look at the blondes behind the bar." She gave a sour look.

"I know men are pathetic."

"I mean – that's not why Stan goes – he's really smart. He loves trivia."

"So, I went there by myself," Morgan continued. Sullivan presumed this protected youngest daughter got a rush exploring the city's grittiness. Little did he know that the crowd at Workingman's Palace were her kind of people.

"He asked me to be on his team – it was all guys except me. So, one of the categories is – you had to guess the movie from a line of dialogue – they were all romantic comedies."

Sullivan saw what had to be a model stroll past the glass door. "We've got to get out of here before lunch," he interrupted.

"So, we're in first place all the way until the last question," Morgan continued eagerly, "It was worth fifteen points. The question was: who wrote a landmark paper about peas in 1865?"

Sullivan rummaged through his memory of high school biology. Nothing.

"I knew it was Gregor Mendel," she said without explanation, "But they kept saying Luther Burbank."

Sullivan remembered that Burbank came later. He could detect some pounding on the other side of the wall. "Let's go – grab your notes."

"They went with Burbank but it was Mendel – so we finished – what's that?"

The panting, the slap of flesh – there was nothing subtle about it.

"Listen," Sullivan said, raising his voice, "We'll head out to Maple Grove right now. We can eat in the car."

"I'm still full," Morgan said, giggling helplessly, as they listened to a woman's deep-throated moans keeping rhythm with a grunting man. "I have to use the bathroom first."

As she opened the door, she almost bumped into the furniture salesman – he extended his arm with a smile. Sullivan had never seen his teeth before. A few were missing. Sullivan deposited essential items into his briefcase a crumpled bag of chips and a can of cola, for the afternoon pick-me-up.

As they headed out on the tollway, he told Morgan what she could expect at the courthouse. He was pleased to see her carefully lettered notes on a yellow tablet. "Here," he said, digging out court file review forms for her from his briefcase. No one at his agency read documents as closely as Sullivan – maybe Morgan would be one of the better ones.

Sullivan searched for something on the radio. He kept landing on commercials.

"So, after trivia – he asked me out – he started talking about a cousin named Charly – Your Charly. She comes to Trivia Night, too and answers all the math and science questions"

Wanting to change the subject, Sullivan asked Morgan what her folks did for a living. She said that they had operated an office cleaning company.

"My dad and mom came from this tiny village in Portugal. It had about 100 people and half of them were my family. I've never been there but there my dad told me there were hardly any jobs. The grocery store was only open two hours a day."

"So, they came to America and ended up living in Justice."

"Really," Sullivan exclaimed, "I had an investigation there once. It was a police brutality case, believe it or not."

"The cops were always at our building," Morgan recalled.

"Were you in one of those high-rises on Roberts Road?" Sullivan asked.

Morgan nodded.

"I used to call that apartment complex the "black hole" because I could never find the people that were supposed to live there."

"Well, you never would have found my parents home," She said coldly. "They got up at 3:00 AM to clean offices in the Loop and didn't get home until 11:00 at night. They left me and my sister, Christine, alone in the apartment. When I was 4 and Christine was 6, a pan caught fire on the stove. I was freaking out but Christine stayed calm. She had me stay low, while she called 911. Luckily, the fire department was right down the street."

Morgan said she and her sister attended the local public school and spent their weekends helping their parents clean offices. "It was the only way to spend time with my parents. I became a good cleaner. After awhile, though, I hated it. I even had to move furniture like a man."

Morgan may have looked delicate but she was no stranger to hard work. That's why she felt so comfortable with the laborers at the Workingman's Palace.

Morgan explained that the cleaning company continued to grow, as they attracted more clients and recruited more workers. "We started taking on Polish women and Hispanic women. I thought my parents were hard workers, until I watched them clean. Anyway, my parents sold the company for a big profit. When I was in high school, we moved to Evanston, so Christine and I could go to better schools."

"Where'd you get your archeology degree?"

"I went to Wheaton College. It was real conservative but I liked my professors."

"Why did you pick archeology? Was it just for the money?" Sullivan teased.

"I know it's not practical but I just wanted to study something that was *different*. Besides, Christine and I used to go to the Field Museum. We loved the exhibits, especially the ones on Africa."

"What do your parents think of you working for me?"

"My dad was actually happy about it. It isn't in my field but at least it requires a brain. He thought waitressing was a waste of my education."

Sullivan dropped her off in the turnaround in front of the sliding glass doors of the courthouse, "I'm heading to the historical society – call me when you're finished."

Sullivan sped west until he hit the outskirts of Maple Grove. He braked toward 35, just as he spotted a black and white peeking from a picnic grove. The Maple Grove Historical Society was housed in a Victorian. It had been handsomely-built but now its decay gave it the charm of the Bates mansion, as drawn by Charles Addams. As he climbed the groaning stairs, Sullivan spied the hours of operation black-lettered on a whitewashed sign: Monday, Wednesday and Friday, from noon to three. It was Wednesday 1:30, the door was open.

As he stepped into the entrance, he was startled by a mannequin dressed in the stark finery of an Imperial Wizard. Sullivan stood transfixed. A balding man in his sixties, deep into a paperback, looked up. "Do you mind signing the register?" He asked brightening into a frozen smile. Sullivan dashed off his signature – only the "S" was legible.

"So," the man said rubbing his hands, he wore a badge that said, "Hello: I'm Alan." "Are you doing genealogy – do you have family from this" – "No family," Sullivan said, "I'm – do you have anything on the history of companies in this town?"

Alan looked lost, "Is there a particular business?"

Sullivan glanced at his file – "Do you have anything on – I mean, do you have a business section?"

"Follow me," Alan said doubtfully, "We have a shelf – you know some of our oldest companies – here's one." He hefted it.

It was the coffee-table saga of the United Can & Seal Co.

"Where do you get your water from?" Sullivan asked, "Do you have anything on that?"

Alan set the book down with a thump.

"Mr. – what is your name?" Alan extended his hand, "Oh, Mr. Sullivan – that doesn't sound like – oh, you said you didn't have family. Water is somewhat of my specialty. I got my degree in hydraulic engineering – spent twenty-three years at the sewage plant."

"I understand," Sullivan said, "But where do you get your drinking water?"

"We used it get it out of Crooked – Carlson Creek," he corrected himself, "But mostly we get it from artesian wells.

Here," he handed a booklet to Sullivan, "The water department put this out." Alan looked down humbly. "I helped."

Sullivan thumbed through pages of rainfall charts and groundwater levels. "You mean you get your water from the aquifer." Sullivan was familiar with a supply of springs that extended from southern Wisconsin across northern Illinois.

"That's right – Mr. Sullivan."

"Is there any problem with it?"

The wrinkles on Alan's forehead deepened as he gazed at his shoes. "Well, it has to be treated, of course." He went to a whisper, "They think there's some contamination from a landfill."

"I heard," Sullivan whispered back – is it paint?"

"Oil-based," Alan confided, "But that's why," summoning a reassuring tone, "We *have* a treatment plant."

"You haven't had any problems with the Trident plant?"

Alan tensed. He had obviously never heard questions like this at the historical society.

"Mr. Sullivan," he said firmly, "I grew up half-a-block from that plant – if there had been any danger" –

"OK," Sullivan said, "I don't want to get – I mean this is my first time here – but I think – don't you think that dummy is offensive?"

Alan had a pat answer. "Our mission is to preserve the history – good or bad- That," he pointed to the figure with the peaked white hat – "Is part of our heritage – whether folks like it or not."

Sullivan did a two-armed curl with the glossy history of the can company, "Did Trident – Universal Bauxite – put out something like this?"

"No," Alan said, wearied by Sullivan's questions, "But we do have a file on the plant – a few newspaper clippings –."

Sullivan sat down at a long table and waited for Alan to bring the folder. He returned with a thin one.

"If you need anything else," Alan said woodenly, "I'll be at my desk."

Sullivan opened it up to find ten clippings in various stages of decay. The most yellowed had a headline trumpeting the arrival of the plant. There was a photo of a crowd assembled to cut a ribbon. Mayor Carlson was posing theatrically at the front with a pair of oversized scissors.

Glancing down the column, Sullivan read the speech given by the president of Universal Bauxite. He promised the company would be a good neighbor and was happy to be part of the Maple Grove family, etc. Sullivan wrote down the date.

The next story came about ten years later. It involved some complaints about the water-treatment plant being inundated with effluent from Crooked Creek. The chief engineer complained that it was being generated by Universal Bauxite.

The company president countered by insisting their waste water was safely stored in settling ponds and it wasn't getting into the creek.

Sullivan considered asking Alan about it but wasn't sure they were still on speaking terms.

Another decade went by before the next article. It detailed claims by a local physicist that radioactive water was getting into the sewers, presenting a health hazard to the entire community. The rest of the story consisted of denials by public officials. Their reactions and the tone of the reporter painted the physicist as an over-educated outsider.

"Alan," Sullivan held up the newsprint, "Can I get a copy of this?"

The docent tore himself away from the paperback with annoyance. "It's a dollar for the first page, fifty cents for each additional page." He added a theatrical sigh.

"I think I need – let me finish these."

The remaining articles marked anniversaries of the plant's opening and retirements of long-time employees. Sullivan copied down their names. He walked over to Alan, "I just need these two," reaching in his pocket for cash. All he could find was a twenty. Alan pursed his lips. Handing over the bill, Sullivan asked if he could donate the change to the historical society. Alan handed him the copies and dropped the twenty into the clear plastic collection box. It had plenty of singles for company.

Feeling pleased with his find, Sullivan called Morgan from his car.

She went first as usual. "I requested all the files I could for today," frustrated they had a limit of twenty. "When are you coming back?"

"Are you anywhere near the library?" Sullivan asked.

"Let me check my phone," she intoned, "There's a county library three blocks from here."

Sullivan gave her the names of the retirees and the physicist and asked her to look them up in city directories. Towns like Maple Grove maintained directories that went back decades. They contained the name, address, phone number and, in many cases, the occupation of the residents.

"Is it OK if I grab something to eat first? There's a cute coffee shop across the street. It's called Legal Grounds." She tried not to sound too desperate.

"Clever name – sure – I have a lot more to do."

Sullivan cruised downtown Maple Grove – getting acquainted with the layout. There was a two-block strip of shops, dotted by two bars and three restaurants – two of which were still serving food. There was a barber shop and several beauty parlors. As for the shops, the main street merchandisers were fighting an uneven battle against the commercial giant Sullivan had passed at the exit ramp. Many were slashing prices.

He found the post office, police station, fire station and city hall, all grouped within walking distance. Sullivan spotted a sign for the library and followed it to an imposing brick edifice; Andrew Carnegie was carved above its entrance. He wasn't intending to duplicate Morgan's efforts. He needed a restroom.

A sign pointed toward the men's room on the lower level. He descended winding varnished stairs – the door was locked. He went back up – the librarian was staring at a computer screen. "Excuse me," Sullivan said, "Can I have" – She wordlessly handed him a wooden ruler, with a key dangling from one end.

As he returned the key, Sullivan asked if they had a phone book for Maple Grove. She gave Sullivan the directory. He was heading toward a table – "Excuse me," the woman stopped him, "I have to hold your ID. You can use a library card, if you want." Sullivan handed over his driver's license.

He copied down the numbers for the mayor's office, sewage plant and other municipal bodies. He searched for a current listing for the physicist and found him at 110 West Galena Avenue. He didn't find the retirees listed. Then he pulled out his black & white photo from the plant picnic. He checked every name on the back and found about twenty still published – at least the last names matched.

On his way to the physicist, Flynn called. "Dad" – Sullivan could hear Ann encouraging him in the background, "Dad, we had regionals today" – his liveliness was palpable. "Really, did you pitch?"

"No – Coach Bob started Andrew." That figured, his assistant choosing his own boy. "I played first. I caught a line drive – I had to jump for it – even the ump smiled. Andrew kept laying it in there. They had two men on – they had this left-handed outfielder – Dad this guy was twice my size. He hit one right at me. I couldn't get out of the way." Sullivan was picturing another dash to the emergency room, his son bleeding in the backseat.

"It hit me right in the chest," Flynn cried out, "But I kept it in front of me. I tagged the base with the ball – the guy was out – the runner on third – I threw – Rahul got him at home."

"Wow," Sullivan exclaimed, "What a play? After a pause, "Did you get any hits?"

"No," he said to the awkward question, "But we won 5-4. Coach gave me the game ball."

"That's great, Flynn – that means you guys advance – maybe I can coach the sectional game. I wish I could have been there today." The only time Sullivan's job got him down was when he drove past fathers playing catch with kids in the dusk. He started to ask if he could talk to his mother but Flynn had already handed over the phone.

"You should have seen it," Ann exclaimed.

"Yeah, I bet you were thinking the worst."

"Oh – when it first happened – I thought he was really hurt – You should have seen him. The ball hit him. It knocked him down. He crawled forward and grabbed the ball. Mike – after he made the play – he stayed face down in the dirt – he didn't want anyone to see him hurt."

"Sounds like Bob did a good job."

"Sure" – she sniffed –"He has an awfully high opinion of Andrew – after he started walking everybody – he put him at short. I know I'm his mother – but Flynn won that game."

There was a silence. "How's your case goin'?" she asked with mild interest.

"Great, actually – had a couple of breakthroughs today – I'm going to see a witness – he could be important."

"Well, I just wanted Flynn to let you know – he's not much of a phone person."

"I won't be home any later than ten," Sullivan said, forgetting, as usual, an 'I love you' before he hung up.

He pulled up to a trim frame, shielded by a fortress of evergreens. There were expansive flowerbeds and a towering pine in the side yard. A Mercedes convertible was crouched on the driveway. The low porch, with gingerbread molding made it look like a farmhouse. He rang and knocked. It was several minutes before he heard stirring.

After some locks were undone, a man in his 60's, scruffy white beard and moustache, mostly bald on top, opened the door halfway. "No solicitors," the man barked, "And, if you're Jehovah's Witness," spotting Sullivan's tie, "You're wasting your time – I'm Catholic."

Sullivan said he was working for the insurers of the plant and the door spread wide – "Well, I hope they have good insurance – they're going to need it," he sniggered.

"I take it you didn't work there."

The man snorted. "I wouldn't set foot in that place."

"I was reading some old newspaper stories," Sullivan said, "You were quoted" –

"Misquoted, you mean," he snarled, "They all think I'm some kind of - but I can prove what I said."

"Do you mind if I come in?" Sullivan asked.

"Yes – I do mind – I'm leaving in five minutes. Got a racquetball game– my partner and I have court time every Wednesday at 5:00."

Sullivan recalled playing racquetball three times – Unaccustomed to rigid surroundings; Each match had ended in an emergency room visit. He pulled out a card. "I come out here a lot," Sullivan said, as the man squinted at it, "Maybe we can talk sometime."

The grizzled little man with the bandy legs looked him up and down, "Do you play racquetball?"

"Sure – I've tried it a few times. I'm not very –"

"Come back here next Wednesday – this time – my partner can't make it – we'll play a couple of games – there's a lounge where we can talk." The man started to close the door. "Mr., I mean, Dr. Leinwebber, can I get your phone number – you know, in case something comes up."

"No – just show up" – he snapped the door shut.

Sullivan called Morgan. She answered in a whisper, "I'm still in the reference department – these directories are so cool. They have them going back all the way to 1859 but I started in 1950 – isn't that when the plant came in?"

CHAPTER 10

The following Wednesday, Sullivan was back at the house with the gingerbread molding. The tan Mercedes convertible was again resting in the driveway. Sullivan knocked and rang. He paced on the porch and heard cabinets and drawers slamming. Sullivan was dressed in sweat pants and scruffy gym shoes with slippery soles. Leinwebber eventually emerged. He had a gym bag in one hand and a half-eaten banana in the other. "Finally found where my wife put the keys," he muttered. He glanced doubtfully at Sullivan's attire.

As they climbed into the Mercedes, Sullivan slammed his door. "There's no need for that," Leinwebber snarled, "This isn't an American car." Sullivan apologized and settled into the soft leather. "Dr. Leinwebber, I wanted to talk to you about the radiation coming from the plant."

"Radiation," he scoffed, "Radiation is everywhere." He thrust his half-eaten banana at Sullivan, "This has potassium, low-level radiation." Leinwebber fumbled with one hand in the back seat and tossed a book at Sullivan. "You should read this." The title was *Radiation for Dummies*. Sullivan started to ask another question but Leinwebber cut him off.

"We'll talk at the club after we play. There's a lounge."

When they stepped onto the racquetball court, Leinwebber looked serious. Wearing prescription goggles and a white headband, he bounced up and down, showing off his sturdy high-tops. "You need shoes with support," he scolded Sullivan. During warm-ups, Sullivan knew immediately he was overmatched. The grizzled, bandy-legged man danced at center court rifling low line drives into the corners.

When the game began, Sullivan lunged from one side to another to return shots. Though Leinwebber was thirty years his senior, the score wasn't close. Sullivan was panting and overheated, while his opponent barely needed his sweatband. They played two more games with the same result. He could tell Leinwebber was disappointed by the lack of competition.

They dressed in silence in the locker room. Sullivan purchased a large bottle of water in the lounge. Leinwebber sipped a fruit drink. Sullivan took a swig of water and asked Leinwebber again about the Trident plant. The doctor didn't answer directly.

"We moved to Maple Grove twenty years ago. It was quiet and not too far from my lab. My wife got a job teaching Kindergarten. Our boys were young. Not long after we moved in, they tracked this red mud into the kitchen. After I yelled at the mess they made, I scooped up some of it. I took it to my lab to analyze it. It turned out to be," he paused for effect, "Radioactive Thorium."

Sullivan grabbed for his pad, "Mind if I make some notes?" Leinwebber waved away the question. "So, the next day, I asked the boys where they had found the mud. They pointed toward the plant. They walked me there and showed me where red mud overflowed from the plant onto the railroad tracks. I went home and got my Geiger counter."

"When I walked back toward Trident, the crackling became louder," he recalled bitterly "I was getting very high readings, it made me mad. It's only two blocks from my house - my sons were exposed."

"Weren't you worried - living so close?" Sullivan interrupted.

"I was just going to tell you," said Leinwebber, annoyed by the interruption, "I took readings on my own property and there was nothing. I took the first flight to Washington. I remember running to make my plane at Midway." He allowed a smile, pleased by the memory of how he rushed to report Trident to the Atomic Energy Commission. "Somebody must have tipped them off," he said resignedly, "By the time I got back, the red mud was cleaned up."

"Is that when you went to the newspaper?"

"Yes," he said sarcastically, "I thought people should know there was radiation in their soil and water. I was getting high readings at the sewage plant. They thought I was nuts of course. The mayor and the council members told everyone the levels were safe. Trident – they treated me like I was some kind of crackpot. So, I gave up."

Leinwebber had finished his drink and stood to go. "I've got to get back for dinner. I'm supposed to pick up the wine." Sullivan rose to his feet as his knees argued against it. When they pulled into the driveway, Leinwebber invited Sullivan to look at his garden. Sullivan didn't know the names of the flowers but complimented their colors.

"All of this is new," Leinwebber gave a broad wave, taking in the evergreens and the tall pine. "Last July, I was at my lab, when my wife called. She was so shook up. At first I thought our youngest, Kurt, had been in a car accident. She told me to come home right away."

"When I got here – my garden, everything was dead. The flowers – they were melted. The lawn was brown, the bushes. My wife told me she had heard a siren coming from the plant. They had an acid spill. Helen described this gray cloud drifting from the plant. She was scared and hurried into the house. It came right over my property –killed everything – even took the paint off my house."

Leinwebber called Trident immediately. He was invited to meet the plant manager the next morning. "He was great," Leinwebber recalled, "He apologized and offered to pay for everything. They sent a landscaper to replace the tree, flowers, everything. They even sent a crew to repaint the house. My wife never had liked the color anyway. It was bright yellow when we bought it."

Sullivan felt pleased. Radioactive and toxic – both reported to the plant. Dr. Leinwebber was going to be his star witness. Sullivan shook the doctor's hand and said he'd stay in touch.

"You know, Mr. Sullivan," Leinwebber's voice softened, "You're welcome to join us for dinner. You have a long drive back."

It wasn't often a witness extended a dinner invitation, but this was the evening he had promised to take Ann out for a prime steak. He heartily thanked Leinwebber, and asked for a rain check. "I'm out here almost every day."

The gruffness returned. "If you buy a decent pair of shoes, I'll give you a rematch."

Two hours later, Sullivan was sitting across a starched white table cloth from Ann. She was sipping a glass of the house wine, while Sullivan nursed a light beer. Ann had just had her brown hair cut and highlighted, and Sullivan made sure to notice. Her makeup accented her deep-set dark eyes. Sullivan was decently dressed, thanks to her, wearing a checked sport coat just this side of loud.

His style of dress, or lack thereof, was what Ann had first noticed about him when they worked together at a savings and loan. Sullivan also caught her attention when he rushed in every morning, just beating the clock, his hair still wet. His mismatched look made her feel sorry for him. Sullivan would take pity any time if it might lead to romance.

As they poked at some miniscule appetizers, Sullivan describe his day with Leinwebber. Ann had little tolerance for his war stories. "Why didn't you have dinner with *him*? The last thing you want is to make him mad."

"Because," Sullivan said, swooping in for a peck on her cheek, "I wanted us to have a meal without interruption. Do you see anything you want?"

Ann had been his superior at the savings and loan and it still shaped their relationship. At first, there was no relationship. She steadfastly refused to go on a date with Sullivan, citing company policy. It took him six months to persuade her to see a movie. He showed up at her family's two-flat, wearing a trench coat.

Ann's teenage sister thought he looked like a doofus. If Ann's mother had been home, she would have objected strongly to her dating a "wild" Irish Catholic. Ann's dad barely looked up from his newspaper and didn't seem to care who Ann went out with. They got to the movie an hour late without realizing it. It ended so quickly they had no idea what it was about.

They repaired to a rustic West Side pub where Sullivan sipped Guinness and poured out the pitiful tale of his childhood. He had found it very effective with certain women. It didn't work with Ann. When he dropped her off, though, she brightened into a smile and insisted she had a good time.

They had had many good times since then. Even after the kids were born, romance survived. They spent a week in San Francisco, without ever uttering their children's names. Sullivan's parents had taught him that escaping kids was necessary to save a marriage. As they sat in the steak house, they could look back on sixteen years of relative bliss and consistent cuddling.

Ann resisted the urge to rail about her job, but Sullivan insisted she vent. After fifteen minutes of hearing about her toxic co-worker, Sullivan was developing indigestion. She stopped when their entrees came. They usually split meals to save money but Sullivan was confident that Trident would pay for two. After tiramisu, Sullivan proposed they take a drive out to Maple Grove.

Ann looked at him funny. "It's too late to talk to witnesses."

"No, I want to take you to Waterfall Glen. We could make out in the car like we used to." During their dating days, they had virtually lived in her green sedan, the only place they had privacy. Ann laughed, "We better get home, they're probably fighting over the remote." With that, the spell was broken and they were back to being parents. On the way home, the radio played *their* song. The first line was perfectly engraved inside their wedding bands, "I Love You Just the Way You Are."

The song was still stuck in Sullivan's head the next morning when he unlocked his office. There was a message from Janet Sterling that the Dream Team was in town and they needed a personal update from Sullivan about

Trident. She apologized for the short notice. "It's tomorrow at 10:00 at my office."

Sullivan wore his emergency suit but replaced the piano key tie with sedate stripes. The defense lawyers were in town for a golf outing and the meeting with Sullivan gave them a tax write-off. There were eighteen of them waiting in the conference room. Some were wearing suits, others had already changed into golf shorts with knife sharp creases.

After Janet introduced him, Sullivan recited a somewhat rambling account of his investigation to date. He led off with the homeowners he had interviewed. One had black stuff coming up from his basement drain and blamed it on Trident. Another tearfully talked of the death of their dog from cancer and claimed it was from the high radiation levels in their back yard.

He recounted interviews with employees from an adjacent plant. They said that Trident was spilling so much acid into the soil that it heated their water lines. The water from their drinking fountain was lukewarm, and they complained to Trident, which had the same problem. Sullivan repeated the accounts of Trident workers, who confirmed these acid leaks and spills. While Trident management insisted their waste was safely contained in storage ponds.

He told the lawyers of hiring his Mexican brother-in-law to interview the low-level employees who scraped out the giant vats after they were drained of acid. They held out their hands to display gnarled fingers and thickened nails. Sullivan could barely look.

Finally, he talked about Dr. Leinwebber. The lawyers did their best to seem unimpressed but the room became very quiet as he described Leinwebber's findings. When he was finished, a tall Texan, wearing a string tie stepped forward and rumbled a question. "Is this doctor alive or dead?" Sullivan waited a beat, "I've only interviewed living people, so far." There was muffled laughter. The Texan wasn't smiling. "You know what I mean – what's he doing living so close to the plant?"

Sullivan told him the readings on Leinwebber's property were safe.

111

Feeling very satisfied, Sullivan was ready to step from the podium. A gentlemanly lawyer from Virginia, with gray hair like spun steel, stopped him. Like a batter who thought the 3-1 pitch was outside, Sullivan awkwardly returned to the podium. "Mr. Sullivan, did you interview a former plant worker named Edith Schauer without reading her the required statement?"

Sullivan was stunned. His very first witness and the only one he had failed to warn. "I didn't know she worked at the plant. She was in the office – she didn't know anything about production or waste. After I realized it, I gave her the disclaimer. I also warned her husband."

"That's all very fine, Mr. Sullivan," the Virginia lawyer continued in his smooth manner, "But Trident's lawyers are seeking sanctions against us for what you failed to do. They're filing a motion to throw out all of the evidence you've just presented here because you talked with Mrs. Schauer under false pretenses. They're claiming you misrepresented yourself."

Sullivan relaxed inwardly. His license entitled him to misrepresent himself, as well as trespass. "I'm very sorry about Mrs. Schauer," he told the courtly Virginian, "Can they really do that – throw out my investigation?" The lawyer allowed a slight smile, satisfied that he had sufficiently scared Sullivan. "Well, we're fighting their motion, of course, and we have a sympathetic judge. But we have more pressing issues right now." The Virginian broke the silence with an announcement.

"Gentlemen!" he announced, "The shuttle is leaving in ten minutes for Pine Meadows. I suggest we hurry."

Sullivan didn't see any need to tell the lawyers about the recent flurry of lawsuits Morgan found against Trident. Their paralegals had already alerted them. These cases had been stirred-up by EPA workers wearing space suits who came to clean-up their yards. Their presence explained why so many Maple Grove residents had come down with cancer and rare blood diseases.

For some members of the Dream Team, severe injuries and death only meant more billable hours. They charged Trident handsomely for filing their appearances.

This cynical view wasn't shared by Morgan, who had spent months reviewing the personal injury and wrongful death cases. She trudged into the office one morning, muscling her shoulder bag. Her olive complexion looked pale, her dark hair was touseld, and her blouse and slacks were rumpled. Morgan sank into her chair with a sigh.

"Sighing is a sign of stress," Sullivan warned, "What's stressing you out now?"

Morgan sipped from her cardboard cup of coffee, "Sorry, I'm trying to wake up. I didn't get much sleep last night."

Sullivan assumed it was too much partying, but Morgan explained.

"These files I'm reading. I just can't get these cases out of my mind. It breaks my heart."

Sullivan knew enough not to get emotionally involved in his cases, no matter how heart-wrenching. In fact, he and his colleagues made dark jokes about the ghastliest auto accidents and industrial injuries. He didn't think Morgan was ready for a joke.

"These twin girls," Morgan continued, "Ashley and Lindsey are only six – they have leukemia. It's the same story all over town. Kids grew up playing in their back yards and came down with these strange blood diseases. It started back in the 30s when the plant first moved in. The bosses were taking the sand home for their kid's sandboxes. Now, we know why so many of their kids got sick. They didn't know what was causing it."

Morgan sipped silently, letting her words sink in. Sullivan said nothing.

"It wasn't just the yards and the sandboxes. It was everywhere. I took a walk from the courthouse to the park. The fence has these old rusty signs, you can barely read them now. They say "Radioactive – with these yellow triangles." The kids don't pay any attention. They climb the fence. I saw a bunch of them playing baseball and football. They were falling in the dirt. I wanted to scream at them to get out but they're not my kids."

"I also checked out the tennis courts. There was an EPA guy with a Geiger counter. Said he was finding plenty of hotspots."

Sullivan reassured Morgan. "There's a citizens group – they're demanding that Trident dig up 587,000 tons of radioactive soil. They found a town in Utah that will take it."

"It's too late for Ashely and Lindsey," Morgan sniffed, "They lost all of their hair. They both need bone marrow transplants – I thought I'd be a match – I'm Type O. The universal donor."

"You look-".Sullivan stopped himself.

"Oh, I stayed overnight with a friend. Didn't have time to shower, or change. Anyway, Trident bulldozed their house and moved the family into a hotel. Their poor parents, wish there was some way to help."

"Morgan, that isn't our job. We investigate and report back to our client. They already know about the cases you found."

Morgan cried softly and fought to stifle her sobs. Sullivan knew she needed a hug but held back. "Listen, you're going to have to get yourself together," Sullivan said firmly, "You owe me an honest day's work and you're a mess. If you can't handle this, why don't you go back home and rest?"

Morgan gazed up at him gratefully. "Really, you don't need me?"

"I need you to get some sleep so you can function tomorrow."

"Oh, thanks, Mr. Sullivan. I'll feel better tomorrow – but please I can't go back to that courthouse. I can't take any more of these stories. Some of the people who are dying – they're my age."

The phone rang. It was Charly. Sullivan put her on hold, while he wished Morgan a relaxing day off.

"Charly, what's up?"

"You won't believe it but they finally picked up Marvin Frye on his warrant. They caught him breaking into cars at a mall in Brown County. They picked him up on the outstanding warrant from Cook County and locked him up. Finally – we have a chance to talk to him."

"OK, get here as soon as you can. I'll call the jail to make an appointment. Maybe we can go today?"

Sullivan called the Brown County Jail and confirmed Frye was incarcerated there as Inmate 30223. He asked about visiting hours and they referred him to the sheriff.

"This is Sheriff Burns, what can I do for you?" The voice was gruff and matter-of-fact. Sullivan explained that he was an investigator and wanted to interview a key witness to a fatal accident.

"Mr. Sullivan, unless you're his lawyer, his next of kin, or on his list of visitors, you cannot see Mr. Frye."

Sullivan played his hole card. "Sheriff, do you consider Brown County to be a Christian community?" The lily-white and prosperous Brown County had been dubbed the "Protestant Vatican."

The sheriff answered guardedly, "Yes, Mr. Sullivan, we've got quite a few church-going families. Why do you ask?"

"Well, Sheriff, Jesus said that we're supposed to visit people in prison. I don't know if Frye will even talk to us but he must be lonely in his cell. Might welcome some company."

There was a heavy silence. "OK Mr. Sullivan," he said in a clipped tone, "You can come see Mr. Frye at 2:00 this afternoon. Come to my office first and I'll escort you."

When Charly arrived, Sullivan gave her a big smile. After he explained how he had finessed the sheriff, she exclaimed, "The Christ card worked!"

Sullivan and Charly drove to the Brown County Correctional Center. In front was a low square municipal building and behind it, the jail. It had guard towers and razor wire atop the walls. It otherwise looked like an airy, modern facility, nothing like the grim monstrosity of Cook County Jail. Sullivan and Charly made it through the medical detector, after removing their belts. Sullivan felt undignified, with his pants drooping. Then they were shown into the sheriff's office. He looked like an Alabama State Trooper. His bullet head was shaved and he wore dark glasses indoors. His uniform shirt was neatly creased. His face was hard.

It got harder. "I thought it was just you Mr. Sullivan, who's this?"

Charly offered her hand but the sheriff waved it away. Sullivan explained that he needed Charly to take notes during the interview and the sheriff grudgingly allowed her to sign in. Sullivan and Charly felt like prisoners themselves, after stashing all of their personal items in lockers and getting patted down. They were escorted to the jail's breakroom and the guard said he would return with Frye. Sullivan bought a candy bar and a can of pop for the prisoner.

When he was brought into the break room, Frye was wearing the standard orange suit and his hands were handcuffed to his waist. Sullivan saw he wouldn't be able to reach the snacks. Frye wore a suspicious scowl as he sat down. "Mr. Frye, we're investigating the death of your cousin, Tamika, in a car accident and – her father said she was meeting up with you that night."

"Yeah, I remember," Frye mumbled uncertainly, "She was at McDonald's that night – Tamika had two girlfriends with – we drank some Courvoisier I had in my trunk. I don't know what happened after that."

"Well, Mr. Frye, she crashed into a tree at Central and Wabansia. Must have been going pretty fast – they all died."

"Of course, I heard about it – what do you want from me?"

Charly bluffed, "Mr. Frye, we have witnesses that say you were dragracing with her car."

Frye became indignant, "I don't even have no damn license, who's telling you this?"

"Mr. Frye," Sullivan continued, "We're not accusing you of being personally involved. But just tell us what happened – off the record – we don't care about the criminal case, we're just trying to get Tamika's family a settlement."

Shorty peered around suspiciously. He commanded Charly to put her pen and paper away. "OK, so after Tamika had a few drinks, she wanted to race. The first car over the Central Bridge. I was in the back seat of my friend's car. There were four of us but I'm not giving any names. We were getting close to the bridge and Tamika was pulling ahead. The guy in the front passenger seat wanted to scare her. So, he fired a shot out the window."

"All of a sudden, Tamika slammed on her breaks. We pulled ahead. We racing up the bridge, when we heard this Bang! We just kept going. We didn't want no trouble." His voice softened, "We didn't mean to hurt those girls. I went to the memorial for Tamika – but I couldn't face my uncle and auntie. I've never seen them like that."

"So, you think the gunshot made Tamika lose control?" Charly asked.

"I don't know," Frye said resignedly. "I'm done talking about this. I'm not saying anything else, without my lawyer here."

"What kind of car were you riding in?" Charly probed.

"I don't know cars. It was brown."

"Who's your attorney?" Sullivan asked. Frye told him it was Marvin Garrett. Garret was one of Sullivan's high school classmates. Sullivan had done some criminal defense work for Marvin, a stylish dresser, who sported a full-length leather coat in the courtroom. Sullivan brightened, "I know Marv, I'll see if I can help him out on your case."

"That's much appreciated, Mr. Sullivan – they say I was breaking in – I just got confused."

On the way back from the jail, Charly scribbled notes from the interview, while they discussed Shorty's account. "I think he's lying," Sullivan said, "The gunshot – I think they hit her car. We're supposed to photograph the vehicle at Serge's Salvage Yard. Have you been there yet?"

"No, I called and placed a hold on it. We have one week, before they crush it."

Sullivan had been dealing with Serge and his junkyard for decades. In the beginning, his dad had given him strict orders to pick up a pint of bourbon on his way to the auto graveyard. Now that Serge was on the wagon that was no longer necessary. Sullivan kept a crisp twenty handy, though, in case he needed "permission" to see a car.

He pulled into Serge's dusty lot. There were forklifts scurrying about with cars that had already been crushed into cubes. Sullivan was careful to stay out of their way. They stacked the cubes of metal onto ever higher piles. Sullivan entered the office and was greeted by Serge's German shepherd, which leapt from behind the counter. Rusty barked furiously but a chain kept him from reaching the customer side of the counter.

There were a few morose workers fetching parts for customers, before arguing the price with them. Sullivan entered Serge's private office where an air conditioner rattled loudly in the window. Serge was on the phone in a heated exchange, with an angry customer. "Our sign says, 'As is' 'No refunds'. Is there something you don't understand about that?"

After Serge slammed down the phone, he greeted Sullivan sharply. Serge hadn't been the same since he stopped drinking. He looked miserable and said that all the fun had gone out of life. His doctor had warned him, though, that to continue would destroy what was left of his liver. Sullivan gave him the last four of the vehicle identification number and Serge paged through a stack of smudged papers.

"Here it is, 4372. The insurance company signed off – it's a total loss. It's in Row Four, Aisle C."

Sullivan offered the twenty to buy Serge's lunch but he waved it away. "How about buying something, instead?" he asked sarcastically. Sullivan was only interested in photographing vehicles not purchasing their parts.

"If I see something I need, I'll let you know."

Sullivan strolled into the yard. He wished it was mandatory for high school drivers to tour a place like Serge's. If teens could see how a car could be distorted by a high speed crash. They were like abstract metal sculptures, barely recognizable as vehicles. He found the Chevy, with the number 4372 crudely scrawled in red paint on the driver's door.

The front end was crushed and the bumper was curved into a semi-circle. The engine block had been pushed back into the passenger compartment. The air bags were pale, rain spotted, and deflated. There were reddish brown stains on the upholstery, a shade very familiar to Sullivan. He bent down to inspect the flat front tires. He found what he was looking for in the driver's side tire.

Sullivan then set about photographing the vehicle from every angle. He climbed on the roof of the adjacent pick-up truck to photograph the roof. The numbers were also painted there. But the most important numbers were on the dashboard. Sullivan took what he called his "money shot," a close-up of the vehicle identification number. Absolute proof it was the car that cost Tamika her life! He finished by photographing all the undamaged parts, the rear end was still in good condition.

He stepped back into Serge's office. "I need the driver's side front tire – how much?" Serge gave him a sour look, "If I had more guys like you, I'd be out of business. You can have it for $40. Normally it would be $10 but you must need it pretty bad. I'll have Tony take it off. You can wait here." Sullivan said he would prefer to photograph Tony removing the tire, for chain-of-custody purposes.

After the tire was removed, Sullivan rolled it on the gravel and could hear a tinkling sound inside it. He fingered a small hole in the sidewall. The flat tire with the bent rim was definitely worth every penny. After Tony placed it in his truck, Sullivan called Charly. "Have you talked to Major Accident yet?"

"No, but I found out Dugan was assigned to it." Sullivan had dealt with Officer Mike Dugan before. He was an accident specialist with a degree from Northwestern University. "Can you find out when he's on, I have to see him." Charly found out Dugan was working the 3-11 shift and would be on the next day.

Sullivan drove to the Major Accident Investigation Unit. It was housed in a small building on the Near South Side. The unit had previously been located in a North Side building, where so much police corruption had been uncovered, the superintendent thought the cops needed a change of scenery. He knew Dugan to be honest and good at his job. When he asked the desk sergeant, he told him Dugan was still in roll call.

As the officers streamed out of the meeting room, he spotted Dugan, wearing bookish glasses on his narrow freckled face. He was not happy to see Sullivan. When Sullivan brought up the accident, Dugan gave him a tired look. "I don't have time for this. I've worked nine fatals in the last seven days," Dugan said exasperated. Sullivan thought maybe the job was getting to him.

"I've got something in my trunk you should see," Sullivan continued, "It's the front driver's tire."

Dugan looked at him blankly. "I've seen the car, I took a picture of that tire."

"Did you check it for a gunshot?"

"Now, why would I do that?" He got official. "If there are no reports of shots fired, I don't check for bullet holes."

Sullivan persuaded him to take a look at the tire, and Dugan's face fell when he saw the jagged round hole. He faced Sullivan, "What makes you so smart?" Sullivan told him Marvin Frye's account of the accident. Dugan said he would have the tire taken to the shop and checked. "Is there anything else?" he asked with some grudging respect.

"Yeah, that car Frye was riding in. He only told us it was brown. Could you have the hot sheet checked for brown cars that were reported stolen that night?" It was a common dodge in Chicago for drivers involved in hit-and-run accidents, or other illegal activities to report that their car had been stolen at the time. Dugan said he would make a few calls and get back to him.

It was later that week that he got back to Sullivan. "There were 33 cars reported stolen on that date – four were brown."

CHAPTER 11

Sullivan didn't hear from Dugan for several weeks. Finally, he got a late-morning call, "Had your coffee yet?" Before Sullivan could answer, "Meet me at the White Palace Grill at 11:00 and you can buy me breakfast. I'll show you how real smart guys work."

As he walked into the diner, Sullivan spotted Dugan at a back booth. He was sipping black coffee and poring over a thick report. Dugan ordered steak and eggs while Sullivan contented himself with ice water.

"I had that tire examined," Dugan began, "they found a 22 slug inside. Then, we got our big break. A witness who was visiting from Cincinnati called us claiming he heard the accident. He said he was with two friends and they were lost on the West Side. They happened to be coming down off a bridge when they saw two cars speeding in the opposite direction. They heard a crash behind them. They turned to look and saw one car had hit a tree while the other car took off up the bridge. The guys from Cincinnati were too scared to stop."

Dugan's meal arrived and he told the rest of his story between mouthfuls. "So, we flew all three of them here and put them up at the Palmer House. We interviewed them at headquarters. They couldn't remember much about the car that took off. So, we had them hypnotized." Dugan paused to slice his steak and let Sullivan catch up with his note-taking.

"They couldn't consciously remember what the car looked like, but under hypnosis all three recalled there was a white object in the rear window. So, remember there were four brown cars reported stolen that night?" Sullivan nodded, "One of them belonged to a guy named Octavius Simmons. Simmons was arrested last year for a smash-and-grab on Michigan Avenue. Guess who he was arrested with?"

"Frye?"

It was Dugan's turn to nod. "Octavius has a Chevy Impala registered to an address on the West Side. I went there with a three-man crew from the Tactical Unit. We found the car parked behind a housing project on Cicero. And, guess what, there was a white Teddy Bear in the back window. We had a warrant and found Simmons home. The 22 was underneath a pile of towels in the bathroom. The gun matched the slug."

"Did Simmons talk?" Sullivan asked.

Dugan gave him a tired look at being interrupted, "He gave up everyone in the car," Dugan continued, "including your boy Frye. We went out to Brown County and persuaded Marvin to talk. He's going to testify that Simmons fired the shot. In exchange, he's going to walk on the auto theft charge– their case was pretty thin to begin with."

Sullivan was pleased that he had helped with the outcome but not as self-satisfied as Dugan. "So, if anyone asks, just tell them how smart *we* can be."

"What's going to happen with Simmons?"

"He's being charged with three counts of homicide and assorted other charges, like fleeing the scene of an accident?"

"Did he have insurance?" Sullivan asked, hoping there might be another source of money for Tamika's family, "No, we're charging him with that, too."

Sullivan gladly picked up the check and promised to call Dugan the next time he had a fatal. Dugan gave him the tired look.

Back at his office, Sullivan and Morgan finished the final report on Tamika's accident. He included all of Dugan's findings and promised at the end to obtain the Major Accident report when it was completed. Knowing Dugan's backlog, Sullivan figured it could take months.

Sullivan charged handsomely for going to Brown County with Charly to interview Frye and for all the other legwork they had done. Morgan had no objection to the size of the bill.

The adjustor had a problem with it. She called from the insurance company's headquarters in Peoria to demand an explanation. "Mike, did you know they only had minimum coverage? Your bill is way too much for such a small policy."

"I didn't know," Sullivan stumbled, "What were the limits on the policy?"

The adjuster didn't answer but plowed forward. "The lawsuits by the other two victims were filed in the Municipal Division." Sullivan knew this division was for cases less than $50,000. Most of the filings were for unpaid rent or credit card debt. It was Cook County's small claims court.

"Like I said," Sullivan explained, "I didn't know the size of the policy, or that these were municipal cases."

"We'll pay this one, but from now on your invoices have to be itemized!" Sullivan hated that word.

"OK, there won't be any more charges. I'm closing my file."

"No, you're not," the adjustor contradicted, "You're going to deliver the settlement check to the deceased's family. You need to get them to sign the Release before they decide to get a lawyer." She overnighted Sullivan a check for the policy limit, $25,000.

Sullivan called Tamika's mother and made an appointment to drop off the check. He returned to their West Side home with the peeling porch. Tamika's father answered the door. His hard eyes were softer and sadder than they'd been before. Sullivan settled at the kitchen table and Tamika's mother again offered him water.

Sullivan removed the check and paperwork from his briefcase but first explained to the parents how the police had arrested a suspect. Tamika's father was incensed when he learned Simmons was his nephew's friend.

"Tamika's own cousin?" he uttered incredulously, "Shorty was always a troublemaker but nothing like this."

"Marvin's going to testify," Sullivan said, doing his best to sooth, "He's trying to make things right."

Tamika's mother broke into a sob and got up abruptly.

"Mrs. Dobbins," he called after her, "I'm going to need both your signatures on the Release."

"We're not signing anything until I talk to my lawyer," Tamika's father declared.

"Oh, who's your attorney?" Sullivan inquired matter-of-factly.

The man didn't answer.

"Well, that doesn't matter," Sullivan continued smoothly, "He might be able to get you more money, but I tend to doubt it."

"Cliff, the only lawyer we know is the one who did our real estate closing," Ms. Dobbins interjected, "What does he know about a case like Tamika's?"

"Even if he can get you more money, you're going to wait five years to get it," Sullivan added, "That's how long the backlog is in Cook County. I have your check right here."

"Just show us where to sign," the father demanded.

"How much is the check for again, Mr. Sullivan?" Tamika's mother asked softly.

"It's for the full policy, $25,000."

The father scoffed, "That will barely cover what we spent on medical bills and Tamika's funeral."

"Cliff," she cautioned him, "That's not Mr. Sullivan's fault."

"How can you do a job like this?" Cliff demanded, "Going to people's houses paying them blood money for their dead daughter."

"It is blood money," Sullivan admitted, "We can't make this right. Money - this is the best we can do."

Cliff grabbed the Release from Sullivan's grasp, signed it with fury in his eyes, and slid it to his wife. She calmly signed it and Sullivan handed her the check. She looked at Sullivan with dark-circled eyes. "I know you did you're best for us, Mr. Sullivan. You'll have to excuse my husband. Tamika was such a daddy's girl."

With the accident investigation finally finished, Sullivan turned his attention to wrapping up Trident. He scheduled a special Saturday morning session to go over the file with Charly and Morgan. They would scour their worksheets for unbilled hours and miles.

Frank Sullivan used to call these Saturday morning exercises "file reviews." He scheduled them yearly, and everyone hated getting up early to go through the files. His dad was determined, though, to find any charges they had failed to bill and send out the invoices. His clients weren't crazy about this, especially when Frank Sullivan charged for the time spent in billing the cases.

Morgan and Charly were in good spirits when they met Sullivan at the office. They were dressed even more casually than usual, in jeans, t-shirts, and gym shoes. They went over their notes and worksheets and were pleased when they found hours they had failed to charge. It would give a nice boost to their paychecks.

After Charly finished her files, she left Sullivan and Morgan to send out the final invoice. Morgan, as usual, had her own opinion about what was fair. "I don't get this," she complained, "We saved our clients from paying for a $5 billion clean-up and what do we get? Our final bill is for less than $5,000!"

"Yes, but we're making a total of $50,000 – more than we've ever made on a single case."

"You're comparing $50,000 to $5 billion?" Morgan asked in disbelief, "You're not charging enough."

"Morgan, we don't get a percentage of a settlement. If we did, I'd be a millionaire. It doesn't matter how big the payout is, we only get our time and mileage."

Morgan was most dissatisfied with this arrangement and reluctantly started typing. "I should have gone to law school," she muttered. Sullivan was long used to being a bottom feeder in the legal process. He was happy with the money they had made on Trident and relieved that he didn't have to make any more trips to Maple Grove.

He was also counting on their success with Trident carrying over into other environmental investigations. The Dream Team gave them rave recommendations. For a year, he and Morgan kept busy investigating pollution from manufactured gas plants and companies that treated wood with creosote. As usual, Sullivan received an education in these industries and felt he could treat a load of railroad ties with no problem.

A new U.S. President was elected. The candidate had won partly on the promise to reign in the EPA. All those regulations were hurting the bottom line of American corporations. When he forced the EPA to back off and not start any new Superfund sites, there were no environmental claims for Sullivan to investigate. Without pressure from the EPA, polluters didn't see any need for clean-ups or suing their insurance companies to pay for them.

Sullivan and Morgan both began to fear for her job security. Charly didn't share their concern. She had brought in her own clients who wanted her to personally investigate their claims. She began to work out of her home and stopped coming to the office regularly. Sullivan missed the camaraderie. Morgan had liked having a woman her age to banter with. Now, Sullivan and Morgan endured lunches with long silences.

Morgan only brightened up when she told Sullivan about her burgeoning romance with an EPA inspector named Evan.

"What happened to Stan?" Sullivan asked.

"He was fun, but no ambition. I felt like he was stuck, hanging out in bars with his union buddies."

"How'd you meet Evan, again?"

"I told you, he was the guy who stayed after work to answer my questions about Trident," Morgan said, a little miffed, "A week later, he asked me to meet him for drinks. You'd like him. He's from this little downstate town. He's close with his family and he's so polite."

Sullivan told Morgan he was happy for her and hoped to meet Evan someday. Inside, he was worried Morgan would be leaving Sullivan Investigations soon and he might never get to meet the guy.

Sullivan was desperate to keep Morgan. It was his old fear of working alone. With their environmental work gone, he hit upon a new job for her. Morgan had showed promise in medical malpractice investigations. She was very adept at reading and summarizing hospital charts. A previous employee hadn't been as selective, writing summaries that were almost as thick as the charts.

Sullivan proposed that Morgan take over the account of their single steady client, Stewart Community Hospital. Frank Sullivan was proud when he landed the account 30 years earlier. Frank had been a pioneer in malpractice investigation. The lawsuits the plaintiff's lawyers filed were seeking millions. Frank Sullivan preferred working on big money cases like these to small matters, like serving subpoenas.

Sullivan's dad stocked the office with an impressive library of medical textbooks, and he had recruited doctors who provided valuable consultations. Frank became knowledgeable in all areas of medicine. This was a necessity because a malpractice claim could be filed against any department of the hospital, from the birth center to the geriatric unit.

Stewart Community Hospital paid a monthly stipend to Sullivan Investigations to investigate any claim it encountered, whether the incident occurred in the parking lot or the operating room. The hospital's steady check covered Frank Sullivan's mortgage. Mike was dismayed, though, when Frank would lower their monthly bill because the hospital was going through a "slow" period. When claims picked up again, Frank never thought of raising it.

Frank was very proprietary about the hospital account and gave Mike only menial tasks. As a result, Mike Sullivan didn't know many people at Stewart, or how to work with the various department heads, When Frank suddenly died from the stroke. Mike was devastated emotionally but determined to keep Sullivan Investigations going.

He made Stewart Community Hospital his top priority. It was his only guaranteed income, and he intended to dazzle them with his dedication. He visited the hospital almost daily and became acquainted with key people. He gained their cooperation to obtain documents, X-ray films, pathology specimens, and other pieces of evidence.

They set him up with appointments to interview nurses, surgeons and employees from every department, including the guy who pushed the laundry cart. He injured a visitor.He now pulls the cart. Sullivan required their help in getting rules and regulations and other documents the hospital lawyers needed. Many cases didn't go to the lawyers. Sullivan settled them himself.

He was accustomed to "practicing law without a license." It had started with a friend asking him to go with her to traffic court. She had rear-ended someone and faced tickets for failure to avoid the accident and no insurance. When it was their turn, the judge asked, "What do you nice people want?" Sullivan admitted he wasn't a lawyer but was representing a friend. The judge threw out the tickets and approved a reasonable payment plan for his friend to pay for the damage. After that, Sullivan wasn't fazed by performing the duties of an attorney.

After a few months of providing stellar service to the hospital, Sullivan was ready to ask the administrator to restore their payment to its original amount. No. He would ask for even more. Sullivan arranged the meeting with Craig Cummings. Craig was a personal hero to Sullivan. He had worked his way up from the loading dock to the executive suite. He had gotten along well with Frank Sullivan and missed him, as did many of the hospital employees. Because of Frank, though, the hospital was paying Sullivan Investigations only $1,500 a month, instead of the original fee of $2,000.

Mike Sullivan brought figures with him that demonstrated the company's services had saved the hospital from large payouts. Sullivan had thought of the hospital as a large ship, with malpractice attorneys firing torpedoes at it. Thanks to Sullivan and the defense lawyers, none of them hit. The big lawsuits were either won or settled for a fraction of the original demand.

Sullivan asked that the monthly stipend be increased to $2,500. Cummings took Sullivan's request to the hospital board of directors and they compromised by raising it to $2,250. This was fine with Sullivan. Now, the check covered *his* mortgage.

Craig Cummings had never met Morgan, and Sullivan thought it was time. She was dressed in her finest white blouse and gray slacks. She had just gotten her hair done and her makeup was just right. Sullivan wore his three-piece suit and shirt with cufflinks. He wanted them to look their best but, more importantly, Morgan would impress Cummings with her grasp of medical malpractice.

The executive secretary showed them into the suite. They were all smiles as Sullivan announced that Morgan would now be responsible for the hospital's claims. The smile quickly fled Cummings' face. He asked Morgan if she could excuse them and wait outside. When he was alone with Sullivan, he broke the news.

"Mike, I don't know if you heard but we were just bought by Fremont Healthcare." Fremont was a large corporation buying up hospitals in the Chicago area. Sullivan never expected them to be interested in a small 250-bed hospital like Stewart. He carefully asked Cummings if it would affect their agreement.

"Fremont has their own Risk Management Department, Mike, so they want you gone as soon as possible. They described you as," Cummings made air quotes, *redundant*. I fought for you. I told them 'Mike knows everyone in the hospital. You're not going to save any money by getting rid of him.' They didn't care. You know the corporate mentality. They want their own people in place. They don't care if they're competent, or it costs them more money. They've agreed to keep you on for four months, until they get up to speed. I didn't want to say this in front of Morgan, but there's no point in her taking over."

Sullivan sat there stunned. His guaranteed money, his mortgage payment, was suddenly gone. But immediately his thoughts turned to Cummings. "Craig, what are you going to do?" Cummings gave a rueful smile. "I'm getting a small severance package and I have a job lined up at the University of Chicago Hospital. I'm going to work in Quality Assurance. But I'm sure going to miss this place. The hospital is like family to me." Sullivan felt exactly the same way.

When Sullivan emerged from the office Morgan gave him a hopeful little smile. Sullivan was in no mood to return it. "Let's go," he said tersely, "I don't want to talk here." As they walked to his car, Sullivan explained what had happened. "I've got to call Ann."

"Let's have lunch first," Morgan suggested, "You don't want to call her when you're upset."

Sullivan remembered he had promised her lunch at a fancy steakhouse to celebrate her taking over the hospital account. He reluctantly followed through on the promise. "Sure, maybe a beer will help?" Sullivan already knew it wouldn't. Drinking beer hadn't helped when his dad died. After they were seated at their table, an overly cheerful waitress took their order. Sullivan ordered a Guinness, Morgan said she would have a Moscow Mule.

"Mike it's going to be OK. You can apply at another hospital." Morgan rarely used his first name and Sullivan felt comforted.

"That's funny you mention that. I saw an ad in the Tribune last week. St. Theresa's is looking for a Risk Manager. The only qualifications I'd need are a couple of degrees." The cheerful server set down their drinks. Sullivan thanked her glumly.

"Really, in what?" Morgan asked brightly.

"Oh, I just need to be an MD and have a law license," Sullivan explained, "If I start now, I should be qualified by the time I'm 85."

Morgan couldn't suppress a nervous laugh. "I'm sorry, it's not funny. I was just picturing you as a college freshman."

"That's my biggest regret, Morgan, I wish I'd gone away for four years. It wouldn't have mattered what I studied. I would have had a great time partying. I'd also have a piece of paper. The way it is now, I don't have a single credential."

"You should be proud of yourself," Morgan insisted, "You were a risk manager – who cares whether you have a bunch of letters after your name."

Morgan's encouragement and the Guinness took the edge off of Sullivan's raw feelings of failure. "Risk Manager – that should be the name of a TV show," Sullivan said lightly, "Maybe I can write the pilot?"

They each ordered another drink before choosing their entrees. Sullivan figured it would be a long time before he dared to splurge on lunch. After he brought Morgan back to her car, Sullivan decided to break the news to Ann in person. He surprised her at her office with a single red rose. Ann looked at him funny. "What's the occasion – why aren't you at work? You said you were having Morgan start at Stewart."

"Can we talk somewhere?"

He followed Ann to her break room. She sniffed, "Have you been drinking?"

"Yeah, me and Morgan had an Irish wake." After Sullivan poured out the story, Ann took his hand. "Thanks for the rose," she said softly, "I'm happy with tulips."

"We've got to tell the kids," Sullivan suggested, "I don't see how we're going to keep up with their tuition." Tara and Flynn both attended the same private high school. Flynn was a freshman and Tara was a junior. It was expensive, but Sullivan considered it money well spent.

"We don't want to worry them," Ann countered, "I'll take a part-time job if I have to."

The thought of Ann taking a second job hurt him. Sullivan had been a good provider for decades. He relished his role as breadwinner.

"I'm going to have to tell our mortgage company," Sullivan continued, "We can apply for a modification."

Ann brightened a bit, "That's the Mike Sullivan I married – always positive. I've got to get back to my desk."

CHAPTER 12

Dealing with his mortgage company turned out to be tougher than Sullivan had anticipated. After navigating a maddening phone menu, Sullivan finally had a woman on the line. He quickly explained his sudden loss of income and asked that his mortgage be modified. He proposed they lower the payment to $1,500.

The woman was not in the least receptive to the idea. "Mr. Sullivan you signed an agreement to pay us $2,500 per month. It's an adjustable mortgage, so your payment may increase even more."

"What state are you in?" Sullivan asked.

"Pennsylvania, why?"

"I just wanted you to know my house isn't on Michigan Avenue, or Lake Shore Drive. I'm living on the West Side. My neighbors are mechanics and union carpenters. We don't play the stock market. We didn't crash the economy."

Sullivan was incensed that ruthless speculators had caused the recession. He had lost three-quarter of his income through no fault of his own. He hoped the government would bail out homeowners like him, but they bailed out the banks instead.

"Mr. Sullivan, we're not going to lower your payment until you demonstrate to us your loss of income. I'll send you the package you have to complete to apply for a modification."

Sullivan didn't know how difficult the process would be. He had to complete forms and send the necessary tax returns and financial statements.

Dealing with the mortgage company would become a part-time job. In the meantime, he considered borrowing from family and friends to save the house.

After he hung up with the mortgage company, Charly called. It was good to hear her voice again. Sullivan hadn't spoken with her in weeks. After a few pleasantries, Charly asked him for a favor.

"I've got a client who wants me to investigate crashes involving their vehicles." Charly now had her private detective license and was taking on her own clients. On paper, she still worked for Sullivan Investigations, but it was only a matter of time before she started her own agency.

"Really, what company are you working for?"

Charly gave him the name of a major auto manufacturer.

Sullivan was floored, "Volkswagen? They fired us before you came on board. We sent them a report about an accident that turned out to be physically impossible. My dad and I never did understand cars."

"They want me to – do you know anything about the black boxes they have in cars?"

Sullivan was aware that cars had devices similar to the ones on planes. They recorded data that showed the speed, RPMs, and braking of the vehicle prior to a crash.

"I need to go to junkyards to download the data," Charly continued, "and I have no idea how to do it."

Sullivan had no clue either but knew who to call.

"Charly, I have a friend who has the equipment to download those boxes. I'll see if he can help you out."

Charly sounded relieved. "Is Morgan there, I'd like to say hi."

"She's off right now. Things are kind of slow around here. We lost Stewart."

"I heard they were bought out," Charly said sadly, "What are you going to do?"

"Morgan and I are looking for work. We've been going downtown to law firms to give presentations. We bring a tray of sandwiches. The partners don't even bother to show up. The guys from the mailroom eat all the sandwiches."

Charly laughed. "I'm sorry, it's not funny. I feel bad, though. I wish I could help."

"I still know how to do scale drawings of accidents. Does Volkswagen need diagrams?"

"Mike, I'd love to give you a piece of the work, but I'm on this exclusive list of investigators and they don't want anyone else to work on their cases."

"What makes you so popular, besides your brilliant intellect?"

Charly gave a small laugh, "A lot of my clients prefer female investigators," Charly explained, "We're less threatening. We get better cooperation."

"Charly, I'm only 5'7" – I'm not scary," Sullivan insisted.

"I know –but these companies have their policies. Who's your friend that knows about black boxes?"

"Jake Houlihan – we grew up together."

"I remember, the guy you took the detective test with. Tell him I'll pay him for his time. Maybe he can teach me how to do it."

"I'm sure Jake will help. This gives me an excuse to call him."

Charly didn't want to hang up. "Let me guess, you're sitting there by yourself. Did you have your shrimp fried rice yet?" She was referring to Sullivan's favorite afternoon pick-me-up.

"Not yet," Sullivan chuckled, "I don't have anyone to send to that Chinese joint. Remember their lunch special?"

"I told you I never liked that place," Charly complained, "I mean, I liked the hot tea and the almond cookie but that was about it."

"I liked the conversation," Sullivan said wistfully, "I don't have anyone to talk to about Russian literature, or French music. Work was fun back then."

"If it's any consolation, I'm not having any fun either," Charly said glumly, "I never did like the real world."

The conversation had turned gloomy. "Hey, when the weather gets better," Sullivan said brightly, "We can sit outside at Phil's and have a drink." Whenever Sullivan passed an outdoor restaurant on a summer day, he'd think, 'That's the good life.'"

"OK, but one Guinness," she chided, "And then back to work."

"Nonsense, once we start day drinking, we can't stop," Sullivan declared, "Remember how sleepy you used to get?"

Charly said she could meet him for drinks in a week or so. He promised to have the information from Jake by then. There was nothing keeping Sullivan at the office, so he called his old friend and said he was coming over.

Houlihan's operation was much larger than Sullivan's. He had a big modern office, in a steel and glass building. He had secretaries and investigators scurrying around. It was a whirlwind of activity compared to Sullivan's office. Jake was on the phone as usual. He was berating a witness into giving him a statement. Jake's voice continued to rise until at last the witness surrendered. The phone call finally ended.

"Why didn't that guy hang up on you?" Sullivan asked, "I would have."

Jake grinned, "You're looking good. Are you planning to live forever?"

Unlike his friend, Sullivan had managed to keep the weight off. Jake had once been a top athlete. Now he was out of shape. His round face often wore a bemused look and he laughed at his own jokes.

"Need any help, Jake, I could use the work."

"Only if you bring us your clients," Jake countered. "Besides, if you *don't* join us, we're just going to put you out of business anyway."

"That is why I couldn't work for you, Jake. You're not even human."

"I'm kidding. What do you need?"

Sullivan explained how Charly had landed a big client but needed to learn a new skill to keep the account. "Sure, we have the equipment," Jake said, "I can show her how to do it in fifteen minutes. In fact, I'm doing a download on Thursday, if you and Charly want to meet me."

"Where at?"

"A Chicago Auto Pound, where else?" The cops pronounced the word "pond" as if there was a river of cars flowing through Chicago and this was where some of them had run aground.

"Sure, if they haven't crushed it yet," said Sullivan, "They have a habit of destroying 'Exhibit A.'"

Jake laughingly agreed, "That's why I gave one of the cops a sawbuck –he promised to keep an eye on it until I get there."

Sullivan called Charly to confirm the appointment. As they were parting, Jake proposed a round of golf after the snow melted.

While driving home, Sullivan received a frantic call from Ann. The way she said "Mike!" made him immediately fear Flynn had been badly hurt. Sullivan was too upset to drive and talk at the same time. He hung up without listening to another syllable. As he approached his house, he saw a squad car calmly cruising in the opposite direction. Sullivan was relieved. At least Flynn hadn't been hit by a car.

Flynn had had a close call when he was younger, racing across their busy street to greet Tara when she got home from school. Close calls aside, Flynn was forever getting hurt. They had made multiple visits to the emergency room for stitches. Flynn's worst fear was to be restrained and the nurses strapped him down to suture his wounds. Tara, cautious from birth, hadn't been in the hospital since the day Sullivan first cradled her.

Sullivan found Flynn sitting calmly in the kitchen. He was holding an icepack to the back of his head. Ann was hovering behind him, spreading his hair to inspect the gash.

"Why did you hang up on me?" she asked, more bewildered than angry.

"I'm sorry. You sounded so upset. Traffic was bad, I had to concentrate. What happened?"

Ann started telling the story. Flynn still seemed a bit dazed.

"Flynn was at the park with his friends. This other boy came up and snatched Flynn's hat. Flynn chased him to get it back."

"I grabbed my hat and I was walking away from him," Flynn interrupted, "He threw his bicycle lock at me. It got me right in the back of the head." Flynn started to cry. He was ashamed of his tears and roughly rubbed them away.

"Do you think it needs stitches?" Sullivan asked Ann, dreading another ER visit.

"It's pretty deep, Mike, I think you should take him."

As they drove to the hospital, Sullivan questioned Flynn, Who was this kid? Did anyone call the police? Why not? The questions brought more tears. Sullivan resumed consoling his son. Sullivan was furious at the boy who had injured Flynn. He was also angry about being back in the ER but kept his cool while they sat in the waiting room. Sullivan spotted a sign on the wall that said, if a patient was a victim of a crime, the Illinois Attorney General would pay their medical bills. Sullivan wrote down the number to call. Flynn was not only a crime victim, Sullivan no longer had health insurance. He would have to pay out-of-pocket.

When they arrived home, Sullivan immediately called 911. The officer who answered listened laconically. "What was the weapon – a bicycle lock? I don't think the detectives will be much interested. You can still come to the station to make a report."

Sullivan brought Flynn with him to help fill out the report. The desk sergeant asked Flynn, "So you're sure that this kid – Anthony Cooper – was the one who threw the lock?"

Flynn nodded.

"Any witnesses?" the sergeant asked. Flynn nodded again. "Make sure you list them on the report."

Finally, the Sergeant asked if Flynn wanted to press charges. Flynn looked to his father.

"Who do we talk to about that?" asked Sullivan.

The sergeant told him someone from the state's attorney's office would be contacting them. Sullivan later got a call from a young sounding assistant state's attorney.

"Mr. Sullivan," he started calmly, "I spoke to the investigating officer. She knows Anthony Cooper. Says he's a good kid. Never been arrested before. She told his parents what happened. They're going to handle this. She doesn't think you should press charges."

Sullivan was stunned. "What if it was your kid?"

"I'm sure you're upset but I don't think this is serious enough – you don't want the kid to have a record. It was just a bunch of teenage boys messing around and someone got hurt. Happens all the time."

Sullivan was seething, but saw he was getting nowhere with the state's attorney. He would report the crime to the Attorney General. The sign in the ER promised they would reimburse him for the ER bill.

After that excitement subsided and Flynn's latest wound healed, time went slowly for Sullivan. Morgan was so bored she made chains from paperclips. Finally, Sullivan received a call from one of his former clients, Janet Sterling.

She was calling from home. She only worked part-time now at her downtown law firm. The environmental work had dried up and she was devoting her energy to her three young children. After the oldest started First Grade, Janet had run successfully for the school board. She was calling Sullivan in her new capacity.

"Mike, have you ever done residency investigations for a school district?"

Sullivan admitted that he hadn't and secretly hoped it wouldn't disqualify him.

"Well, after the difficult work you did for us, this should be relatively simple. My son's school has a major problem. Kids are sneaking in from other districts. They're not only stealing tuition – about $7,000 in our district – but they cause the most trouble. They're a drain on our resources."

Sullivan listened quietly. He had no idea how he would go about catching these kids but was desperate for work.

"We had a retired FBI agent investigating these students," Sterling said, "We paid him a lot of money to sit in his car all day. He did surveillance on the students but never did prove where they lived. His reports were inconclusive. So, at our last board meeting, we terminated his contract. We're looking for a new investigator and I suggested we try you."

"Thanks for thinking of me, Janet, you say this is a contract?"

"Yes, the district pays a monthly stipend. It adds up to about $25,000 a year. How would you like to audition for the job?"

"Sure, my assistant Morgan can help. If you want surveillance, we'll need at least two people."

"So, Janet, do you miss working full-time?"

"I miss the people but it's nice to finally have a life. No more weekends and late nights at the office. I don't know how I did it with young children. And, if I ever want to hear an oral argument, I have a four-year-old who can argue with the best of them."

When Sullivan told Ann about the possible job, she demurred. "I know we need the money, Mike, but I feel kind of funny. These parents, they're just trying to get their kids into decent schools."

"They're stealing from the district and making their kids live a lie," Sullivan countered, "We would never do that to our kids."

A week or so later, Sullivan and Morgan were sitting in the office of the school superintendent. He spoke in a frustrated manner. "Mr. Sullivan, I watch them with my own eyes getting off trains and buses. We need to prove they live out-of-district so we can kick them out. Are you planning to do surveillance like the last investigator we used?"

"We'll give it a try," Sullivan said hopefully.

The superintendent tossed an inter-office envelope to Sullivan. It contained packets of information on two Fourth Grade boys. Sullivan handed one packet to Morgan and read the other. The boys were cousins and their parents claimed they lived at the same address.

After they left the district office, Morgan was thrilled about the assignment. "I've always wanted to do undercover work."

"It's not exactly undercover, though we could pass for teachers."

Sullivan and Morgan went to meet Sterling at the school office. She provided them with yearbook pictures of the two boys and their class schedule. "Good luck Mike," Sterling said, "We hope you nail them."

Their first day on the job, Sullivan and Morgan arrived at the school a half hour before dismissal. Sullivan had persuaded Charly to help out. She was stationed in a car outside the playground, in case they lost the students. Sullivan had dubbed them "Frog 1" and "Frog 2" in the spirit of the *French Connection*. He took "Frog 1."

When the bell rang, both boys bolted out the door onto the playground. Sullivan hurried after "Frog 1" but immediately lost him. Outside on the playground, there was a sea of students wearing backpacks. The boys all looked the same to Sullivan.

Morgan was having the same problem, searching the playground for "Frog 2."

Sullivan called Charly, "We lost them. See if you can pick them up."

Charly called back in less than five minutes. "Mike, I've got them. They're walking north down Caldwell toward a park."

Sullivan waved for Morgan to join him and they set off at a brisk pace to catch up to the boys. They finally spotted them a half block ahead. They fell in behind and followed them from a safe distance. The boys were oblivious to being followed. Charly pulled over to the curb. "Do you still need me?"

Sullivan shook his head, "We've got them. Thanks. It would have looked bad if we had lost them the first day."

Thus began several hours of following two Fourth Grade boys. At the park, they were play-fighting with their friends. They also taunted girls, but Sullivan could see it wasn't serious. His behavior at that age had been far worse.

Morgan soon learned how boring surveillance could be. She sat on a park bench, scrolling through her phone, glancing up occasionally to make sure "Frog 2" hadn't left the park. As it started to get dark, students left the park one-by-one or in groups. The two Fourth Grade boys eventually left and walked toward a library.

Inside the library it was warm and Morgan picked up a bestseller she had wanted to read. The boys had gone down to the children's level. Sullivan and Morgan stayed upstairs, keeping an eye on the exits. When the Fourth Graders left the library, Sullivan and Morgan followed them to a nearby Wendy's restaurant. Things were looking up. Now they could have something to eat and drink as they watched the boys.

Finally, it became pitch dark outside. The boys went out to the parking lot and stood waiting. A car pulled up and a woman got out. They waited until the driver entered the restaurant. Morgan took out her phone to photograph the car's license plate and the boys climbing into the back seat. Sullivan suddenly heard a sharp voice behind them. "Who gave you permission to photograph my son?"

Sullivan whirled around to face the woman driver. She looked to be in her 30s and her mouth was set hard. "We're residency investigators for the district," Sullivan explained hesitantly. "They assigned us to make sure your son and his cousin live in the school district."

"Are you calling us liars?" she cried, "I gave them our lease and the utility bills."

Sullivan and Morgan felt the heat of embarrassment and didn't know what to say.

"OK then," Sullivan assured her, "If you have the proper documents, we can close our file. We just needed to make sure."

Early the next morning, Sullivan got a call from the superintendent. "I had an angry mother in here this morning, Mr. Sullivan. I didn't expect you'd get caught photographing students. She's threatening to sue the district for invading her son's privacy. We have to be very careful about photographing students. We need permission slips from their parent."

"I'm sorry it didn't go better but it was our first assignment. We did run the mom's license plate and it's registered to an address in Chicago." Sullivan paused, "From now on, we'll be more discreet."

"I'm sorry Mr. Sullivan but, if this is how you conduct residency investigations, we'll find someone else."

Morgan had already resigned herself to them not getting the contract. Sullivan called Janet Sterling to apologize. "Mike, what were you thinking? Don't you know anything about how careful schools have to be? I'm *not* looking forward to the next board meeting."

Sullivan couldn't believe they had blown a chance at steady money. Ann was more philosophical. "I know you wanted that contract but — following kids?" She made a face, "It's just too creepy."

CHAPTER 13

A misty drizzle was falling the day Sullivan and Charly drove to Auto Pound 3 to meet Jake. Chicago was in the grip of its usual gloomy spring. The pound was located beneath an expressway and was guarded by a forbidding fence. Jake drove up and parked next to them. Two more cars parked. One contained Jake's client, James "Cotton" Weaver.

Weaver was a legendary trial lawyer in Chicago. His hair was white and he was getting a bit stooped. Age, though, had not slowed his hard-drinking nor quieted his booming voice. The other car had Michigan plates and was driven by a lawyer for General Motors. After introductions were made, they walked toward the office.

Weaver had filed a lawsuit against GM alleging the brakes on his client's car had failed. "This was a completely avoidable accident," he thundered more than once.

"Sure, Cotton, if your client had kept his eyes on the road," the GM lawyer responded.

"It should have been survivable, too," Weaver added. He turned to Jake, "Are you certain you can do the download in this weather?"

Jake thrust an umbrella at Charly, "Sure, if *she* can keep my equipment dry." Charly was taken aback by Jake's brusque manner, but Sullivan was never fazed by Jake's antics. Jake had been a force of nature since they were four. Charly dutifully shielded the device as a pound employee led the group to the car. It was a red Impala with heavy damage to the front end. Jake pulled a pair of mechanics overalls over his clothes. He suggested Charly buy herself a pair.

Jake slid underneath the car to hunt for the black box. It was formally called an SDM, sensing diagnostic module. Sullivan asked Weaver what kind of data it recorded. "Speed is the main thing we're interested in. It starts recording about 10 seconds before the accident. Jake, what are you doing down there?" Weaver was impatient, as the lawyers huddled under their umbrellas in the chilling rain. Mud was spattering Weaver's Italian loafers.

"I found it," Jake announced, "It's under the center console." The SDM was still connected to a bundle of wires. Charly crouched down to watch as Jake disconnected it. He finally emerged from underneath the car, proudly holding up the box, oblivious to his mud-covered overalls.

Charly continued to hold the umbrella, as Jake plugged his device into the SDM. "This is going to take a while," he explained to the small gathering. Jake turned to Charly and stared at her intently. "You don't remember me, Charlevoix?"

Charly was baffled. "No, I just know you're an old friend of Mike's."

Jake wore his usual mischievous grin, "I talked to you about ten years ago," Jake continued, "You were the witness to that bus accident." Jake explained that the bus company had hired him to identify and interview witnesses. "I found about ten people, besides you."

Slowly, the circumstances dawned on Charly. "You're the guy who wouldn't stop calling my work!" Jake chuckled, but Charly wasn't smiling. "You were a hard case," Jake told her, "I usually get cooperation – ask Mike – but you were a piece of work!"

"Cut the bullshit, Jake," Weaver interrupted, "When are you going to finish the download?"

Jake directed his attention to his device and started to read the data. "This doesn't look good, Cotton. Your client was traveling 120 in a 30 mile-per-hour zone. He didn't apply his brakes until eight seconds before the crash."

Weaver was uncharacteristically speechless, while the GM attorney took the opportunity to gloat. "Well, gentlemen – I believe that concludes our business here." Jake disconnected his equipment and started packing. Weaver reminded Jake to send him his bill. The well-heeled lawyers trudged through the mud back to their cars.

Sullivan had been silent during the download, but now he turned to his old friend. "Jake, I knew you were working the other side of that bus case. I always wondered how you got those witness statements."

Jake grinned, "A well-placed buck or maybe a bottle and they said whatever I wanted."

Sullivan had done his own share of "reimbursing" witnesses. He found it distasteful and worried it would taint their testimony.

"Is that right?" Charly snapped angrily, "Is that the way you treat people? Your calls –I almost got fired."

Sullivan watched Jake's grin fade.

"She doesn't mean it," Sullivan hurried to add.

Charly recovered her composure and smiled hopefully at Jake, "I'm sorry – I have no right to judge how you do your job."

"Hey, I've been called an asshole before," Jake grinned, "No hard feelings. I'll rent you my equipment any time you need it – for 50 bucks. Don't forget those overalls."

On their way back to the office, Sullivan explained his long relationship with Jake and how fiercely loyal he had been. "Jake thinks you're OK, you can count on him," he assured Charly. Sullivan told her about the night Frank Sullivan suffered his stroke. Jake had searched everywhere for him and found Sullivan sitting stunned in a friend's backyard, absently sipping a beer. "Jake was bringing up all these old stories about my dad – I was laughing and crying at the same time. You might think Jake is full of shit, but he has a good heart. If you really want to get in good with him, buy him tickets to a Hawks game."

Sullivan dropped Charly at her car and returned to his empty office. Morgan was away on a two-week vacation to Montana with her new boyfriend from the EPA. Evan was looking more and more like a keeper.

There weren't any new files to open, so Sullivan spent his time assembling paperwork for his upcoming hearing at the Attorney General's office. After his claim to be reimbursed for Flynn's medical bills had been rejected, he had to come up with something to say.

The day of his hearing, Sullivan entered a waiting room packed with females. They were relatives of crime victims. Sullivan was the only male among them. The rest were mothers of sons and daughters who had been murdered. Along with their grief, they faced crushing debt and prayed the state would pay their bills.

They spoke freely with Sullivan and he learned most had been afraid to help the police with their investigation. If an arrest was made, they declined to testify against the assailant. Sullivan could sense their fear. They were stuck in crime-ridden neighborhoods, and any attempts they made to attain justice for their children – it would be like signing their own death warrants.

In the presence of their fear and sorrow, Sullivan felt small and insignificant. Flynn had been a victim of a crime – not a CRIME. They tried to stay positive as they waited their turn to plead their case. Several asked Sullivan what he planned to say. "I'm going to tell them the truth. The cops asked me not to press charges against the kid, so I didn't. Now, they won't pay my bills, because I didn't prosecute. It's not fair."

Several women thought Sullivan's argument sounded good and wished him luck. Sullivan's hearing was brief and the outcome seemed preordained. The Attorney General would not pay his bills unless he pressed charges. The incident with the bike lock now seemed so trivial, and Flynn appeared to be unaffected by it. Sullivan emerged from the hearing room wearing a beaten look. He wished the women in the waiting room better luck.

When Sullivan got home, he told Flynn the outcome. His son was utterly unconcerned. He had never wrestled with paying bills of any kind, least of all medical expenses. Flynn was more focused on trying out for the freshman baseball team. He dreamed of being their starting lefthander.

Tara had taken a different direction at school. She was blessed with an athletic build but lacked the talent and coordination of her brother. She tried out for the debate team and chose other scholarly pursuits. Tara was in a good mood when she arrived home late from school.

"Mom, I just got asked to the spring formal," Tara announced. Ann was happy for her but wondered if she could wear last year's dress. Tara made it plain that it was out of the question. She would also need new shoes.

"Who are you going with?" Sullivan asked.

Tara told him the boy's name, Chris, but it didn't register.

"He's really smart, Dad, he's on the chess team."

"How did you meet this guy?"

Tara looked at her dad as if he had no idea who she was. "Don't you remember, Stephanie and me are managers for the chess team?"

"Chess teams have managers?" Sullivan asked perplexed.

"Yeah, we carry all the equipment, set up the boards and the clocks. We get them water if they need it. Mostly, we keep their spirits up. When they're losing, some of them look like they're going to cry." Tara smiled, "We thought it would be a great way to meet boys."

"What about the chess part?"

"Oh, between tournaments, they practice against us. I beat Chris in ten moves. He was mad and said it was a trick checkmate. But it got us talking – he's really nice, Dad. You're going to like him."

Ann and Tara found a dress that was still fashionable at a discount shop. They splurged on some delicate sandals and the costs mounted with the purchase of a boutonniere. The night of the dance, Chris came to pick her up. He was quite the gentleman. Sullivan hadn't been addressed as "sir" since he was being scolded in high school.

Sullivan decided to use Frank Sullivan's strategy for sizing up boyfriends. His dad believed that a person's true personality came out in the way they played chess. Sullivan, for example, was an unrelenting attacker who never backed down. He proposed a quick game with Chris.

Tara flounced down in her dress, giving Sullivan her "Aw, Dad" look."

Chris, though, eagerly set up the pieces. Sullivan not only planned to win but, when he was ahead, he intended to turn the board around and beat Chris with the inferior position. This didn't happen. Chris chatted amiably with Ann while he decimated Sullivan. Tara moaned, as Sullivan stubbornly refused to resign.

"Dad, we're going to be late. We're supposed to do pictures at Stephanie's house." Ann already had her coat on. Sullivan tipped his king over and congratulated Chris on his win.

"It was a pleasure, Mr. Sullivan, hope we can do it again."

Sullivan shook Chris' hand and held on for an extra beat. "Get her home by 11:00," he said tersely. Chris looked a bit panicked as they left.

Tara walked in at 11:00 on the dot. "What did you say to Chris?" she demanded, "He acted like he was in a hurry all night." She stomped off.

While Morgan was away, Sullivan took on any assignment he could find, including some that would have been beneath her standards. One of the low points was when Sullivan was asked to serve a summons on a psychic. He had to pick up the summons from a rival fortune teller.

Sullivan's new client, Madame Z, operated out of a brick bungalow on a busy street. Her greatest expense was the garish neon sign in her picture window. Madame Z was very businesslike as she handed Sullivan the papers and a $100 bill. She had psychically selected Sullivan's name from a list of local process servers. She hoped the lawsuit would knock her rival out of business.

Sullivan didn't always carefully read the summonses he served, but this was a page-turner. The plaintiff was a friend of Madame Z's who had visited her rival on a lark. The plaintiff didn't take fortune telling very seriously but was chilled when the fortune teller predicted she would be dead within six months.

The plaintiff was only 35, and in excellent health. After six months of dread, the woman was still in good health. The lawsuit accused the psychic of causing emotional pain to the plaintiff and demanded $50,000 in damages. Sullivan agreed to serve the summons for a $100, no matter how many trips it took.

On his way to serve the summons, Sullivan fought a frustrating battle with stop-and-go traffic. The busy street was lined with tacky businesses like Madame Z's and assorted fast-food joints. Sullivan parked in front of a small house displaying stars in the front window. He had no problem serving the psychic. She never saw it coming.

Sullivan took on more questionable assignments, like watching a women's backyard to make sure a neighbor wasn't poisoning her dog. He charged a flat fee for such matters, as he couldn't command his usual fee, but some assignments were beneath him.

A young downtown attorney called to ask Sullivan to spy on his ex-girlfriend. "We had a one-night stand," he claimed in his cocksure manner, "and she got pregnant. She demanded I pay for the abortion. I was fine with that but she wanted it done by a surgeon in Paris. I flew her there and paid for everything. I'm worried she just kept the money and didn't get the abortion."

"What do you want me to do?"

"I need you to go see her. I don't care what pretext you use. I just need you to see if she's still pregnant."

Sullivan recoiled at the request and the attorney's cavalier attitude. Once someone had insulted him by suggesting Sullivan would do anything for money – including retrieving a $100 bill from a toilet. This assignment felt just as disgusting and he turned it down.

After Morgan returned from vacation, they received another dubious assignment. A woman in Detroit offered them $500 to follow her husband. He was spending the weekend at a conference in Chicago, and she wanted to know his movements. It was obvious they had a marriage built on trust. Though she didn't spell it out, the woman thought it would be better if Sullivan had a young attractive female with him.

Morgan balked at the very idea. "Mike, this is pretty low. You want to use me as bait? Isn't this kind of like one of those prostitution stings?"

"You mean entrapment? I would never ask you to do something that makes you uncomfortable. I just thought we could hang out at his hotel and see what this guy is up to. It's probably nothing, but we could use the five hundred bucks."

Morgan reluctantly agreed to meet Sullivan in the hotel lobby. "Don't expect me to wear anything slutty," she said curtly, "I don't own anything like that."

When they met in the lobby, Morgan was dressed conservatively in a long-sleeved blouse and Capris. Morgan's beauty would stand out, Sullivan thought, regardless of what she wore. Sullivan and Morgan studied a photograph of the husband and wandered the lobby looking for him. The wife had even supplied them with his room number.

They finally spotted him in the hotel bar. He was fattish and appeared to be in his 50s. He was wearing some kind of badge he had picked up at the conference. There were other badge-wearers in the bar, but the man sat alone drinking something that looked like scotch with empty stools on either side of him.

Morgan strolled in alone and took a seat at the bar, while Sullivan watched them from the lobby. The man glanced more than once at Morgan. She had begun a spirited conversation with the bartender, who had kidded her about ordering a cosmopolitan. The bartender kept up the banter as he mixed the drink. Sullivan could see that Morgan had brightened his day.

The husband continued to sit there quietly, until he finished his drink and paid his bill. Morgan's attractiveness had been wasted on him. As he left the bar, Sullivan fell in behind. The man waited for a glass elevator to take him to his room in the atrium. Sullivan got on the same elevator. They got off on the third floor and Sullivan saw him enter 317. Sullivan and Morgan took up a position in the lobby where they could watch the elevator. They never saw the man again that evening.

Sullivan called the woman in Detroit and reported that her husband had not hit on his assistant and had retreated early to his hotel room – alone. The assignment had been boring and didn't prove much, like most surveillance jobs. The personal check they received, though, somehow made it worthwhile. Something else came in the mail that day. Sullivan's credit card bill that contained charges for the high-priced drinks they had at the hotel.

Ann was furious when she saw it. "What kind of drink costs $15?" she demanded.

"A cosmopolitan?" Sullivan answered weakly.

"I know you were working, but I don't like the idea of you and Morgan hanging out at a hotel. I especially don't like the drinking. I trust you, Mike, but I think you and Morgan are getting a bit too friendly."

"Besides, we can't afford her anymore," Ann stated flatly, "I'll take over the typing and filing. You're going to have let her go. We just don't have enough work."

Sullivan knew she was right and didn't argue. He dreaded breaking the news to Morgan, who was so excited about being back at work.

The next morning, Morgan was in a great mood. The sun was shining and people had shed their winter coats. His dad had taught him to make firings short and direct. Sullivan hesitated, though. He didn't want to hurt Morgan and didn't want her see how much losing her was going to hurt him.

Seeing the strange look on his face, Morgan asked what they had on the agenda.

"We made some changes while you were on vacation," he said grimly.

Morgan was still in good spirits but sensed something was coming.

"We gave away your job," Sullivan continued. "Ann is going to take over the typing, all the clerical work."

Morgan stared at Sullivan in disbelief. "What?" Sullivan could see her eyes begin to glisten and her lower lip tremble.

"It's for the best, Morgan. You've got a great future ahead. You don't want to be stuck here," indicating their shabby surroundings.

Morgan stoically swallowed her tears. "There's not much for me to say, if you and Ann have made up your minds."

"This is hard for me, Morgan, I've loved working with you. You've made my job fun again. Nobody makes me laugh the way you do."

"I somehow don't feel like laughing," Morgan said softly, "What do I tell my parents?"

"Just tell them we ran out of work. I'll give you two week's pay and the best references you've ever had. No one can write a recommendation like me."

There wasn't much else to say, so Morgan silently collected her belongings, sniffing back a tear or two. She tried to put on a brave front but she was too hurt. "I hope we can still get together – you know for lunch."

Sullivan assured her they would but wondered if it would ever happen.

CHAPTER 14

With Morgan gone, Ann came to the office in the evenings to take over the typing and work on the books. It became a nightly routine and Sullivan was grateful for her company. She was savvier about spelling than Morgan had been and was experienced at writing business letters. They proved to be a good team. Ann deferred to Sullivan on billing and didn't interfere in the investigation side of the business.

Unlike Sullivan, Ann had a good head for numbers, and her banking background helped her balance the checkbook. In short, she was more of a business person than Frank and Mike Sullivan had ever been. Ann knew how to cut costs and keep their overhead low. It was necessary, because the flow of new assignments had slowed to a trickle.

Finally, they had to eliminate their biggest unnecessary expense, the office itself. Looking around, Ann pointed out what they didn't need. "Mike, there's no reason for having three desks and all these file cabinets. We also can't afford $500 a month. We'll move your office back into the basement."

During some lean times, Sullivan Investigations had been headquartered in Mike's basement. He hated it but dutifully put on a suit every morning and descended the stairs. Frank would already be down there, hogging the space heater. Sullivan felt like he was working for "Scrooge & Marley" and he was Marley.

When Frank proposed cutting their overhead even more, Sullivan protested. "Dad, we can't get any smaller, or we're going to disappear."

They weathered the tough times until they could afford the small office overlooking the train tracks. Now, it looked like Sullivan would have to abandon this sanctuary, where he could concentrate on his cases, undistracted by family.

"I'll go see Carleton about breaking the lease," Sullivan responded, "I still have four months left on this one."

Harry Carleton operated a real estate office a few blocks from Sullivan's office. This is where Sullivan brought his monthly check. He called Carleton to say he would be stopping by. Sullivan found Carleton parked behind his desk. Though he was only in his 30s, Carleton owned several building's in the neighborhood. They were all upscale compared to Sullivan's.

He greeted Sullivan warmly. He had always been gracious, even when Sullivan had to postdate a rent check. Sullivan wore a sheepish smile. "Harry, I don't know how it's going for you but we're hurting." Carleton nodded, "I understand, Mike, half of my tenants are behind on their rent. What can I do for you?"

"I know I have four months left and I appreciate that you haven't raised my rent in five years but I just can't afford it anymore."

Carleton smiled knowingly, "You don't have to explain, Mike. Most of the business owners in your building have one foot in their spare bedroom. I'll let you out of the lease, but I'm afraid I'll have to keep your security deposit."

Sullivan was relieved. "That's fair, Harry, we've caused our share of damage over the years. We'll clear everything out before the first of next month."

Carleton rose to shake his hand. "I'm sorry to lose you Mike. You've been one of my steadier ones."

When Sullivan told Ann the news, she proposed recruiting Tara and Flynn to help. "We're not paying for movers."

Sullivan dreaded the move. In the past when Sullivan Investigations changed addresses, it disrupted business and they lost clients. He would have to endure it again, but it would save him so much in the long run. He also thought of a way to make the move a positive experience.

"I'll get Charly and Morgan to help. Morgan can bring her new boyfriend. All I have to give them is beer and pizza."

On his final day in the building, Sullivan made the rounds to say goodbye to his neighbors. The hotel furniture salesman, as expected, had no comment. But the insurance agent was still grateful for the whole life policy Sullivan had taken out and said he'd miss him. The artist didn't answer his door. The couple who ran the classy clothing store took it hard. The husband exclaimed, "You mean, even after that big case you told us about, you still can't afford this place?"

Sullivan explained that the work had dried up and he no longer had a use for fine suits. He thanked them and wished them well. As usual, there was not a single customer in the store. Sullivan rushed to a grocery store to pick up boxes. The crew would assemble at his office at 6:00 PM.

Tara and Flynn were decidedly unenthusiastic about the move, while Ann had collected some cleaning supplies, determined to leave the office in the best shape they could. Charly, Morgan, and Evan had also promised to help. In fact, they were already at the office when the Sullivan family arrived. Morgan's boyfriend, Evan, shook Sullivan's hand. Evan's hand felt surprisingly rough.

He had been a farm boy from Galva, Illinois. A tall Swede, who had been a star of his high school basketball team. One of Sullivan's treasured memories was driving through small towns in central Illinois during basketball season. He saw banners stretched across main streets and signs painted on barns. High school basketball was the center of life for each of those towns.

"Mr. Sullivan, I thought of an easier way to do this," Evan volunteered with a slight country accent, "There's a dumpster below the back window. We could just toss everything out, instead of carrying it down."

Flynn suddenly perked up. The prospect of pushing desks out a window promised to be spectacular. The back-saving idea equally appealed to Sullivan. Morgan was concerned. "We're going to toss everything – even the files?"

"She's right, Mike, aren't these confidential?" Charly added.

Sullivan seemed unconcerned. "Most of those cases are over. There's no reason to keep the files."

Ann didn't have an opinion. She was busy holding Tara's legs to keep her from falling, as she washed the outside of the windows.

"Let's have a beer first," Sullivan suggested, handing cans to everyone on the crew, except his kids. He chatted with Evan about his basketball career. At 6'3", Evan had been the starting center. His team had made it "downstate," the nirvana for high school athletes, but had lost in the quarter finals of the state tournament. He later tried to be a walk-on for his college team but wasn't nearly good enough to play for Purdue.

Flynn steered the conversation to baseball and demanded to know whether Evan was a Sox fan, or a Cubs fan. "Neither, I grew up in Cardinal country. How about you?"

"Sox all the way," Flynn replied.

Evan smiled and gave Flynn a fist bump, "Great, we both love it when the Cubs lose."

Drinking beer took the sting out of shutting down the office. They became kind of boisterous. It was exhilarating flinging files out the window into the dumpster. Every now and then, Charly or Morgan would glance at a file and recall the case. "Remember this one?" Charly asked, holding up a hit-and-run pedestrian case they had investigated. "Yeah, he got knocked out of his shoes, like they all do," Sullivan replied evenly.

Charly became animated, "Yes, but the best part – remember it happened in front of that high rise?"

"That's right," Sullivan recalled with a laugh, "a building full of optometry students. All of our witnesses wore glasses!"

Morgan was wistful, when she came across the Trident files. "Mike, you should save these. You could write something, like a letter to the Maple Grove newspaper. These are part of the town's history."

Finally, the office was empty, except for one desk and two file cabinets. The pizza had been eaten and most of the beer cans were empty. Ann was sweeping, while Tara chatted with Morgan about their favorite TV shows. Flynn basked in Morgan's presence, too tongue-tied to talk to her.

Evan chatted easily with everyone. He asked Charly if she was dating anyone. "No, I don't have a life right now. It's so much work starting this agency. The license, the insurance, and the questionnaires I have to fill out – do I carry a gun, do I use guard dogs?" She sighed, "Mike, how did you do it with a wife and two kids?"

"Poorly sometimes, but it was worth it to have the freedom. I got to coach Flynn's sports teams. I never missed one of Tara's debates."

It was almost 10:00 when Sullivan turned off the lights for the last time. Carleton had told him to push the keys through his mail slot.

The crew re-assembled at Sullivan's house to carry the remnants of his office into the basement. Some were yawning by then, as the beer had worn off. Sullivan told them to leave everything and he would set up the office in the morning. He thanked Evan for his help and wished him well. Sullivan could see by the way he looked at Morgan he would treat her well. He also noticed how Morgan laughed when she was with Evan, a special laugh Sullivan had never heard before. Sullivan gave Charly a hug. It was the first time he had hugged her since the time he had consoled her in her kitchen. This time, it felt comfortable.

Sullivan tried to adjust to working out of his house but felt so isolated. Sitting in his basement made him stir-crazy, especially on fine summer days. One afternoon, he couldn't take it any longer and surprised Ann at her office. "Don't you have *any* work?" she asked.

"I'm all caught up. C'mon, let's get out of here. It's too nice outside – can't you take a half-day?"

Ann asked and her boss gave her the afternoon off. "So, what are we going to do?"

"I promised to show you Waterfall Glen Park," Sullivan replied, "Remember?"

It was a long drive, but their stroll through the park was worth it. Sullivan saw that the creek was flowing clear now. The soapy film he had first noticed was gone. When they got back to their car, it was starting to get dark. There was no one around, so they climbed into the backseat and did their best to steam up the windows. Afterwards, they felt relaxed, tired, and hungry. Sullivan drove to the all-you-can-eat Chinese buffet. Ann called Tara and Flynn on the way to warn them they were on their own for dinner.

After they piled their plates high, Sullivan and Ann sat and talked about everything but their kids and the business. Ann was excited about the book club she had joined and described the romance novel they were reading. Based on her description, the men were impossibly handsome and the heroine frequently required a new bodice. While she was talking, an elderly woman made her way to Sullivan's table. She was carrying a doggy bag.

He dimly recognized her from the Trident investigation but couldn't place her name, "Mr. Sullivan," she began, "I'm sorry to interrupt your meal." Sullivan rose to greet her. "You don't have to get up. Is this your wife?" Sullivan introduced Ann.

"Mrs. Sullivan your husband is a wonderful man. You have no idea what he did for this town. You don't remember me, do you?" she asked Sullivan. "My granddaughter, Elizabeth" -

"Now I remember," Sullivan said recalling a ten-year-old who had developed a tumor in her leg. Her family had lived near the plant and they feared the aggressive cancer. "How is Elizabeth doing?" he asked, fearing her response. "Mr. Sullivan, thanks to that payout from Trident, we got her the best oncologist in the county. We were worried it was going to spread to the bone but she's been cancer-free for three years. She's on her school's track team." The woman beamed. "Again, I'm sorry to bother you two. I just thought you should know."

After she left their table, Ann looked at Sullivan with something approaching admiration. "Mike, this makes it all worth it. Those nights you were gone, you weren't *really* at a casino," she teased, "You were saving lives."

"And getting well-paid for it," Sullivan added, "But without you at home -Tara and Flynn wouldn't be doing so well."

"You're right," Ann agreed, "But let's not talk about them until we get home."

The summer crawled by for Sullivan. He filled his time with lawn work, cooking, and taking an increasing number of naps. Finally, he got some work from an unlikely source. Charly called him with an urgent request to tackle a terrorism investigation.

"Mike, I just got a call from a New York firm. They represent victims of the attack on Flight 782."

Only tribes in the Amazon were ignorant of the incident. A bomb had been slipped on the plane at the Hong Kong airport. It exploded over a small village in Thailand, killing all 101 on board and 11 people on the ground.

"I can't take the case," Charly explained, "The airline is one of my biggest clients. The lawyers filed a lawsuit claiming lax security. They're alleging that the former head of security at Hong Kong International was hiring screeners in exchange for sexual favors. One of these screeners allowed an unattended package on board."

"What do they want me to do?" Sullivan asked.

"They believe the security director left Hong Kong and is hiding out somewhere in the Midwest. They want you to serve a subpoena on him. His testimony is crucial to their case. I really talked you up. They should be calling you soon."

Sullivan thought it ironic a former underling providing him with work. He was grateful for Charly's loyalty, though, and earnestly thanked her.

"If you get this guy served, Mike, that would be thanks enough for me. Otherwise . . ."

"Don't worry, I would never make you look bad."

The next morning, Sullivan found himself on a conference call with a team of lawyers, who spoke with thick New York accents. He wrote down the security director's name as Khe Tong Zhuang. "We believe he may be living on the second floor of his father's house in Rockford," the lead attorney said, adding the father's address. "We're emailing the subpoena to you. It has to be served as soon as possible."

Sullivan indicated his schedule had suddenly been freed up and he would immediately start his search. After he received the subpoena, Sullivan drove the ninety miles to Rockford. He pulled up to the father's address and immediately knew Zhuang didn't live on the second floor. The house was a small, frame bungalow.

When he rang the bell, a middle-aged Asian man came out to talk to him. He denied knowing his son's whereabouts and claimed he hadn't spoken with him since he took the job in Hong Kong. Sullivan didn't believe a word but didn't argue. He left a card with the man in case he heard from Khe Tong.

After he left the father's house, Sullivan called his source for vehicle information. For years, Carl Sawyer had run plates for him and had never raised his rates. CS Services was still charging five bucks per plate. Sawyer would give him a hard time, though, if the car happened to be registered to a young female who listed an ideal height and weight on her driver's license.

"Let me guess, you spotted her at a stoplight?" he would say.

Sullivan would never misuse the information but knew investigators with fewer scruples. This time, he ran Zhuang's name to see if he owned a vehicle in Illinois.

"He's got a pickup registered to a rural route address outside Starling." Sawyer rattled off the make and model, along with the address. It was only thirty miles away and Sullivan headed there. He arrived at a gravel road that was posted with several "Keep Out" signs. It reminded Sullivan of the signs on the way to the Wicked Witch's castle. He ignored them and sped down the road raising a cloud of white dust.

As he neared the end of the road, he saw a house sitting not far from a river bank. A car was parked in front – no pick-up truck. Seeing it was a dead-end, Sullivan drove away from the house, looking for a hiding place. He found a small clearing and backed his car into it. He was shielded from the road by trees and planned to sit there until the pick-up came down the gravel road.

Sitting in the woods was hot and uncomfortable but Sullivan was willing to wait. A half hour went by, before he heard a car and saw the sedan that had been parked in front of the house. It was driven by a young woman. Sullivan was relieved that she didn't look at him as she passed. More time crawled by, as Sullivan worked a newspaper crossword puzzle.

He later heard a car coming and hoped it might be the pick-up. It was the sedan, again, returning to the house. This time, the young woman stared directly at him as she drove by. Sullivan felt exposed and became very uncomfortable. A few minutes later, Sullivan heard a car hurtling down the road at a high rate of speed. When it reached the clearing, the car made a sharp turn off the road and drove directly at Sullivan. It stopped a few feet from his front end, trapping his car in the clearing.

A short squat man with white hair climbed out through the passenger door. He approached Sullivan in a menacing manner. He wore spectacles, which didn't hide the anger in his eyes. Sullivan stayed in his car and lowered the driver's window.

"Who the hell are you?" the man demanded.

Sullivan wanted to ask him the same question but thought better of it.

"I'm an officer of the court," Sullivan announced with authority, "I'm serving a subpoena on the man who lives in the house near the river."

"I own that house," the man growled, "This is my property and you're trespassing. You're also scaring the hell out of that man's wife. She called me, all shook up."

"I'm sorry – I didn't mean to upset anyone," Sullivan said softly, "I just need to speak to her husband."

161

"First, you're going talk to *her*," the man insisted.

Zhuang's wife was the last person Sullivan wanted to meet. He wanted to save what was left of the element of surprise to serve the subpoena.

The landowner pointed down the road with emphasis. "You're going there now. That poor lady is losing her mind."

The man returned to his car and backed it up to the road. He blocked it, so that Sullivan had to drive toward the house. Sullivan slowly approached the small frame. It had a pleasant porch and the summer sun was shining, but Sullivan sensed a darkness coming from the house. He rang the bell and a woman came to the other side of the screen door. She made no move to unlatch it.

Sullivan could barely make out her features through the screen, but he could tell she was young. Her fear was apparent in her quavering voice as she asked Sullivan who he was. She spoke like a home grown Midwesterner. As his eyes adjusted to the gloom inside, Sullivan could she had a face with fine features and her brown hair had a stylish cut. He wished she would let him in but held out little hope for an invitation. Sullivan gave his name and explained he needed to meet with her husband for a few minutes.

This statement did nothing to diminish the worry in her eyes and Sullivan knew he'd have to tell her more. Whatever she was afraid of was far worse than what Sullivan had in mind.

"I'm here about Flight 782. There's been a claim made by families of the victims. Your husband is a key witness and we need to take his deposition."

"Mr. Sullivan, our life has been a living hell since the day that plane went down." Tears were forming in her eyes. She tried her best not to cry in front of a stranger.

"I understand," Sullivan said, though he had no clue what she was going through, "We'll make this as convenient as we can for your husband but we need his testimony. I take it he's not home."

"He doesn't live here," she stated coldly. "I have no idea where he lives. I can only get in touch with him through a third-party. I wish they would leave us alone but they won't."

Sullivan took out a card to hand her but she wouldn't open the door. "Here, I'll leave my card in your mailbox. If you hear from your husband, please ask him to call me?" If there was ever a wasted business card, this was one.

Sullivan drove back down the gravel road. There was no sign of the angry landowner. The afternoon was fading into dusk and Sullivan wanted to drive back to the city but he felt dissatisfied. He had come all that way to not only fail in his mission but to tip off the witness that he was wanted. Just before he got onto the interstate, he visited downtown Starling. He thought the local police could be persuaded to help him.

He found the sheriff's office with no problem. It was 19th Century and quaint like every other building on the main drag. A bell tinkled as he walked in. It felt homey for a police station. The sheriff was standing behind the counter. He wore a crisp brown uniform shirt that prominently displayed a star. He had an easy manner and welcomed Sullivan to state his business.

Sullivan explained he was working for some New York lawyers and looking for a Mr. Zhuang, who lived on the dead-end road to the river. He didn't mention Flight 782 or the subpoena. The sheriff called his deputy over. They both spoke in drawls. Sullivan felt like he had stumbled on Mayberry.

"Kirby, doesn't Edith have an Asian son-in-law?" the sheriff asked.

"Sure he married her youngest, Eileen, but I think they moved away."

The sheriff looked at Sullivan, "What do you need him for?"

"It's an insurance claim, he's a witness. I need to meet with him for a few minutes."

"If that's all you need, we can probably find out where he is."

"How?"

"I'll call Edith right now," the sheriff said, "She'll tell me. Kirby, get Edith on the phone."

Kirby used an old push button phone. When Edith answered, he put her on speaker. The sheriff greeted her and didn't disclose Sullivan's presence. The sheriff and the elderly-sounding woman engaged in about fifteen minutes of small talk. It seemed they attended the same church and were preparing for their yearly picnic. Most of the conversation was about what flavor pie Edith would bring.

"Say, Edith," the sheriff suddenly cut in, "Where's that Asian son-in-law of yours?"

Edith was silent, stunned by the question. When she spoke again her voice was cold and remote.

"Why do you want to know?"

"We just need to talk to him about something," the sheriff said off-handedly.

"He's at work right now," she said guardedly, "I don't know when he gets off."

"Where's he work?"

"I don't know, some company in Rockford."

"He's not in any trouble, Edith, just tell him to call us, or come to the station."

Her voice relaxed a bit and they returned to discussing pies for a few minutes. Edith promised to give her son-in-law the message but said she had no idea if he would call.

After he hung up, the sheriff assured Sullivan they would soon be in touch with his witness.

"I'm having breakfast with Edith tomorrow morning," the sheriff said confidently, "If I don't hear from her son-in-law by then, she'll tell me where he lives. Now, what exactly do you need from him?"

"I have to serve him with a subpoena," Sullivan finally admitted.

This interested Kirby enough to come to the counter. The sheriff's eyes narrowed.

"Do *you* need to give it to him, or can anyone give it to him?"

Sullivan thought about the statute, anybody over the age of 18 could serve the subpoena.

"Anyone can serve it," Sullivan answered, wondering where this was going.

"How about we give it to him?" the sheriff said with his easy smile.

Sullivan asked how they would do it.

"Easy, I'll get his number from Edith. I'll tell him we've got something for him. We can either bring it to him, or he can come here to pick it up."

It sounded simple but what about their pay? Sullivan was thinking in the thousands when the sheriff piped up.

"We'll do it for a hundred bucks."

Sullivan didn't carry that kind of cash but they took his check. Sullivan promised to call the next day to see how things worked out. When Sullivan called, the sheriff answered in his cheerful manner. "After you left, Edith called back and gave us his number. We *persuaded* him to come pick it up. He was not too happy about it. He does live in that house down by the Kishwaukee."

Sullivan was ecstatic. He would have the sheriff sign the affidavit of service and send a large bill to New York. He also felt pleased that he had made Charly look good.

When they later made a movie about Flight 782, the terrorist who built and placed the bomb was, of course, the villain. But, when it came to bad guys, the head of security at Hong Kong International ran him a close second. No actor portrayed Sullivan in the film.

CHAPTER 15

A few days after Sullivan completed the Flight 782 case, Charly called to congratulate him. "Great job, Mike. The guy's cooperating. They're flying him to New York. The attorneys are really impressed. They may be throwing you some more business."

"I could use it," Sullivan admitted. His days were either too busy or too slow. There'd be a flurry of activity when he got a new case, and then nothing for days. He wasn't used to spending so much time at home. He enjoyed cooking dinner, but Flynn and Tara had tired of the three or four recipes he had mastered. One evening, it was just about dinnertime, when his doorbell rang.

Sullivan opened the door to find a nattily dressed man. He was wearing a three-piece suit and a matching hat. His manner was very polite, as he asked if he were Michael Sullivan. Sullivan readily admitted but wondered what the man wanted.

"Here, Mr. Sullivan, this summons and complaint is for you." The man handed him a thick stack of court papers. Sullivan glanced at them and saw they were from his lender. He was being served with foreclosure papers. He thanked the overdressed man. Sullivan would never disrespect a process server. Serving papers was one of Sullivan's principal activities.

Sullivan walked into the kitchen holding the papers. Ann, Flynn, and Tara were already seated at the table, passing mashed potatoes for another pork chop dinner. Ann saw the perplexed look on his face.

"Who was at the door?"

"I just got these," Sullivan said showing her the papers, "It's from the mortgage company. We have thirty days to respond."

Flynn and Tara stared at him, wondering what was going on and fearing the worst.

"Does this mean we have to move, Dad?" Flynn asked apprehensively.

"Not right away," Sullivan assured him.

"Are we losing our house?" Tara asked gravely.

"I don't know. I have to get some advice."

Ann asked who he planned to talk to.

"I'll go to Pete DeSantis, he handles foreclosures, bankruptcies . . ."

"And *divorces*," Ann added.

"Mr. DeSantis?" Tara interrupted, "Remember when I had to go to traffic court, dad? Mr. DeSantis went with me. The place was packed and I was so scared. My name got called first and I didn't even have to talk to the judge. Mr. DeSantis must have known someone. We were only in court for a few minutes."

Sullivan had paid DeSantis $400 for getting Tara out of her speeding ticket. When she had started driving, Sullivan had hoped she'd have a minor violation or a fender bender as a learning experience. Tara was scared enough to slow down after being pulled over and going to court.

"I'll go see him about this tomorrow," Sullivan said, putting down the papers and sitting down at the table. "Flynn, can you pass the gravy?"

Being served with foreclosure papers was not unexpected for Sullivan, but still devastating. His family had a history of being forced off their property, starting with the English seizing their farm outside Cork in the late 19th Century. Sullivan's great-grandfather was forced to flee Ireland with only the proverbial clothes on his back.

Sullivan never forgave the English for how they treated the Irish, his family in particular. But long after Cornelius Sullivan was forced to abandon his native land, the Sullivan family still struggled to save their property. Frank Sullivan had lost his first house before Sullivan was born. Now, it was happening again.

Sullivan had done his best to forestall it. He had completed all the arduous steps to apply for a mortgage modification. He finally satisfied all the lender's requirements and was notified of his new payment. They had modified it *upwards,* increasing his monthly payment to more than $3,000. Sullivan angrily called his loan officer and declared he wasn't making another payment until they reduced it to something reasonable. The officer warned him not to do it. Now, Sullivan was facing the consequences.

Pete DeSantis had a corner office on a busy street, only a few blocks from Sullivan's home. When Sullivan walked in, he saw files stacked everywhere, including on the leather chairs. DeSantis' long-time secretary, Trisa, was holding down the fort. She told Sullivan that DeSantis was "in court." This only meant one thing. DeSantis was at his favorite haunt, holding court at Sansone's.

The bar was conveniently close to DeSantis' office, an easy walk for Sullivan. As he entered the dimness, Sullivan could hear DeSantis' booming voice before he spotted him at the bar. There was a game show on and DeSantis was competing with another patron to guess the correct answers. As was his custom, DeSantis had a pint of draft beer and a shot of whiskey in front of him.

DeSantis had a year-round tan and a magnificent head of black curly hair, now shot with gray. He wore a rumpled suit and his tie hung loose.

Sullivan settled on the stool next to him. "Pete, I've got some more business for you."

DeSantis turned to face him, "It's not your little girl again?"

"No, this time it's me. I just got served with foreclosure papers."

"No, you didn't," DeSantis said firmly.

"What do you mean, I have them right here?"

DeSantis didn't even glance at the papers. "No one served you, Mike, you found those papers in your bushes. And that's not considered proper service. Stella, get my friend a Peroni. Put it on my tab."

Stella was blousy blonde with a world-weary manner. "Sure Pete, but one of these days you're going to have to settle up. Sansone is getting mad."

Pete patted her hand, "Tell Sansone not to worry. I've got a big one going to trial. My client lost his leg in a motorcycle accident. For some reason, the adjustor won't settle."

Sullivan guessed that DeSantis had a client with a severe injury but questionable liability. Sullivan had investigated a few cases for DeSantis. He didn't attract the best class of clients, and some of the personal injury suits he filed were desperate.

Stella brought Sullivan his drink and DeSantis' attention shifted back to the game show. "What's the Spanish Flu?" DeSantis announced triumphantly beating his rival, "It didn't start in Spain but they were the first to report it," he added, showing off.

After Sullivan finished his beer, DeSantis suggested that he come to his office the next day. "I'll write up a Motion that says you didn't get the papers. You can sign it. I'll notarize it, but *you* have to file it with the court."

When Sullivan came the next morning, DeSantis was on the phone. Trisa had already prepared the Motion. It was a simple statement, denying service. Sullivan signed it and DeSantis stamped it. "This will stall it for a while," the lawyer said, "But once they get service, we'll start a foreclosure file for you. We'll put you in the foreclosure pile," he said pointing to a tottering stack of folders piled on the carpet, "In the meantime, don't answer the door."

Sullivan knew that DeSantis was saving him money by having him file the Motion but feared it would be unpleasant. Sullivan searched for a seat in a courtroom packed with people facing foreclosure. Sullivan heard their whispered conversations. About half were speaking Spanish, Polish, or some Asian language. They were completely bewildered by the proceedings. They were in terror of losing their houses and two-flats. The others, like Sullivan, who understood the legal process, were filled with the same panic. About ten defendants had retained lawyers and their cases were called first.

After the judge granted continuances to the attorneys, he addressed the remaining throng. He told them which room they should go to file their responses. If they couldn't afford the $150 filing fee, they could fill out a form pleading financial hardship. Sullivan immediately left the courtroom to beat the rush. He completed a form claiming he was destitute and filed his Motion. Sullivan had no idea what would happen next but warned his family to be cautious about answering the door.

Sullivan was still reeling from the foreclosure when he received a call from a new client. He was a young attorney from a reputable firm. "Mr. Sullivan, you were highly recommended by our office in New York. We have a large volume of summonses to serve and wondered if your firm would be able to help us."

Sullivan tried not to sound too anxious. "I'm free temporarily. I just finished a big case."

"Yes, we heard about your work. That's why we're willing to give you a try on these. Can you come downtown next week to pick them up? They're too bulky to mail. In fact, you should come directly to our loading dock."

"Oh, I forgot," the young lawyer interposed, "I first have to get the OK from our partners. What are your charges, Mr. Sullivan?"

Sullivan gave him his hourly rate and his charge for mileage.

"That won't be acceptable, Mr. Sullivan," the attorney said in a clipped manner, "The most we ever pay is $75 per summons."

Sullivan hated serving papers for a flat-rate. Who knew how many trips it could take? But he was in no position to be picky. After the young lawyer got Sullivan's fee approved, they scheduled a date to pick up the summonses. It happened to be the same day as the hearing on Sullivan's Motion.

That morning, Sullivan picked up DeSantis and they drove downtown to the Cook County Courthouse. As they crawled through the morning rush, Sullivan asked DeSantis what he was going to say to the judge.

"I'll just tell him I didn't know anything about this and that I'll need six months to review your documents before I can proceed."

"Really? Won't that make him mad?"

"No, I stall all the time," DeSantis said casually, "It's like your daughter's case, I kept continuing it until we got the right judge."

When they walked into the courtroom, Sullivan spotted the process server. He was dressed in khakis and a sports shirt. Maybe he only dressed up to ambush people with papers. When Sullivan's case was called, he walked up alongside DeSantis.

"Your honor," DeSantis began, "I've known Mr. Sullivan personally and professionally for years, but he never told me he was having financial problems. I'll need six months to review his mortgage documents, before we can move forward."

The lawyer for the lender jumped up, raising aloft a copy of Sullivan's Motion. "What do you mean you didn't know about it," he exclaimed, "You *notarized* his signature!"

DeSantis didn't even look at him. "Your honor, Mr. Sullivan lives in the neighborhood. He comes by my office to have things notarized. I never read them."

Sullivan could see the judge wasn't buying DeSantis' hastily improvised explanation. "We're going to need testimony to determine whether the defendant was properly served," the judge ruled, "Is the process server here?"

The man who had served Sullivan came forward and took the witness stand. The attorney for the lender led him through his testimony. The only mistake the witness made was saying Sullivan's house was brick, when it was frame. The lawyer then asked the process server how many summonses he served a year.

"About 2,000."

The judge interrupted "You serve 2,000 summonses a year. How could you possibly remember this one?"

"You don't forget it, your honor, when a guy yells at you and throws the papers in the bushes!"

Sullivan was called next. The lawyer again held up a copy of his Motion.

"This is a lie, isn't it?"

"No," Sullivan said without much conviction.

"And being a process server yourself, Mr. Sullivan, you would know how to lie about being served?"

The lawyer then picked up Sullivan's mortgage papers.

"This a lie too, Mr. Sullivan. You promised to pay my client. This is your signature."

"It wasn't a lie when I signed it," Sullivan replied with as much insolence as he could muster.

The judge ruled that the service was valid but allowed DeSantis six months to file his answer. Sullivan was shaken by being called a liar in open court. DeSantis was unflappable. "Don't worry, Mike, we'll drag this out as long as we can. After you lose the house, we'll kick your file into the bankruptcy pile."

They got Sullivan's car out of a parking garage and drove to the loading dock behind his new client's building. There were several cardboard boxes stacked on a pallet. When he opened a box, Sullivan could see they were foreclosures. He was glad to have DeSantis' help, as they loaded his trunk and filled his backseat. "I bet some of my clients are in here," DeSantis said cheerfully, "I'll be filing more appearances."

When Sullivan arrived home, he described the humiliating hearing to Ann. She felt deeply sorry for him.

"I wish I could help you with this, Mike, but you know so much more about the legal stuff."

Sullivan sighed, "I got us into this mess. I'll deal with it. I just wish DeSantis could have come up with something better. I felt like we were a tag team of liars." On a brighter note, he told her of all the summonses they had picked up. "I'm leaving them in the car, I only have a month to serve them."

The next morning, he started a new routine, serving summonses on defaulting homeowners. Sullivan began his journey at the Wisconsin border and worked his way south. He felt like he was spreading misery throughout the Chicago area. He gave papers to whoever answered the door. Most wore the same stunned expression, except for the few who turned instantly angry.

It was heartbreaking work, but Sullivan was determined to serve the summonses before they expired. Some of the defendants had already abandoned their homes, and Sullivan had to track them down. In one case, he found the house burned to the ground. The homes ranged from hovels to mansions. It was particularly memorable when Sullivan drove up to a palace on a private lake to serve a defaulting doctor.

Sullivan's cutoff time for serving papers was 7:00 PM. He returned home most evenings around 8:00. He spent mornings filling out affidavits and adding to his bill. As usual, he advanced all the money for gas and tolls and wouldn't collect for weeks. He was careful not to complain to Ann. The one thing she couldn't tolerate was people moaning about their jobs.

Ann, Tara and, Flynn felt the pressure of the impending foreclosure. Tara now handed over her babysitting money to the family, and Flynn had found a job stocking shelves at a local grocer. Ann was determined to keep them in private school. She found a second job at a local clothing store, folding clothes three nights a week.

Meanwhile, Sullivan's bill mounted as he raced to serve the papers before the court deadline. In the end, he still had a small number left. For these, he filled out affidavits of non-service and hoped the client would still pay him.

Sullivan brought the unserved summonses, along with the affidavits and his bill to the downtown law firm. He finally got to meet the young attorney in the firm's fancy reception area. His name was Todd and he was fresh out of law school. Todd assured Sullivan that he would present the bill to the partners and Sullivan would be promptly paid.

Weeks dragged by while Sullivan waited for his money. Whenever he called, Todd would reassure him that his payment was being processed. Finally, Todd confessed that they had to await payment from the mortgage companies before they could pay Sullivan's bill. Sullivan used Todd's word to tell him this was *unacceptable* and demanded to speak with one of the partners.

A smug-sounding lawyer came on the phone. "Mr. Sullivan, we're having cash flow problems like everyone else. We simply can't advance the funds to you until our clients pay us." The firm occupied an entire floor of a Loop high-rise and they couldn't pay Sullivan the few thousand he was owed! He remembered a tactic one of his colleagues used to get his bill paid. "I go to their office with some high-smellin' people and we sit there until I get the check." Sullivan wouldn't consider doing anything like that, but he kept up the pressure on Todd with calls and emails. There wasn't much else to do.

Tara announced one evening that she had made the honor roll. Ann wasn't home to hear the news. She was stuck at work until 9:00. Sullivan congratulated Tara and they discussed her dream colleges. "I want to go to U. of I. in Champaign," she declared, "That is, if I can't get into Stanford." Tara had been setting high standards for herself, and the rest of the human race, since she was six.

"Those are great schools. I hope they're giving scholarships. It would be cheaper to take your required courses around here."

Tara gave him a sour look. "I'm not expecting you and mom to pay for college," she said resolutely, "You've already spent so much on high school, but I'm not going to some community college. We went to California for our class serve trip and that's where I'm going to school." Sullivan knew better than to try and talk Tara out of anything.

Flynn was a bit more realistic about the family's finances. "Dad, plenty of my friend go to Harrison. I could play baseball there. They don't have a million rules, and I wouldn't have to wear a uniform."

"I know but your mother is determined that you and your sister graduate from St. Scholastica. As soon as I get paid, we'll catch up with your tuition."

Suddenly, their doorbell rang. Tara looked alarmed. Sullivan went to see who it was. Peering cautiously through a side window, Sullivan saw Jake

Houlihan standing on his front steps. Jake was pounding on the door and ringing at the same time. He burst into the house with his usual exuberance.

"Mike, I need you right away. I've got a surveillance tonight and the rest of my people are tied up. The client told us we have to use two people on this."

"Tonight?" Sullivan asked incredulously.

"Yeah, his flight is landing at O'Hare at 8:30 and we have to catch him when he leaves the terminal."

Jake had a cop at O'Hare who gave him the flight information on people he was tracking. The cop was expensive, but his information was solid.

"Alright, but let me grab a book to read if we're going to be sitting at the airport."

Jake scoffed, "A book, on surveillance? I'm paying you for this. You can't be reading."

By this time, Tara and Flynn had been drawn by curiosity into the living room. Sullivan introduced them and Jake peppered them with questions about school. When Flynn said he was a pitcher, Jake demanded to see his form. Flynn did a pantomime wind-up and pitch. Jake quickly corrected him, showing him the proper arm angle.

Tara wasn't intimidated by Jake's impertinent questions about her classes, she gave it back just as hard. "Why are you wearing green sweatpants and red shoes?" she demanded, "It isn't Christmas."

Jake loved it. "Mike, you don't have to worry about this one," he said, giving Tara a warm grin.

"We better get going," Sullivan said, "His flight could come in early."

Jake drove like he was possessed as usual, while chattering away on his cell phone. They settled into a no parking zone in "Arrivals." Jake treated every rule as a suggestion. "I've been working with Charlevoix," Jake recounted, "She really caught on quick. You must miss her. She talks about you all the time."

A cop rapped on Jake's window. Jake pulled a handicap placard from his glove box and lowered his window. "We're picking up my mom, she's in a wheelchair," he explained. The cop let them stay.

"Someday, you're going to believe your own bullshit," Sullivan warned Jake, "What are we doing here anyway?"

"There's a guy flying in from Atlanta. He claims he has to use a cane at all times. We're supposed to follow him from the airport and see if he uses it. If he doesn't, we're supposed to get pictures." Jake pulled out a photograph of a heavy-set, middle-aged man. "This is the best picture we have of him."

Sullivan was the first to spot him walking slowly out of the terminal. He was leaning heavily on a cane he held in his right hand. They watched him climb into a cab and Sullivan wrote down the license number. The cab sped away into traffic and Jake got into position two cars back.

They sped down the wide-open expressway toward the South Side. When they got off at 79th Street, Jake's driving got even more reckless. Sullivan steeled himself in the passenger seat, as Jake cursed the cars in front of them, darting into the opposing lane to pass them.

Jake knew the address where the man was headed and arrived within seconds of the cab coming to a stop. They watched the heavy-set man climb clumsily out of the back seat, while the driver fetched his suitcase from the trunk. The man settled with the cabbie and extended the handle on the rolling suitcase.

He started walking toward the entrance to his apartment building. It began to rain and apparently he got fed up with using the cane. He slipped it through the handle of the suitcase and strode confidently to the entrance, pulling the suitcase behind him. Jake was madly taking photos with his phone. The lighting wasn't ideal but he got some great shots when the building's motion-activated lights snapped on.

Jake was very pleased with the pictures. He calmly drove Sullivan home, chatting about how their old friends were doing. "Mike, we never see you at McGaffer's. If you're that broke, I'll buy you a beer."

"First pay me for this job. Am I getting your rate, or mine?" Sullivan charged $75 an hour, while Jake's rate was $100.

When they got to Sullivan's house, Jake peeled off $200 in 20s. "Mike, thanks for coming with. We might need you as a witness."

As he handed Sullivan the bills, Jake said, "We usually meet at McGaffer's on Friday nights. *Now*, you don't have any excuse not to come."

CHAPTER 16

S ullivan was feeling flush when he walked through the front door, thanks to the unexpected windfall from Jake. Flynn was watching the late innings of a White Sox game. "Are the Sox playing tomorrow night?"

Flynn glanced at his phone, "Yeah, the Red Sox."

"Good, you and I are going."

"Really?" The Sullivans had attended Sox games regularly during good times, but now it was a rare treat. When they did go, they perched in the cheap seats far above the action. Sullivan also had to adjust to watching baseball sober. There was no way he could afford what they were charging for beer.

They drove down to the game and parked for free in an out-of-the-way spot Sullivan had discovered close to the stadium. Flynn was wearing his full Sox regalia and pounding his mitt. They walked up to the box office and were shocked to find the game sold-out. Big crowds were rare at White Sox games, but the Red Sox drew a full house thanks to all the New England transplants living in Chicago.

Sullivan and Flynn trudged toward the "L" station where shady scalpers did their business. One of them looked Flynn up and down and smirked at Sullivan, before demanding twice the face value. Sullivan reluctantly handed over the cash. There was one bright spot. Their seats were only a few rows behind the White Sox dugout.

Flynn was excited to be so close to home plate and to have a chance to catch a foul ball. "You can have whatever you want to eat and drink," Sullivan announced grandly as he stopped a vendor for a $12 beer. Flynn was into every pitch and actually snagged a foul pop-up while his father cowered. The wrong Sox team ended up winning the game, but the summer night had been exhilarating. Sullivan drove home broke but happy.

Later that week, he decided to take Jake's offer to meet at McGaffer's. The bar was a true neighborhood joint, popular with union members and softball teams. It was rundown and smelled of stale beer. Jake was on one of the stools talking with a high school classmate Sullivan hadn't seen in years. He couldn't even remember his name.

"Mike, you remember Terry?" Jake greeted him. Then he addressed the bartender, "Chubs, get this man a Guinness."

"Terry, what are you doing these days?" Sullivan asked.

"I'm at Illinois Disposal," his classmate replied.

"Oh, in the office?"

"No, I'm a driver. I belong to the Teamsters." Sullivan tried to conceal his surprise. Most of his classmates had gone on to become lawyers, several were doctors, and one was CEO of a national clothing chain.

Terry sensed Sullivan's shock and felt the need to explain. "I've made some mistakes in my life," he confessed.

"What are you talking about?" Jake jumped in, "You're making a ton of money. You're going to have a pension. Mike and I will never be able to retire. Tell Mike about that case against your company."

Terry was happy to switch the subject. "There's a woman friend of mine, Debbie, who owned a small trucking company. Illinois Disposal wanted to buy her company so they could put a transfer station there. They low-balled her on the offer but promised her a big job if she sold."

Terry paused to take another sip of his straight whiskey.

"After she sold, they gave Debbie the worst job they could find, collecting debts from customers that didn't pay us. She was in a basement office with no windows. I used to stop by to see her. She was miserable trying to squeeze money from these deadbeats. Finally, she quit. She called me a few days ago and said she had found a lawyer to sue Illinois Disposal."

"On what grounds?" Sullivan asked.

"She's got a woman lawyer who's claiming Debbie was discriminated against on the basis of her gender. She's also alleging fraud – that they bought her company with a promise of a good job. Instead, they practically forced her to quit, so she can't collect unemployment. Debbie's lawyer is looking for someone to serve the CEO. The sheriff gave up."

Sullivan knew that the sheriff had probably not tried very hard. The head of a garbage company would face countless claims for property damage and personal injury. Serving the chief executive should be a snap.

"Can you believe this guy's ducking it?" Jake chimed in. "*You* should serve him, Mike, you need the money."

Terry looked hard at Sullivan, "I made some mistakes, too," Sullivan said with a shrug, "I'd be glad to serve him. I have a wife and a daughter. I hate assholes who take advantage of women."

Terry said he would give his name to the attorney. "I'll even help you serve the prick. I don't care if they fire me. Garbage companies are always looking for drivers."

With that, their attention shifted back to the baseball game on TV and Jake bought Sullivan another drink. Sullivan asked Terry, "How come you don't show up to the reunions? I didn't see you at the 20th."

"Because the guys who come to reunions are the same ones who didn't talk to me in high school," Jake replied, "They thought they were better than me then and I doubt they've changed their minds."

Chubs set another pint in front of Sullivan. He knew he lacked the capacity to keep up with Jake and Terry. Sullivan's friends kidded him for being a "high-bottom" drinker who would be the first to call it a night. Sullivan's weakness, however, was he was powerless over free beer. Chubs kept pouring while Jake kept paying.

It was late when Sullivan left his friends. His house was only a brisk walk from the bar, but Sullivan found it impossible to walk in a straight line, so it took twice as long. He was relieved to see the house dark and assumed that Ann and the kids were asleep.

As he quietly opened the front door, a lamp lit up the living room. Ann was sitting on the couch in her bathrobe. She scowled at Sullivan and said in a hurt voice, "I thought you and I were a team."

Sullivan steadied himself and tried to straighten up. He sank into a chair and insisted, "We *are* a team," with too much emphasis.

"I thought we were working together to get out of this mess," Ann continued, "You waste our money in a bar and come home drunk."

"Jake paid for everything," Sullivan countered, "Plus, I might have picked up a new case."

Ann was unmoved. She stood up and pulled her robe tight. "You can sleep here. You smell like a brewery. I don't want you in my bed."

"Our bed," Sullivan called to her as she climbed the stairs. Sullivan resigned himself to sleeping on the sofa. He comforted himself by having a conversation in his head with Ann, in which he defended himself for the handful of times he had come home drunk. Even in his dreams Ann wasn't buying it.

Early the next morning, he heard Ann in the kitchen filling the coffee maker. Tara and Flynn stumbled down the stairs and were surprised to find their father on the couch. This didn't stop Tara from blasting the TV. Sullivan was startled into a sleep-deprived stupor as he went upstairs to his still-warm bed. Ann remained disgusted with him while she readied herself for work. Before she left, she sat on the edge of the bed and stroked his hair.

"I suppose the way you feel is punishment enough," Ann said gently, "Just don't make a habit of it. We're a team, remember?" She kissed the top of his head and encouraged Sullivan to go back to sleep.

It turned out that Terry's conversation about a possible case for Sullivan wasn't just the beer talking. He recommended Sullivan to the plaintiff's attorney. Sullivan was appointed special process server and the attorney mailed a summons and complaint for him to serve. Sullivan immediately called Terry. His old classmate gave him a physical description of the CEO and told him what kind of car he drove including the license number. "I'll show you right where he parks," Terry promised, "You should get to our company lot in the morning. This guy goes to lunch every day at 11:30."

When he arrived at Illinois Disposal, Sullivan alerted Terry that he was in position. "Do you see that green SUV parked by the employee entrance?" Terry asked. Sullivan confirmed it was there and hunkered down to wait. He flipped on sports radio and opened a newspaper.

11:30 came and went but the SUV never budged. Every time the employee entrance door swung open, Sullivan hoped the CEO would emerge. He didn't see anyone matching the CEO's description and employees wearing suits were scarce. Hours crept by as Sullivan reread the paper three times and then perilously worked the crossword puzzle in pen.

The company parking lot began to empty out in the late afternoon. Sullivan was weary of waiting and worried he wouldn't be able to charge for all his time. Finally, there were only two vehicles left in the lot. Sullivan's car and the green SUV.

A security guard tooled up to Sullivan's car and motioned him to lower his window. "Lot's closed," the guard declared matter-of-factly, "You've got to leave."

Sullivan was crestfallen. He had no doubt the CEO had called security to make him move. He resignedly agreed but when Sullivan turned the key his starter gave only empty clicks. All those hours of sports banter had drained his battery. Sullivan told the guard his car wouldn't start and sheepishly asked for help.

The guard retrieved jumper cables from his trunk and quickly had Sullivan's car running. Sullivan drove toward the exit, searching for a spot where he could stop the SUV from leaving the lot. The company driveway, though, was way too wide to block with his car. Sullivan parked across the street and walked back to the driveway clutching the papers.

It wasn't long before he spotted a tall man wearing a pricey suit climb into the driver's seat of the green SUV. Sullivan stood in the center of the driveway, determined to stand his ground. The SUV backed out of its spot and headed for the exit. Sullivan didn't move as the SUV barreled toward him. At the last second, Sullivan stepped aside and flung the papers at the CEO's windshield. They bounced off and fluttered everywhere.

If the CEO had been smart, he would have kept going. He could claim some homeless man had thrown an issue of "Streetwise" at his car. The CEO, though, was incensed and screeched to a stop. He lowered his window and glared at Sullivan. "You gotta' problem, buddy?" he asked through clenched teeth.

"No, *you've* got a problem," Sullivan shot back, "Your business is all over the parking lot." The sight of the legal papers floating upward was quite comical. The CEO had nothing more to say and peeled off. Sullivan was worried that the service might not be considered valid.

The next morning he called Debbie's lawyer. Sullivan was surprised how pleased she sounded. "Mr. Sullivan, that was quick-thinking on your part. The lawyers for the garbage company have already filed a motion to quash your service. We have a friendly female judge, though, and I think she'll allow it. We have a case management conference this afternoon. Can you come?"

Sullivan completed his affidavit of service, report, and invoice, and took the "L" downtown to the courthouse. He met Debbie's lawyer in the corridor and they walked into the judge's chambers. Three lawyers for Illinois Disposal were already assembled. They cited case law as they sought to have service quashed. The judge put up her hand. "Speaking of cases, how many lawsuits were filed against your client last year?"

"Our client is the victim of many frivolous lawsuits like this one," the senior attorney replied.

"How many?" the judge repeated.

One of the younger attorneys spoke up, "We had over fifty cases, your honor. They were mostly for minor accidents involving my client's trucks."

"Gentlemen, in that case, you should have waived service. There was no reason to waste this man's time. If lawsuits against your client are that common, the registered agent or the CEO should make themselves available to be served."

Sullivan was jubilant when the judge ruled his service had been valid. She specifically cited the brief exchange between Sullivan and the CEO as proof that the defendant knew he was being served. Sullivan was even happier when the plaintiff's lawyer wrote him a check on the spot without questioning his charges. $750 was ten times the going rate.

The money helped but Sullivan couldn't escape the shadow of foreclosure. He feared being evicted and dreaded where they would end up. Would it be a sterile suburban condo? Or worse, an apartment in one of the low-income complexes Sullivan frequented to serve deadbeats. Sullivan used to refer to the deadbeats as "turnips," in the sense that you can't get blood from a turnip. They had few financial assets, so they didn't fear lawsuits and bill collectors. After he lost his house, Sullivan would join the ranks of the turnips.

In the meantime, he continued to torment Todd to pay his bill for serving summonses. One day, Todd exploded. "Mr. Sullivan, if you don't stop this harassment, we're going to file a restraining order against you!" Sullivan wasn't a bit intimidated. "Let me talk to that lead partner again? What's his name?"

"I'll see if Mr. Swanson is in," Todd said tersely.

Sullivan again heard the partner's smug tone. "Mr. Sullivan if you're calling about your bill, we are still awaiting payment from our clients."

"Your clients didn't hire me, Mr. Swanson, your firm did. I have a proposal. Pay me half and I'll stop calling."

"That sounds reasonable, Mr. Sullivan. I'll have our accounting department prepare a check and you can pick it up. By the way," he added gravely, "We're closing our Chicago office in two weeks. Thankfully, I'm close to retirement but – well we haven't told Todd yet."

Sullivan didn't feel a trace of sympathy. "Let me know when the check's ready, Mr. Swanson, I can be here in a less than an hour." Sullivan later made a special trip downtown to pick up the draft and deposit it. It was his second trip to the firm and he was shocked to see all the empty desks. Somehow, it was appropriate. The firm that was forcing people out of their homes had now been forced out of their offices.

The demise of the law office reminded Sullivan of the vacuum monster in the animated Beatles film, "Yellow Submarine." The creature literally sucks up the entire universe. Then it sucks itself up and implodes out of existence. What it did to others it finally does to itself. As the law firm imploded, Sullivan felt fortunate to get fifty cents on the dollar.

Ann, pleased that he was bringing in some income, socked it away in their savings. She worried, though, that her husband's empty days were having a debilitating effect. She would catch him napping in the middle of the day and he seemed listless. Flynn was playing summer league baseball and Ann encouraged Sullivan to catch one of his starts.

Sullivan sat in the stands with a handful of fans. They were all related to the players. Flynn was on the mound and Sullivan looked forward to watching him pitch. After striking out the first two batters, Flynn walked the bases loaded. The opposing batters had stopped swinging and Sullivan felt the umpire was squeezing. He loudly let the umpire know how he felt and the other fans seemed disturbed by Sullivan's behavior.

Flynn was still trying to get out of the first inning and had two strikes on the batter. The ball got away from the catcher and Flynn raced toward the plate. The runner was streaking home from third and Sullivan cringed at the impending collision. The catcher flipped the ball to Flynn just in time and he had the ball when the runner crashed into him. As he lay in the dirt, Flynn proudly held his mitt up to show he had hung onto the ball. The umpire ruled the runner safe.

It was all a bit of a blur but Sullivan suddenly found himself on the field confronting the ump. He was screaming about the call while Flynn's manager restrained him. Flynn was mortified trying to calm his dad. The opposing manager was so alarmed he called the cops. By the time two officers arrived at the diamond, Sullivan had settled down. He had turned his back to the field, deeply embarrassed. He couldn't even watch Flynn, who shakily walked one batter after another until he was mercifully removed.

The officers demanded Sullivan's ID and escorted him from the field. One of them gave him a ticket for disorderly conduct and said he could pay the $50 fine by mail. They warned Sullivan that he was no longer permitted on park property. Sullivan felt like seeking solace at McGaffer's but decided to go directly home to face Ann's wrath.

"Mike, it was a high school game," she said worriedly, "What got into you? Flynn called me crying. He said you were so mad at the umpire you didn't even check to see if he was alright."

"Was he hurt?" Sullivan asked emptily.

"Only his feelings," Ann said softly, "He doesn't want you coming to any more games."

"That's one thing he doesn't have to worry about. I'll take him out for pizza or something and try to make it up to him."

"Mike, I don't want you to beat yourself up about this. I'm just worried. You don't know how scary you get."

Sullivan consoled Flynn over pizza and finally got him laughing. "I definitely tagged him dad, so at least you got that right. Only not so loud next time. The guys on my team thought you looked like a quiet guy. Now they think you're crazy. I told them that we didn't just watch the "Cookie Monster." We had a *real* monster!"

Flynn asked about Morgan and Sullivan said he hadn't spoken to her since the night they cleared out the office. "She's really nice, dad, I like her boyfriend, too. It's too bad she doesn't work for you anymore. Did she get a new job?"

"I have no idea," Sullivan confessed, "Maybe I'll give her a call."

Sullivan was planning to telephone Morgan the next day but she called first.

"Mr. Sullivan, Evan and I wanted to talk to you about an idea we had. I also might need to use you as a reference."

"I'll give you a glowing recommendation, Morgan. Do you guys have time to have lunch at Phil's?"

"Sitting outside, eating seafood, we have time for that," Morgan answered excitedly. "I'll check with Evan and get back to you."

"When you talk to Evan, tell him lunch is on me. I want to treat you guys for helping with the move."

They met at Phil's on a bright breezy afternoon. Their table had an umbrella that kept them comfortable. After their drinks came, Morgan ordered her favorite entrée, lobster rolls. Sullivan and Evan were content with cheeseburgers.

"So, was there some idea you wanted to discuss?" Sullivan asked.

"Mr. Sullivan, what do you think of us taking jobs overseas?" Morgan asked excitedly.

"Now is the time to do it. Once you have responsibilities, travel isn't so easy. What do your folks think?"

"I haven't talked to my parents yet. Actually, it was Evan who came up with the idea for us to get jobs with the U.S. Geological Survey."

Sullivan looked confused.

"Mr. Sullivan, they don't just have projects *here*," Evan explained, "They have jobs everywhere that are in our fields." He said that the survey worked on issues involving biology, geology and hydrology.

"What's hydrology?" Sullivan asked.

"You know, clean water," Morgan explained, "They report on earthquakes and volcanoes all over the world."

"I'm hoping to focus on climate change, Mr. Sullivan," Evan said, "The EPA – we don't do enough."

The more Evan explained the more he boggled Sullivan's imagination. Besides climate change, the survey dealt with wildlife issues, oil and gas investigations and even space exploration.

"What don't they do?" Sullivan asked.

"Wait, I forgot, they also analyze minerals and make topographic maps," Evan added.

"We want to go to Australia," Morgan declared, "There having a terrible drought there. It's hurting the koalas."

"Well, you have my blessing, it sounds like a perfect fit for you guys. I'll be glad to write you a recommendation, Morgan. Just tell me where to send it. I'm sorry I can't do the same for you, Evan, unless - do you need a recommendation for throwing confidential files out the window?"

"My boss said he would recommend me," Evan said, "He thinks it's a great opportunity. He knows a couple who joined the survey when they were newlyweds. They just celebrated their 50th Anniversary."

Sullivan couldn't be happier for the couple and ordered another round of drinks to celebrate. His finances were so bad, they were absurd. Why not a little spree, now and then? When they got up to leave, Morgan impulsively hugged Sullivan.

"I'm so glad you came into Delaney's that day, otherwise I might still be stuck there."

"C'mon Morgan, give yourself some credit. You're a smart, well-educated woman."

"I know but I used to have zero confidence."

"Morgan, you're the only person who doesn't know how wonderful you are."

She nodded, "Thanks, I'll work on it."

"You and Evan are going to go far together – literally. The only favor I ask is that you invite me to your wedding. I'll come to Australia if necessary."

"Mr. Sullivan, thanks again for lunch," Evan said with his easy smile, "Morgan can really use your help getting her that job."

"I could write a long letter about Morgan's qualifications, but I'll keep it short. I'll just say, "If we had more people like Morgan, the world would be a much better place!""

CHAPTER 17

Sullivan received a call from another New York law firm that had been impressed with his work on Flight 782. A woman attorney with a nasal New York accent offered him the assignment. "Mr. Sullivan, our client operates a well-known gentlemen's club in Manhattan called Pirate's Booty," she pronounced the name with some distaste, "He learned a club with the same name has just opened outside Chicago. We're planning to file an injunction against the club for trademark infringement. First, we need proof. Before we discuss this any further, what is your hourly rate?"

Sullivan cited his charges.

"Really," she replied, "Private detectives in New York are charging $250 an hour. They're mostly ex-NYPD. Your fees are reasonable compared to theirs."

The lawyer launched into her list of requests, while Sullivan took notes. She gave him the name and address of the club and asked that he visit it as soon as possible. She instructed Sullivan to photograph the exterior to show the signage. He was then to go there as a customer, and collect any matches or napkins bearing the club's logo. He was also requested to take note of the color scheme, the layout, how many seats, etc.

"We also want you to pay for a lap dance, Mr. Sullivan. According to Illinois law, if there is any physical contact between a dancer and a customer, any rubbing or touching, it constitutes prostitution. We want you to prove there is prostitution taking place on the premises."

Sullivan accepted the assignment, hoping this firm would be more prompt in paying his bill. He already had plenty of experience doing investigations that involved strip clubs. He had no illusions about them. The clubs were downright depressing, nothing like the glamorous nightspots portrayed in movies. Pathetic men watching bored dancers.

Several times, Sullivan had to track down insured drivers who danced for a living. One of these was a woman who listed her occupation as "executive assistant." When Sullivan visited her workplace, he found her strutting on stage wearing high heels and little else.

Another time, an exotic dancer claimed her daughter's finger was injured by a sharp surface in the trunk of her car. When Sullivan showed up at her house for a 10:00 AM appointment, the woman sleepily answered the door in her robe. Sullivan sat beside her on a couch, purposely not peeking at her loosely closed robe. The dancer said she had to take a shower, before she could talk.

"While you're taking a shower, I'll take pictures," Sullivan said, "Of your *car*," he hastily added.

Sullivan was careful not to cut himself when he examined the trunk. He used an old trick, running a ripe peach over the metal edges in the trunk to check for a sharp surface. He found it and photographed it. He later interviewed the little girl and asked her to bend her finger, so he could photograph her scar. Bending her finger showed she wasn't having problems moving it.

Finally, he had a case involving a "house mother" for the dancers at a strip club. When Sullivan walked into the club with his briefcase, dancers swarmed around him asking if it was full of money. Sullivan strode toward a small office and interviewed the gravel-voiced manager. She was wearing a walking boot, having broken her fibula in a fall at his client's hospital. They quickly agreed to settle the case for $10,000. Before he left, Sullivan couldn't resist asking her one more question.

"Are these girls, are they normal?"

"Normal, honey?" she rasped in response, "No, none of them is normal."

Sullivan rarely discussed new assignments with Ann and didn't feel the need to tell her about this one. He simply said he had an assignment in the same direction as St. Scholastica. After he was finished, he would meet Ann and Tara at Flynn's basketball game.

Sullivan pulled into the club's gravel parking lot. He got out and took photographs of all four sides of the club. One wall had a sign that displayed Pirate's Booty in violent purple and yellow. As he walked back to leave his camera in his car, Sullivan spotted a familiar vanity plate "LAW WON." It was attached to the yellow Cadillac that Pete DeSantis drove.

After placing his camera in its case, Sullivan emptied his pockets of identification. He didn't want any of the employees to know who he was. He grabbed a debit card and walked into a world of loud colors and throbbing music. He saw a handful of men gathered close to the stage, gawking at the dancers. He spotted DeSantis sitting at the bar with his usual shot and beer.

"Mike, you should be ashamed of yourself – a married man with two kids," DeSantis scolded.

"Would you believe me if I said I was working?" Sullivan replied. They both burst out laughing.

"I'm the only married guy in this place who doesn't feel guilty," Sullivan said with some pride. "What's your excuse?

"My client owns this place," DeSantis explained, "I helped get him his permits to open. It was a bitch getting him a liquor license, because this joint is within 200 yards of a park. I knew the village attorney and figured he didn't want to do any actual work. I told him I'd take him to court if the village council didn't grant me a zoning variance. It passed 5-4."

"How's *my* case coming?" Sullivan asked.

DeSantis rumpled his hair, "The judge is starting to get pissed about all my continuances. The other attorney already hates my guts. He keeps filing motions to move the case forward. I think I can string it along until Christmas."

"What do I owe you?"

"I'll have Trisa send you a bill – I'm charging you $200 a month. Consider it cheap rent."

Just then, a young Asian woman sidled up to Sullivan. She was short and a bit plump, but had a sweet round face. Her hair was short, and her breasts were obviously not the original model. She seductively asked Sullivan if he would like a private dance, and said it would cost him $100. DeSantis couldn't help staring at Sullivan. It took a lot to shock him, but Sullivan was succeeding. Sullivan excused himself and said he would get the money from an ATM.

Sullivan withdrew $100 in 20s and rejoined the girl at the bar. She took him by the hand and led him into a dim private room. The room was already occupied by one of the largest men Sullivan had ever seen. The man was neatly dressed in a suit but that failed to disguise his muscular frame. His head was shaved and his face was mean. Sullivan mentally nicknamed him "Bruno."

"Bruno" explained the rules to Sullivan in a stern manner. He specified where he could touch the dancer, the sides of her waist only. If he touched her anywhere else, he would throw him out of the club. The young woman started gyrating to techno music while she removed her pirate get up. She rubbed against Sullivan with abandon.

Sullivan didn't know what to do, or say, but chose to push the envelope on prostitution. "What are you doing after work?" he asked her, "Maybe, we could meet somewhere?" The woman continued to grind against him and didn't respond to any of Sullivan's questions. She offered views that belonged in a doctor's office. Sullivan found it more clinical than titillating. Sullivan kept his hands at his side. When his right hand accidentally touched her butt, "Bruno" gravely shook his head.

After the dance, Sullivan stopped at the bar to say goodbye to DeSantis. The lawyer was gazing at his "family man" client in a whole new light. On the way out, Sullivan grabbed a book of matches and a clump of napkins. They bore a purple and yellow logo similar to the one used by the New York club. He felt a tap on his shoulder and turned to face "Bruno."

"Are you Michael Sullivan?" he asked in a menacing manner.

Sullivan could barely conceal his panic as he nodded. "Bruno" held up a slip of paper, "You left your receipt in the cash machine."

Sullivan grabbed it gratefully and hurried to his car. How stupid could he be? It had been bad enough running into DeSantis. Now, "Bruno" knew who he was. He dreaded the idea of "Bruno" paying him a house call.

Sullivan drove to the high school and arrived during halftime of the basketball game. It was surreal walking into the brightly-lit gym after the tawdry dimness of the strip club. The pom squad was dancing at center court. Their wholesomeness added to Sullivan's feeling of arriving from another planet. He found Ann and Tara sitting in the stands and saw Flynn's team was trailing by sixteen points.

When the second half started, Flynn remained glued to the far end of the bench. Flynn had too much "street" in his game for the coach's liking. Flynn's coach ran a plodding offense that required five passes before each shot. Fast breaks were practically forbidden. Flynn's team kept pounding the ball inside to their big men. They weren't good shooters but ferocious on the boards.

It wasn't working, though, as Flynn's team fell behind by 20. Sullivan started to seethe. He figured Flynn could miss shots with the best of them, why not put him in? Ann sensed his frustration and suggested Sullivan leave before he boiled over. Sullivan grimly stayed in his seat. With 30 seconds left in the game, the coach finally cleared the bench. Flynn promptly grabbed a rebound and flung a full-court pass to a streaking teammate for an easy layup. The father of the benchwarmer who scored was beaming. "This could be the start of something special, Mike?" Sullivan hoped he was right.

The next morning couldn't have been more unpleasant. Sullivan was still bleary-eyed when Ann confronted him with the matches and napkins. She didn't say anything but glared at him, waiting for an explanation.

Sullivan sat up in bed, "Oh, those are pieces of evidence," he said dismissively, "You know that case I was working on yesterday."

"There's also a small matter of a hundred dollar withdrawal you made," Ann said accusingly, "What was that for?"

"Part of my assignment was to get a lap dance," Sullivan answered weakly.

Ann's eyes were round at this point. "Mike, I know you need the work but I don't even want to touch you after you've been in a place like that."

Sullivan stood up and tried to hug her. She pulled away. "Ann, you've got to understand. I can't turn down any work these days."

"Well, as long as you get paid for your time and they reimburse you for – please don't tell anyone else about the lap dance, especially my parents."

Sullivan promised to bill out the case immediately. He didn't mention DeSantis had been at the club. Ann's opinion of him was low enough. The New York lawyer had instructed Sullivan to give a verbal report before putting anything in writing. Sullivan calmly narrated what had happened and she seemed satisfied. She told him to mail the photos, matches, and napkins, along with his invoice. He could testify at a later date about the club's décor and the antics of the lap dancer.

Sullivan felt panicky again. "I can't testify," he pleaded, "One of the security guards knows my name. I also ran into the owner's attorney. When you file your injunction, they're going to know I was behind it."

"If you don't testify, we're not going to pay you," she said flatly.

Sullivan felt trapped. He needed the money but was still in fear of what "Bruno" might do to him. "Can't we do it another way?" he asked the lawyer, "What if I sign an affidavit instead?"

Sullivan preferred a quiet affidavit to testifying in open court.

"OK," she relented, "Put together a report that contains all your findings and we'll use it to prepare an affidavit. Make sure you include your bill. I want to pay you right away. That way we can claim your report as work product and don't have to turn it over to the other side."

Sullivan was relieved he didn't have to testify and happy that prompt payment had been promised. He promised to warn Ann about sleazy assignments in the future.

Tara told him she was having a change of heart about attending college in California. She wanted to visit a small college in Michigan that had been recommended to her. "My English teacher, Ms. Forbes, went there and thought it would be a good fit for me." Tara had a three-day weekend coming up and asked her dad to drive her. Ann worked retail and wouldn't be able to join them.

Before they left, Sullivan got a call from Charly. "I just got a postcard from Morgan! She and Evan are doing their training in Australia. They love it there so far. What are you up to?"

Sullivan told her about the road trip he planned with Tara. "You're going to Michigan, really?" Charly said, "I just got a new case in Indiana. It's a plane crash and I can't get to it right away. It's right on your way back. It would pay for your trip."

Sullivan liked the sound of that but wasn't sure Tara would be on board. Charly went on to explain her client was a manufacturer of small planes and one of them had gone down shortly after takeoff, killing the pilot and two passengers. "There's no claim yet but it's going to take the NTSB a year to investigate and the company wants to know right away if there was mechanical failure."

Charly sent Sullivan the particulars by email. First, he had to clear it with Tara. "I don't mind as long as it's on the way back," Tara said resignedly, "I already made an appointment with the admissions office. We can't be late."

They packed for an overnight stay and headed toward Visitation University. Tara kept to herself during the drive, listening to her music and scrolling through her phone. For Sullivan, it felt good to escape the city and be back in farmland. It took them three hours to reach the school. Sullivan was taken aback by how tiny it was.

The campus contained a one story administration building and a row of three story cinder block dorms. There was also a prominent chapel but no signs of a sports facility. They arrived for a lunch-time meeting with the head of admissions. Tara and Sullivan were ushered into his office. He was a young man wearing a white short-sleeve shirt and a brown crew cut. Sullivan thought he looked like a Mormon missionary.

His name was Brad and he gave them a gracious welcome. He had Tara's transcript in front of him and was quite impressed with her grades. "Tara, you will qualify for one of our academic scholarships. We also can arrange a job for you on campus. We have openings in the cafeteria and coffee shop. That would help pay for your room and board."

Sullivan was pleased by the numbers Brad was presenting. He certainly made it sound affordable. He was very unimpressed with the campus. It looked like a junior college stuck in the middle of a cornfield. Brad gave Tara a packet of materials to study and proposed that they have lunch at a nearby restaurant. He would use the university credit card to treat them.

They repaired to a casual dining spot near the interstate. Brad explained the history of the university. "We started out as an all-female women's teaching college," he said, "We still have a majority of female students but lately we've been attracting more males." Tara didn't like that the student body was 60% female but Sullivan thought the ratio was just fine.

Brad outlined the college's philosophy, which as a liberal arts school offered a diversified course load on all general studies. Students declare their major when they're sophomores. When asked what her focus would be, Tara quickly responded, "Early childhood education." Brad smiled and said that Visitation was especially strong in that area.

After lunch they toured the campus. Each dorm bore the name and image of a saintly woman who had taught there. They all wore tight perms. Sullivan sensed this was a very conservative college. Brad explained the strict rules for early curfew, no drinking and limited visiting hours for boys. Sullivan could sense Tara already chafing against the constraints. Their final stop was the cafeteria which was serving "Chicken Surprise."

"Tara, we have a spare dorm room you can stay in, to get the feel of the place," Brad offered. Tara thanked him and agreed to stay the night.

While they were walking back to the car to get her stuff, they encountered three co-eds along the path. They stopped to welcome Tara to the school. They were dressed stylishly like her and had long flowing hair. He could tell that Tara was instantly comfortable with them. They promised to show her to her room. Sullivan wished her good night and headed to a motel.

He had found a cheap room along the frontage road close to the interstate. Sullivan stopped at a liquor store to pick up a six pack. With Tara staying in the dorm, he could spare her the sight of one of his road trip rituals, filling the bathroom sink with beer and ice. Sullivan went to bed early but the noisy trucks roaring by made it difficult to sleep. The next morning, he called Tara. She sounded groggy. She confessed to staying up late with her new acquaintances. They planned to have a late breakfast at the cafeteria, and Sullivan asked if he could join them.

Tara and two of the girls were chowing down on cereal when Sullivan arrived. She introduced her father to Kelly and Jennifer. They were both juniors. Sullivan dined on scrambled eggs that had obviously been made from a mix, while the two students talked up the university to Tara. They described an odd tradition that called for female students to ring a certain bell if they became engaged. The bell would summon their friends to help celebrate.

It sounded corny to Sullivan. He boasted to the girls that he was a private detective, while Tara rolled her eyes. "As a matter of fact, Tara and I are working on a case right now," Sullivan said. Tara's stock instantly shot up, when they learned she helped her dad with investigations.

It was all hugs when Sullivan and Tara hit the road. When they were alone in the car, Tara confided, "I can see myself going there, dad, the girls are so nice, and they said there were a lot of fun things to do."

"Like what?"

"Bowling," Tara offered uncertainly, "It won't cost me a lot of money, especially if I get a scholarship." Sullivan agreed that the university was certainly affordable but questioned Tara about her change of heart.

"What happened to Stanford or was it U. of I.?"

"I was thinking I'd get lost in a big school like that," Tara replied, "I'd rather go to a small school, where they actually care about you. Besides, most companies just want to know you have your degree. They don't care what it says on the diploma."

Sullivan wasn't going to argue with her, as they sped down country roads toward Euphoria, Indiana. Sullivan enjoyed driving the old state routes and county highways as they passed through one small town after another. Euphoria had an old fashioned downtown. It had a Main Street, with a few side streets on either side. The airstrip was located on the outskirts of town.

Sullivan drove through the open gate of a community called Horizon Airpark. It was a small subdivision surrounding a grass airstrip. It consisted of about twenty frame houses sitting on sizable pieces of property. Each frame house had a metal canopy in back for parking a plane. Most of these were occupied by small prop planes. Sullivan spotted a few residents tinkering with their engines.

Another plane was taxiing for takeoff and they watched it climb into the sky above the cornfields. Sullivan planned to canvass the residents to see if anyone had witnessed the recent crash. Having Tara with him might be a plus. They may not trust a stranger knocking on their door, but a dad and his daughter would be less threatening.

According to Charly, the plane that crashed was a small used Cessna. The crash killed the plane's owner and two prospective buyers. The customers wanted to take the plane up for a test flight, before deciding whether to buy it. The owner was at the controls. The newspaper report contained the names and ages of the three fatalities. The owner, Grant Richards, and his wife had a small house in Horizon Airpark. Sullivan was instructed not to talk to Grant's widow, for fear of stirring up a lawsuit. The customers were from Illinois.

Sullivan and Tara started going door-to-door. The folks they met were friendly enough, but none of them had witnessed the crash. Most had heard a loud noise about a mile to the north but didn't learn until later that it was caused by Grant Richards' plane going down. They found one man outside working on the engine of his turboprop.

He stopped to wipe his hands and said he had seen Grant taking off that afternoon. "He had two guys with him, big guys" the man recalled, "Grant had been trying to sell that Cessna for months." Sullivan asked if they could go inside to talk. The man invited them in and offered glasses of lemonade. Tara was smiley and polite. She listened intently to the conversation without commenting.

The witness' name was Spencer and he described the takeoff in detail. "I was outside changing a cylinder when I heard Grant start up and taxi to the strip. It was ideal flying weather, no ceiling. There wasn't much wind either. Grant used every inch of runway to get that thing off the ground. He barely cleared the trees at the end of the runway. Then I think he lost ground effect."

"What's that?" Sullivan asked.

"You said you were an aviation investigator and you don't know about ground effect?" Spencer asked warily.

"I'm kind of new to this," Sullivan admitted.

"My dad just got this job," Tara hastily explained, "He's used to investigating car accidents."

"Ground effect," Spencer explained, "happens when your plane is still close to the ground after takeoff. It gives your plane more lift. But when you get to a certain altitude, you lose it and your plane can stall. Like I said, Grant barely cleared those trees but then he dropped a hundred feet or so."

"I stopped what I was doing," Spencer said, "because I thought Grant might be in trouble. It looked like he was stalling when he made a sharp turn to the north. I couldn't hear it, of course, but I'm sure his stall horn was blasting. He was still losing altitude when he turned back toward the airstrip. I think he was planning to land."

"Did he have his landing gear down?" Sullivan asked.

Spencer found the question insulting. "We all have *fixed* landing gear on our planes, Mr. Sullivan, including Grant."

"Did you see or hear any signs of engine trouble?"

"No I didn't," Spencer said, annoyed by Sullivan's persistence. "If I had, I already would have mentioned it." Spencer resumed his story, "I watched him circle back about a mile north of here, but he was still losing altitude. If you and your daughter want to take a ride, I'll show you where he ended up."

Father and daughter piled into the front seat of Spencer's pickup and headed north on a gravel section road. The road made a ninety degree turn to the east and a few miles down they saw a blackened structure on their left. Spencer parked near the remains of a cabin that had burned down. The smell of charred wood was still in the air.

"After I heard the crash, I called 911," Spencer recalled, "I beat the fire truck getting here. The plane and the cabin – it was burning so hot you couldn't get close. It looked like Grant had gone nose first. I'm hoping for their sake they was all killed on impact. It took the fire department a half hour to get the flames down, what with all that fuel. I couldn't stand to watch after a while, and I'll never forget the smell."

They headed back to the house in the pickup. No one said a word, imagining the horror of seeing the plane burn.

As Sullivan was leaving, he thanked Spencer for his time. "Has anyone else talked to you about this?" he asked.

"The sheriff stopped by to ask me a few questions," Spencer recalled, "but there was nothing official. He said it was all in the hands of NTSB. They came out and hauled away what was left of the plane. I heard they brought it to a hangar at Indianapolis Airport. I don't know what they're going to do with it."

Sullivan extended a card. "If anyone else bothers you about this, Mr. Spencer, just have them call our office. There's no reason you should have to answer more questions."

"I have a question, Mr. Spencer," Tara interrupted, "Do you know if anyone else saw the crash?"

Spencer smiled, "You've got yourself a good assistant, Mr. Sullivan. No, young lady. I didn't see anyone else around." Spencer wished them a safe trip back to the city.

When they were back on the road, Sullivan called his license guy, Carl Sawyer, to see if the two victims from Illinois had any vehicles registered there. Sawyer came back on and said they both owned vehicles registered to addresses in an affluent Chicago suburb. "Say, these are big boys," Sawyer exclaimed, "According to their driver's licenses, one guy is six feet, 221 pounds, the other guy is only 5'9" but close to 300. Who are you working for, Weight Watchers?"

During the drive back, Tara busied herself with her phone. "Dad, I found a picture of the kind of plane they were flying," she said excitedly. Sullivan couldn't look because he was driving. "It was a 1970 Cessna. That's old isn't it?"

Sullivan had no idea what constituted an old plane, unless it was a biplane.

"Does it list the specs on it?"

"Yeah, it has the wingspan, maximum speed, range – Dad, it lists the maximum weight load as 900 pounds!"

"Do you think it was overloaded?" Sullivan asked hesitantly.

"Those two passengers alone, that's over 500 pounds. I wonder how big the pilot was, or what else they had on board."

"I'll get Richards' height and weight off the coroner's report," Sullivan said, "Good work. I thought you only used that thing for texting."

CHAPTER 18

When father and daughter arrived home, Sullivan found a fat envelope waiting for him. It was from the New York firm and contained a detailed affidavit for Sullivan to read and sign and a check paying for his visit to the strip club. Ann was pleased by the check and relieved the case was over.

Sullivan called Charly to give her a verbal report on the aviation case. "I knew you'd come through," she deadpanned. "Seeing you had Tara with you. I bet she was the brains of the outfit."

"Don't tell *her* that. She'll want to get paid."

"Seriously Mike, do you see her taking over some day?"

"She'd be perfect," Sullivan replied, "She's fearless and has a PhD in reading people. The only problem is she doesn't want to have anything to do with my company."

"How about Flynn?"

"The jury is out on Flynn. He's too young. But I don't think either one wants it. They've watched me work my butt off and then wait months for my money."

"That's the part of this business that stinks," Charly agreed, "but this aviation company is the best. They pay me within one or two days of getting my invoice."

Charly would get back to him if they needed more work done.

After hanging up, Sullivan realized he didn't have a single assignment left. Later that week, though, he received a call from Worldwide Insurance

Company in New Jersey. Sullivan already knew their reputation. They were a substandard insurance carrier that issued policies with minimal limits. The woman who called, though, acted very self-important.

"Mr. Sullivan, we are considering retaining your firm to locate our clients in the Chicago area. We have strict guidelines, though, before we enter into any arrangement. First, you must provide me with a complete copy of your private detective policy. If it meets our requirements, we can start assigning cases to your office."

Sullivan had never read his policy, which ran to over a hundred pages. It contained all kinds of arcane clauses, plus random exclusions for "Unmanned Aircraft," "Certified Acts of Terrorism," and "Liquor Liability," among others. They didn't remotely relate to his business, although the last one excluded coverage if Sullivan was found drunk on the job.

After he put together a package and sent it off, Sullivan wasn't sure he would ever get any work from Worldwide. However, the company representative was satisfied with his million-dollar policy and placed him on its list of approved investigators. An adjustor named Spaulding called him with his first assignment. His manner was borderline rude, as he barked instructions at Sullivan.

Spaulding's case involved a cab driver Worldwide insured named Mohammed Al-Malicki, who had struck a pedestrian in a crosswalk. His last known address was on the North Side. Spaulding cautioned that it was only a $20,000 policy, so Sullivan's charges to locate him should not exceed $150.

Sullivan invited Flynn along on a Saturday afternoon to look for Al-Malicki. Maybe it would trigger his interest in the business. They talked sports nonstop on their way to the address. When they arrived at the block where the apartment building was located, taxis were parked up and down the street. In the lobby, they found many Middle-Eastern names listed, but no Al-Malicki.

Sullivan rang the apartment number Al-Malicki had listed on his insurance application and hoped for the best. A woman answered the intercom and buzzed them into the building. Sullivan and Flynn reached Apt. 203 and knocked politely. No one answered. Sullivan used the metal knocker to add more volume. Still no response.

"Let's go, Dad, they're not home," Flynn said anxiously.

"What do you mean they're not home?" Sullivan growled, "She buzzed me into the building!" He kept up the knocking and called, "Anyone home?" Several tenants opened their doors and peeked at Sullivan suspiciously. When he asked them if they knew Al-Malicki, they didn't answer. Sullivan was ready to leave a card, when a young woman bounded up the stairs and strode toward them.

She wore a purple hijab and loose flowing slacks of the same color. Her face was angry.

"Who are you?" she demanded. Sullivan explained he worked for an insurance company and they were trying to locate Al-Malicki.

"Well, you're scaring the hell out of my cousin!"

"But she buzzed us into the building," Sullivan pleaded. Flynn stood speechless during this uncomfortable situation. The woman shouted some Arabic words through the door and it finally opened. A visibly frightened young woman allowed them to enter. She wore a heavy veil and only her terrified eyes were visible. There was a pungent odor of cooking coming from a pot on the stove.

"She thought you were someone else," the woman in purple explained, "I told her you're trying to find our uncle."

Sullivan questioned the young woman, using her cousin as a translator. She admitted that Mohammed Al-Malicki had lived there. She had no idea where he had moved. Sullivan assumed she was lying. The English-speaking cousin also denied knowing where he had gone. Sullivan left a card with each of them, on the chance they might hear from Uncle Mohammed.

Before leaving the building, they searched for something identifying the building's owner. Sullivan spotted a "For Rent" sign and copied down the name and number. Sullivan suspected it was a Romanian name. Every ethnic group in Chicago had found an economic niche. The Irish started out as cops and firemen. Now, they were lawyers and politicians The Greeks ran restaurants. Romanians managed apartment buildings.

Sullivan got the property manager on the phone. He consulted his list of tenants for the building. "He moved out of 203 two years ago," the manager said routinely, "Didn't leave a forwarding. I remember the guy, though, he drove a cab, always paid in cash." Sullivan thanked him and wondered what to do next. When they were outside, Flynn had an idea.

"Dad, let's check all these cabs and see if we can find his." Sullivan thought it was far-fetched but didn't have an alternative. He took one side of the street and Flynn the other. They peered inside at the cab licenses hoping to find Al-Malicki's. They checked every cab in a two-block radius and were getting discouraged. Then he heard Flynn cry out, "Dad, I got him!"

Sullivan crossed the street to join him. The license bore the insured's name and the photo of a forty-something man in a full beard. He looked forbidding in the photo. Sullivan copied down his cab registration number and the license plate number.

"Why don't we wait until he shows up," Flynn suggested. This also seemed unpromising to Sullivan. Who knew what shift he drove?

"OK – we'll give it a half hour," Sullivan said agreeably, "I think there's two mitts in the trunk, we can play catch."

Father and son tossed the ball back and forth, pausing for passing cars. When the half hour was up, Sullivan placed a card under a windshield wiper, with a message for Mohammed to call. On the drive home, Sullivan thanked Flynn for his idea.

"What are you going to do next, dad?"

"The city has an office, where the cab drivers have to register," Sullivan said thoughtfully, "I'll go there next week. Maybe they have his address."

Sullivan was interrupted by a call from DeSantis. "Mike, I tried to stall your case until Christmas," DeSantis began, "But there's a mandatory hearing on December 15th. You're required to be there."

Sullivan's heart sank at the thought of going back to court. "Sounds like I have no choice," he said sullenly, "Thanks for the heads-up."

DeSantis' voice became cagey. "Mike, you didn't do anything to mess with my new client."

Sullivan couldn't think of anything to say.

"Seeing you at the club might have been a coincidence, but I got wind there might be an injunction filed to shut down Pirate's Booty."

Sullivan wasn't comfortable discussing the strip club on speaker with Flynn in the car. "That's news to me – Pete, I got another call – keep me posted about the hearing."

When they arrived home, Sullivan spotted fresh flowers on the kitchen table. Ann was in an unusually good mood. After greeting Sullivan with a kiss, she smiled mysteriously. "You're looking at the new office manager of VisionClear," Ann announced. "I knew I was getting my evaluation today but had no idea they wanted me to replace Marianne."

"Is there a raise involved?" Sullivan asked hopefully.

Ann nodded, "Ten percent!" she announced triumphantly. "Now I can quit the clothing store."

"What's going to happen to Marianne?"

"She's going to take my job answering phones. My boss thought the job was getting to be too much for her. He said that I had become much more efficient and I was ready to take over. I think working for you really helped."

"Let's celebrate," Sullivan said, as he embraced Ann and held her close.

"Oh, so you love me even more," Ann said coquettishly "It can't be because of the pay raise."

"I'm serious, we should go somewhere nice."

"As long as it isn't all-you-can-eat Chinese," Ann teased, "There's a pizza in the freezer for the kids."

Ann's raise had taken some pressure off Sullivan. They felt comfortable dining at an upscale seafood restaurant. He didn't ruin the evening by bringing up the mandatory hearing. He clinked his stein with her wine glass as they toasted her promotion. Sullivan knew that the highlight of his day was still to come. Climbing into a warm bed to cuddle with Ann.

On Monday morning, Sullivan drove to a particularly gritty neighborhood where the city office regulating taxi drivers was located. The customer line featured a kaleidoscopic of colors. Some looked like they were from Central Africa, others seemed Eastern European, and there were many Hispanics. Sullivan could hear a cacophony of accents, as the drivers stepped forward to renew their registrations.

When it was Sullivan's turn, he was directed to an office in the back. It was occupied by a tired-looking civil servant sitting at a small desk. Sullivan introduced himself and the purpose of his visit. The man's impassive expression perked up a bit. This was something new.

"So, you need the address of this cabbie?" the man said, "You know, these guys never give anyone their correct address. These countries they come from, they're so afraid the authorities will come knocking."

"I understand but I'm trying to help this guy."

The man typed Al-Malicki's name into the computer.

"They lie about their address to the DMV, or anyone else who asks," the man said, "But they don't lie to us. If they get caught giving us a phony address, we take them off the street. Let's see, there's more than one. Here we go, Mohammed Al-Malicki. He rattled off the address as Sullivan copied it down. It was a short walk from where Flynn had found his cab.

Sullivan thanked the man sincerely for his help.

He surprised Sullivan with his card. "From now on, don't waste your time going to bad addresses. Just call me and I can look up their name. It will save you the trip coming down here."

Sullivan marveled at his level of cooperation.

"OK, but is there anything I can do for you?"

"I'll think of something," the civil servant said with a secretive smile.

Sullivan finally found Al-Malicki at his new address. Mohammed was so suspicious of his visitor, he wouldn't open his apartment door.

He denied being served with summons, and thought the accident case had been resolved. He grudgingly gave Sullivan his cell phone number. Sullivan alerted Al-Malicki to expect correspondence from Worldwide. He slipped a card under the door and instructed Mohammed to refer any further inquiries to his phone number.

Completing the assignment had taken Sullivan more hours and miles than he was allowed to charge. He had to stick to the $150 limit. As Frank Sr. often warned, "You can always get work at the wrong price."

After Worldwide discovered Sullivan could track down their insured cab drivers, they sent more assignments his way. Some he solved with a simple phone call to his new friend at the city office. John Schneider didn't ask for much in return but had a weakness for premium cigars.

Meanwhile, Charly was true to her word and Sullivan was paid promptly by the aviation company. She said they might be sending him back to Euphoria to interview the owner's widow. They needed to find out what kind of payload the plane was carrying.

He also got a call from DeSantis, who offered to buy Sullivan a beer if he stopped by Sansone's. Sullivan assumed they would discuss his case. Maybe DeSantis needed fast money for attending the upcoming hearing. When Sullivan walked into the bar, DeSantis was sitting on his usual stool. It was just like the time before, with the game show blaring above the bar.

Stella brought Sullivan his usual and DeSantis finally revealed why he wanted to see him. "Mike, my new client just got shut down," he began, "I told the owner there was no way to fight the injunction. There was an interesting affidavit attached to it. You'll never guess who signed it."

Sullivan's face flushed. "Pete, there was no way I could tell you why I was there."

DeSantis waved away the excuse, "Don't worry about it. I'm happy to know you aren't as big a scumbag as I thought you were."

"Is this going to get you in trouble?" Sullivan asked with concern.

"You kidding? You just gave me more billable hours to get the joint reopened."

Sullivan asked if they had a plan. DeSantis confessed they had no choice but to change the name.

"Any ideas?"

DeSantis smiled, "I came up with Treasure Chest. That way, they don't have to change the pirate theme. They just have to dress the girls like wenches and maids instead of pirates." A few weeks later, the club reopened with the new sign. Sullivan saw no reason to check if the roly-poly Asian girl had made a costume change.

Sullivan slogged along finding foreign-born cabbies for Worldwide, mailing them minuscule bills by his standards. He recalled how his father reacted when they received checks for small amounts. "Why are we sending invoices for $65?" he'd ask in disgust. Finally, though, the cumulative cost of locating the cab drivers got Sullivan's adjustor in hot water. Spaulding called Sullivan to tell him they were going to go with someone less expensive. Sullivan wished him luck but knew from experience that you get what you pay for with cheap detectives.

Sullivan now had so much time on his hands he proposed the family make their annual fall pilgrimage to a state park, a few hours west of the city. He had started the tradition with Ann before the kids were born. There was something comforting about retracing the same route year-after-year. After hiking the trails, they stopped at farm stands to buy apple cider, pumpkins and fresh maple syrup. He worried this could be Tara's last fall trip with them.

While he walked through the woods alongside Ann, Tara and Flynn lagged behind. It was a crisp day and the fall colors were at their brightest. When they stopped to rest at an overlook, Sullivan asked his kids if they had ever thought of taking over his company. Tara scoffed at the idea.

"I know you don't think much of the company," Sullivan said, "But we had some good years. Remember the trips we took? How many times we ate out?"

Tara nodded and chimed in with some memories of her own. "I'll never forget when you bought me a whole lobster for lunch! Remember when we drove straight through to Disneyworld! I still can't believe we went skiing in Colorado."

After a thoughtful silence, Tara admitted she had no desire to take over. "Flynn, you should think about it."

"Why me?"

Sullivan didn't have an answer but Ann interjected. "Didn't you like your father coaching your teams and coming to the games?

"Sure," Flynn agreed uncertainly, wondering where this was going.

"In a normal job, your father could never have taken off time during the middle of the day."

"What does this have to do with me?" Flynn asked perplexed.

"Someday you could have a son yourself," Ann continued, "Wouldn't you want to hang out with him? Take him golfing and do all the other things you do with dad."

"I guess," Flynn said uncertainly, "But I just did a case with dad. It was scary. I don't want to talk to strangers."

"I understand," Sullivan assured him, "It took me ten years to get over my fear of talking to strangers."

Tara scoffed, "I've never seen *you* scared."

"That's because I never brought you along on those kind of cases."

Frank Sullivan hadn't been so considerate. He didn't hesitate to bring his kids to rough neighborhoods. At a young age, Sullivan had accompanied his dad. They entered decrepit buildings and were face-to-face with some very creepy people.

"Dad didn't take you, because you're a girl," Flynn taunted in a patronizing tone.

"I don't run like a girl," Tara retorted, "First one across the creek," she challenged, pointing to a shallow spot with stepping stones. Tara beat Flynn to the creek. They jousted with their walking sticks, trying to push each other off the stones. The scene reminded Sullivan of Robin Hood battling Little John at a stream crossing.

Ann put a stop to the skirmish before anyone got soaked. Ann tended to be more careful concerning the kids. One time, he was roughhousing with Flynn when Ann warned that someone was going to get hurt. Sullivan responded, "That's how we know when to stop."

Sullivan had never dreamed that he'd take another road trip with Charly but she called to invite him on a journey back to Euphoria. "The company wants me to get a signed statement from that witness, Spencer. I told them that no one is better at taking statements than you."

Sullivan was touched. "They want me to go with because I know more about the plane's specs," Charly continued, "They also want us to talk to the owner's widow. They figure she's going to get a lawyer anyway, so maybe we can pin her down on some details."

"OK," Sullivan agreed, "But we better get an early start." He didn't think Ann would be happy about an overnight stay.

Charly picked him up that morning at 6:15. They took her late-model luxury car. It was more reliable than Sullivan's. As Sullivan settled in, Charly handed him a cardboard cup of coffee. She also gave him the plane's owner's manual to study on the way.

"I have the autopsy report," Sullivan said, "Grant Richards was 53. Let's see, he was 5'11," 170. His occupation is listed as clerk at a feed store. His widow's name is Connie Richards. Her occupation is hairdresser."

Sullivan was nervous as they merged onto an interstate. Sullivan didn't trust Charly's driving. Once they had hit a parked car and they often had close calls. He had no choice, though, as they beat the morning rush to escape the city.

As they headed east, Sullivan and Charly settled into an easy conversation about an exhibit they had both seen at the Art Institute. Sullivan felt instantly comfortable, grateful for Charly's companionship. He could tell she felt the same way. He also took time to skim the manual and ask occasional questions.

"How much was he asking for the plane?"

"I don't know," Charly replied, "But the Blue Book value was $69,000."

Sullivan whistled, "I won't even ask what a private jet costs."

As they crossed into Indiana, Sullivan asked if she was still working with Jake.

"That guy - how did you put up with him all these years?"

"Jake's harmless. He just loves to needle people. If you give it back to him, he'll stop."

Charly recounted some adventures with Jake in junkyards and at auto auctions. "He shows up in the craziest outfits," she recalled, "He's got so many things going at once. He's like a three-ring circus."

"You know he's divorced," Sullivan cautioned.

"He's never actually hit on me," Charly said, "But he loves to flirt."

"So, no one special yet?"

"I don't have time to date," Charly claimed.

Sullivan was suddenly filled with an overwhelming tenderness for Charly. He had no idea what her reaction would be but couldn't hold back his words.

"I love you, Charly." he said simply. She was so startled, he thought she might go off the road.

"What?" she stammered, "You mean, in a romantic way?" she asked in a trembling voice.

Her question caused Sullivan to recoil.

"You didn't have to do *that*," Charly snapped angrily.

"I'm sorry, I just never thought of you that way. I love who you are, that's all," he said softly. Sullivan's definition of love meant appreciating people for their good qualities, as well as their faults. The way he felt toward Charly fit that meaning.

"I like everything about you," Sullivan insisted, "Even the things that bug me, like the way you drive."

Charly sighed in relief. "Thanks for explaining. I was worried. I guess I feel the same way toward you -but the "L" word? I'm not sure." Desperate to change the subject, Charly asked, "So, are you still sleeping with your best friend?"

Sullivan smiled, "Ann and I are getting along better than ever."

The discomfort subsided. Sullivan didn't regret what he had said and could tell Charly was privately pleased. His other definition of love was the ability to endure boring tasks with the person while still enjoying their company. Driving together across the flat landscape of Indiana certainly qualified.

Finally, they pulled into Horizon Airpark and headed for Spencer's house. As usual, they hadn't called ahead and simply hoped he would be home. As he opened his door, Spencer gave Sullivan a questioning look. "Never expected to see you again."

"This is Charly."

"Another daughter?" Spencer exclaimed.

Charly laughed, "No, we work together."

"I hope you're as sharp as that other young lady he brought here," Spencer added.

Spencer invited them in and they sat in his breakfast nook. He offered them coffee but they were both caffeinated enough. Sullivan pulled out his notes from the previous interview.

"Mr. Spencer, I want to write up a statement about what you told me last time. You can look it over to make sure it's correct. Then, if you sign and date it, we can use it in court if necessary. It could save you a trip to the courthouse."

Spencer was agreeable and Sullivan started writing, pausing to ask a question now and then. Charly struck up a conversation about small planes. Spencer was impressed by her expertise. He warmed to her quickly. She asked if he knew whether Grant was carrying any cargo.

"Beats me. But, when we're through here, I can introduce you to his wife, Connie. She does hair out of her house, so she's probably home."

Sullivan composed a very detailed statement for Spencer to sign. He made his usual deliberate mistakes and asked Spencer to initial the corrections. Spencer read it slowly and was satisfied. After he signed it, he said he would accompany them to Connie's. Her house was a short distance away. "She's home," Spencer confirmed, "That's her car in the driveway."

Sullivan was leery of interviewing a grieving widow. Charly's cover story was that the aviation company had seen a newspaper report of the crash and wanted to know the facts, even before the NTSB report came out. When the widow answered her door, Spencer greeted her warmly. "Connie, if you're not busy with a customer, these folks want to talk to you about Grant's crash."

Connie was a neatly-groomed woman in her 50's. She had a fashionable hairstyle but looked haggard. "Where are you folks from?" she asked warily.

"Chicago," Charly answered.

"No, I mean who do work for?"

Charly gave her story in a way that depicted the company's concern about her husband's crash. "Mrs. Richards, we're so sorry about your loss. But the company wants to find out if there were any mechanical problems with the plane. If there is, they want to rectify it, before another tragedy happens."

"I like your hair," Connie suddenly said, "When you're young, you can wear it short like that."

Charly smiled and thanked her for the compliment, as they stood waiting to be invited in.

"Connie, these folks are good people," Spencer interjected, "It's OK to talk to them. You should have met Mr. Sullivan's daughter. Very well mannered, didn't talk much but took in everything."

The woman didn't seem completely sold but politely invited them inside. Spencer said goodbye and wished Sullivan well. He looked at Charly, "This little girl knows her stuff. Maybe she can teach you something about airplanes."

Connie fussed with clearing off two chairs for them. "Ever since the crash, I haven't felt much like cleaning," she said apologetically. If only she knew about some of the hovels Sullivan and Charly had visited. "Your place looks great," Charly said, "I love your curtains."

After the small talk subsided, Sullivan asked if she knew how the crash happened.

The woman seemed reluctant to discuss it. It was too painful. She did her best to compose herself. "If you ask me specific questions, maybe I can answer them. But I don't know where to start."

Charly asked about how and when her husband had purchased the plane. "Grant's been wanting a plane since he graduated college," she recounted, "He went to an aviation school you know. He wanted to be a FedEx pilot, but he never did get instrument-rated. So he just flew for pleasure."

"He was only rated for daytime flying?" Charly confirmed. Connie nodded, "He used to tell me that flying made him feel fully alive," she said with a sniff. "Anyway, we moved here about five years ago. He picked the plane out of a catalog of used aircraft. The local bank here gave him a loan and he made monthly payments."

"Why was he trying to sell it?" Sullivan asked.

"Frankly, we couldn't afford it. It wasn't just the payments but the fuel, repairs, and they charge us here for using the runway. It was breaking his heart to sell it but we had no choice. He placed an ad in that same catalog."

Charly asked if he had had any problems with the plane. "He had to have a part replaced now and then but nothing major. That plane was his baby. He treated it better than me." She related how he meticulously completed his check list before every flight. "He was so careful about everything. I always felt safe when he took me up."

Sullivan finally posed the question that had brought them there. "Was he carrying anything that day?"

Connie gave him a funny look. "As a matter of fact, he had some 50-pound sacks of feed. After he took the test flight with the two gentleman, he was going to drop the feed off at his dad's farm. There's a big clearing he used for landings and takeoffs but . . ." her voice trailed off.

"One last question, Mrs. Richards," Charly said, "What company did he use for repairs?"

"A local outfit called Avionics. They came out and did all the work on the plane."

As they stood to leave, Connie expressed her sorrow about the two passengers. "Do you know if they were married, had kids?"

"We don't know," Charly said, "The article didn't mention their families."

"No one should have to go through something like this," she said firmly, "Some lady at the wake told me Grant's in a better place. I wanted to tell her, "No, his better place was right here with me.""

Sullivan and Charly again expressed their condolences. As they drove back to Chicago, Charly said she would get the plane's maintenance records from Avionics. There was no further talk of love.

CHAPTER 19

Sullivan was well-compensated for his return trip to Euphoria. Charly had continued to work on the assignment by obtaining the plane's maintenance records. They were mostly bills for routine repairs. She also interviewed the pilot's father, who said he had been expecting his son to deliver six feed bags to his farm.

Now, as Sullivan entered the bleak days of November he was feeling empty inside. He was fine when family was around but, otherwise, his days dragged. It was getting dark earlier and the Chicago winter loomed ahead.

He contacted a counselor he used to see before he married Ann. Betty was retired now but still giving practical advice. "Mike, you've got to get out of that house," she said in a motherly way, "Sitting around is going to kill you. Why don't you go back to your old job?"

"Driving a cab?" Sullivan asked incredulously.

"It will give you something to do, until you find something better. You told me how much you liked talking with the passengers. Besides, you'll be bringing home cash. It will make you feel like you're helping out."

Sullivan couldn't picture going back to cabbing, a dead-end job that demanded more and more hours. Twice he had been robbed. Even when passengers didn't try to steal his money, they knew how to scare him. "Where's your safe?" a sinister-looking man once asked from the backseat, knowing full well that Sullivan stashed his cash in the yellow envelope lying on the front seat.

He ran the cab driving idea past Ann. She gave him a worried look.

"That's your choice, Mike. I'm not going to tell you to go back to driving. Betty may be right, though, moping around here isn't doing you any good. It might be good timing. Tips are better during the holidays."

Sullivan drove to the cab company and parked near the garage he had worked out of in his 20s. As he entered the office, he recognized a few of the old-time dispatchers. They answered the phone with a mechanical, "Cab. What's your address?" The dispatchers didn't care much for the drivers. They used to yell at Sullivan for being late picking up fares.

Sullivan knocked on the owner's office door. He was surprised to find a young man with brown hair and glasses, wearing a crisp white shirt and tie.

"Are you the one who called about a job?" the man asked pleasantly.

"Yeah, I used to drive – where's Leonard?"

"My father retired five years ago," the man said reverently, "I'm Paul." Leonard had been an irascible boss, who gave him nasty looks when Sullivan suffered a mishap. Once, Sullivan sideswiped a parked car. Leonard stared at the latest dent in Sullivan's cab in disbelief. He once awarded Sullivan the "Golden Tow Truck Award" for being the first cabbie to get stuck in the snow that winter.

"My chauffer's license expired," Sullivan explained.

"No problem, I'll have someone take you to the Secretary of State. We have a special relationship with one of the supervisors."

Sullivan easily renewed his license and was assigned to a late-model Prius that was equipped both with a computer to notify Sullivan to pick up passengers and GPS to guide Sullivan through the city streets. Sullivan already knew the city better than most. He became angrier at the computer than he had been with the surly dispatchers. "She" gave maddening directions that forced Sullivan to make difficult maneuvers in heavy traffic.

Sullivan started every day rolling over rough pavement waiting for the computer to ping him with pick-ups. He wouldn't know the passenger's destination, though, until they climbed in. The city enforced a strict law that once the passenger gave their address, the driver had no choice but to take them there. Several times, Sullivan would be reaching the end of his shift, when he suddenly had to make a long haul to the far suburbs.

Rides like these would extend his workday, but Sullivan had no intention of working late hours. The free spending bar crowd offered an opportunity to make good money, but Sullivan knew from experience drunks were more trouble than they were worth.

Sullivan chose the evening rush instead and started work in the late-afternoon. He quickly discovered he wasn't the daredevil driver he had been in his 20s. He no longer took chances just to get to an address a few minutes earlier. Some passengers complained about his slow driving.

His daily goal was to make $100. Sometimes it took four hours, other times six or more. Either way, he wasn't home for family dinners and missed the easy conversation around the kitchen table. After his final fare, he'd pick up fast food on the way home. Sullivan spent most of his driving time in the "underserved" neighborhoods on the South and West Sides. Unlike many drivers, he was comfortable in these neighborhoods, where he knew there was a steady demand for cabs.

He enjoyed the back and forth with passengers and saw that lively conversation led to better tips. The driving was exhausting, though, and he couldn't help feeling that he was going backwards career-wise. What was next, a job in a mailroom?

Ann appreciated the money he was earning but said he could quit any time the job became too much. Sullivan continued grinding his way through the city streets until he reached his daily quota. Thanksgiving was approaching and Sullivan toyed with the idea of driving that day. Cabs would be busy with passengers anxious to get to grandma's house.

Sullivan called his younger sister, Clare, to see what she was doing for the holiday. She lived in Minneapolis with her husband, Malik, and their two young children. Sullivan was still close with his little sister. They spoke by phone several times a week but rarely got together. Clare had gone into medicine as her parents suggested but became a pharmacy tech, not a nurse. During her training, she confided to Sullivan she hoped to marry a doctor and, sure enough, she fell in love with a pediatrician.

Sullivan considered himself lucky to have Malik as a brother-in-law. He had emigrated from India and was one of the kindest men he had ever met. He treated Clare like a goddess and was a hands-on dad with his sons. Sullivan, though, used to tease him about his heavy accent. "Mike, I *am* speaking English," he would insist. "I know, Malik, but I'm only getting every other word."

Clare was shocked to hear Sullivan was back driving a cab. "Isn't that dangerous?"

"I don't have a lot of choice these days," Sullivan said morosely. "Say, have you heard from Patrick?"

"No," she said hesitantly, "In fact, I was going to call you about him. I'm worried."

Sullivan rarely spoke with his big brother. When Patrick did call, he would start by saying, "This is Pat, your brother."

Sullivan would laugh, "Patrick, I've been hearing your voice for forty years, I think I can recognize it."

He usually called Mike when he needed a favor. This wasn't often, because Patrick was living well in a palatial house in a North Shore suburb. His wife, Carolyn, had come from money and her parents had bankrolled a seat for him at the Chicago Board of Trade. They had three daughters in their teens.

"Why, what's wrong with Patrick?" Sullivan asked.

"Carolyn says he's drinking more than ever," Clare continued in her worried tone, "Not just beer but hard stuff. He goes to a bar downtown after work. Some nights, he doesn't come home at all. Have you talked to him?"

Sullivan grunted, "He calls me once in a while. Do you know Patrick hasn't asked me a question since we were kids?"

"I know, Mike, but you should give him a call."

"I'll do better than that. I know where he drinks."

The Stock Exchange was the favored watering hole for traders and runners alike. It was close enough to the Board of Trade for a quick one during the workday but the real rush came after the markets closed at 3:15. Sullivan parked his cab nearby and walked into the bar, his eyes searching for Patrick.

He wasn't difficult to spot. Pat was slapping his gold credit card on the bar, loudly announcing that the next round was on him. Bartenders and patrons alike we're always happy to see Patrick. Sullivan noticed his suit was rumpled and his skin more lined than the last time he had seen him. Gray was creeping into his dark hair. Sullivan was surprised to see Patrick's eyes light up, when he settled on the stool next to him.

"How's my little brother doing?" he asked in his patronizing way, "What are you drinking?"

"Sparkling water and lime," Sullivan replied, "I'm working."

Patrick was astonished that Sullivan was back driving a cab.

"It's parked outside, if you need a ride," Sullivan said, "I hear you sometimes forget where you live."

His eyes narrowed, "Did Carolyn send you?" he asked tersely.

"No, but Clare's worried about you."

Sullivan had his own worries about Patrick. He was well-known at the Board as a bold trader. Patrick was able to get away with it during the Board's heyday in the 80s. Back then, there was still "open outcry" in the pits. Pat used his hands for more than signaling trades. He was notorious for getting into fistfights. Those "Wild West" days ended on a "Black Monday" in 1987, but somehow Patrick had kept his seat. Now, the Board had become a sedate place where computers had replaced the shouting and gesturing.

"So, Pat, what's hot these days, pork bellies?"

His face clouded, "Don't bring up commodities. I lost my shirt once on soybean futures. I'm trading something safe for a change, treasury bonds."

"You sound like a solid citizen. Is everything OK with Carolyn?"

"She says I'm never home. It's such a pain in the ass to fight the traffic. I usually stop here for a quick one before I hit the road."

Sullivan knew from experience that Patrick never had a "quick one."

"You know, Mike, I've been a lousy husband and father," Pat confessed, "But I've had *so* much fun." Patrick's eyes glowed at the thought.

"That's true, but you missed out on the dad fun, like soccer, baseball – that kind of thing." It was the closest Sullivan had ever come to scolding his big brother and Patrick didn't care for it.

"I hate soccer," he said testily, "Is that why you came here? This is worse than listening to Carolyn complain."

"What are you guys doing for Thanksgiving?" Sullivan asked, softening his tone.

"We always go to her folks," he replied glumly, "Why?"

Sullivan asked about his three nieces. One was in college, the other two were still in high school. Patrick rarely talked about his family. He treated it like a painful subject.

"Well, I was just making sure you're alright," Sullivan said, "If you ever need anything, let me know?"

Pat resumed his cocky persona, "Sure, Mike, I'm going to ask a cab driver for help."

Sullivan smiled, "Call me next time you have trouble getting home."

"How's the company doing?" he asked abruptly, "Are you still doing detective work? I might be able to use you. There's something going on at the Board."

Sullivan assured Patrick he would give him the family discount.

After he left the bar to return to his car, Sullivan reflected on the conversation. Pat would never admit he was in trouble, but something was bothering him. He could read the worry in his eyes. Maybe it was a trade that had gone sour? If Patrick had lost money on a trade, he would never disclose it. One thing he knew about Pat was that he had never admitted a mistake.

Owning up to his mistakes was part of everyday life for Sullivan. Losing his house was the latest one. When he got home, he proposed to Ann that they host her folks for Thanksgiving. "It will be one last party," Sullivan said with enthusiasm, "Who knows where we're going to be next year?" Ann agreed to prepare the spread, if Mike did the cleanup.

Sullivan warmly welcomed his mother-in-law, Phyllis, on Thanksgiving along with his flinty father-in-law, Kurt. Phyllis was a nurturing earth mother and Kurt had mellowed since he retired from truck driving. They were thoughtful grandparents, who lavished affection on Tara and Flynn. There was much hugging, as the kids were excited to see them.

After dinner, Sullivan gloomily speculated that this might be the last party they'd have in this house. Ann looked at him with alarm. Her parents had no idea they were in trouble. She was very private when it came to their finances. Kurt gave Sullivan his usual withering look when Tara proposed a game of Charades.

Playing the game was the perfect tonic for Sullivan's troubles. His pathetic attempt to act out "Beauty and the Beast" drove his family to hysterics. Afterwards, they told the family stories that never got stale. Like the time, he and Ann were hosting Thanksgiving and the oven started on fire.

The next morning, Sullivan felt a little groggy from staying up late, scrubbing plates. Drinking more beer, while he cleaned the kitchen, might also be to blame. He sat in his bathrobe, quietly sipping coffee, trying to gather the energy to shower and shave. Sullivan Investigations was not receiving any calls or emails.

The holidays had always been slow for Sullivan. Clients were too busy partying to assign cases. Jake startled him, though, with an early call. He asked Sullivan's help with an asbestos investigation. There was no conflict this time. Jake simply had too much work.

"Mike, have you ever worked an asbestos case?"

Sullivan admitted that he hadn't.

"They're a gold mine," Jake said enthusiastically, "I've got more work than I can handle. The one I'm giving you. The guy alleges he was exposed to asbestos in his high school auto shop class. He claims they were grinding brake pads and the machine gave off asbestos. I'm working for the manufacturer of the machine."

"How long ago was this guy exposed?"

"He graduated with the Class of 1967," Jake explained, "After high school, he worked in a foundry for thirty years."

"What do you want me to do?

"They need you to track down every student in his auto shop class and ask them about asbestos."

"They must be in their 70s by now," Sullivan exclaimed, "This is going to be tough."

"You said you needed work," Jake said wearily, "Now, you're complaining?"

"Sorry, Jake, you just kind of took me by surprise. This is something completely new for me."

That was the nature of detective work, becoming an expert in something you had hardly heard of like asbestos. Jake sent him a manual for the machine and directed him to a suburban high school. Sullivan visited there and talked an administrator into letting him look at some yearbooks. Sullivan claimed he was doing it for family history.

Sullivan concentrated on the 1967 yearbook and got a kick out of the shaggy hairstyles and hippie fashions. He found the plaintiff's stiff picture and copied down the names of his male classmates. He assumed girls were not taking auto shop in 1967. Sullivan then performed painstaking searches to locate the former students. A sizable number were dead.

Sullivan conducted phone interviews with the surviving classmates. The conversations were brief, especially when they hadn't taken auto shop. When he did find someone who had been in the plaintiff's class, they denied seeing any asbestos. They also couldn't recall the brake grinding machine. Finally, he stumbled on three classmates who had clear memories of auto shop and dim memories of the plaintiff.

One was a retired auto mechanic who flatly stated there had been no brake grinding in the classroom. "We took the drums to my dad's repair shop. That's where we grinded them. My dad made us wear masks. None of us were exposed to asbestos. If you ask me, he's got bad lungs from breathing in all that sand at the foundry."

After Sullivan finished his list of witnesses, he reported back to Jake, who was pleased with Sullivan's work. "We're proving he's a damn liar about how he got it," Jake said approvingly, "Send me your bill. I'll try to get you paid before Christmas."

Sullivan liked the sound of that. He had been fretting about buying presents. He and Ann had stopped exchanging years ago, but he didn't want to disappoint the kids. Tara had expensive taste in teenage outfits and Flynn wanted the latest video games. Sullivan was grateful to get Jake's call that he had his check. He could pick it up at McGaffer's that evening.

When Sullivan walked in, Jake was watching a run-of-the-mill Bulls game. Jake handed him a window envelope with a check inside. Sullivan pulled out his wallet to buy him a drink. Jake had no objection. He told Jake about his adventures with Charly.

"Charlevoix does aviation, too?" Jake said with admiration, "Maybe she can get me work downloading *those* boxes?"

Sullivan asked Jake if he knew anyone at the Board of Trade.

"I know a couple of traders, why?"

"I'm just wondering if my brother Patrick is in some kind of trouble."

"Remember when Pat was the center on my rec. league basketball team?

"Sure, I went to some of your games. Did you foul out of every game, or is that just my imagination?"

Jake smiled at the memory, "Pat never finished a game either. He'd either get ejected for screaming at the ref, or he'd pick a fight with the other team. "

Jake suddenly became somber, "Actually Mike, one of my buddies was telling me the Board's going to set up a whole new set of rules because of your brother. He was caught hiding his losses on trades and still taking a six-figure salary."

Sullivan was stunned. "The money belongs to his in-laws."

"That might save his ass," Jake said, "Anybody else would have him in handcuffs."

The thought of Patrick being in trouble upset Sullivan. He suddenly stood up to leave. "Thanks again for the check. If I don't see you, have a Merry Christmas." Jake was surprised by Sullivan's abrupt departure.

Ann was pleased he was home early and very happy about the check. "Tara wants these jeans. They cost more, because they already have holes in them." They both had to laugh.

Ten days before Christmas, Sullivan was driving downtown with DeSantis for his final foreclosure hearing. He confided in DeSantis about Frank's problems. "Sounds like he can use a good criminal attorney," DeSantis said gravely, "I've seen guys do time for that."

Sullivan and DeSantis walked into a crowded courtroom, where the desperation was palpable. Sullivan saw the panicked look on the faces of homeowners. He also spotted the smug face of the lawyer for his lender. He looked confident that he had a slam dunk. DeSantis had run out of ways to stall but promised to beg the judge for mercy.

When their case was called, Sullivan and DeSantis came forward like they were walking to their own execution. The opposing lawyer made his motion for judgment against Sullivan and taking possession of his house. The judge asked DeSantis if he had a response.

"Your honor, can we place a six-month stay on eviction," DeSantis pleaded, "So that my client's kids can complete their school year?"

The lender's lawyer delivered a harsh rebuttal. "Your honor, the defendant's children attend a private school. Moving to another school district will not disrupt their education."

The judge didn't like the sound of Sullivan paying private tuition while defaulting on his mortgage. He asked Sullivan what school his kids were attending. Sullivan explained that Flynn was a freshman and Tara a junior at St. Scholastica.

The judge sighed, "This court has already shown you great patience, Mr. Sullivan. I believe the plaintiff has satisfied the law in presenting their case. I'm going to rule in their favor of their motion, but I will put a *three-month* stay on eviction. That should be sufficient time for you to find suitable housing for your family."

As they drove back, DeSantis asked Sullivan if he had any prospects for finding a new home.

"Pete, I'm scared to death. I can't picture us crammed into an apartment."

"I have a client who owns some property in the neighborhood. I do his closings. I can ask him if he has anything available."

"That would be great," Sullivan said with some relief, "I don't want us to end up in some condo in the suburbs."

Sullivan was desperate for some Christmas cheer and it came in the form of a phone call from Charly.

"Mike, Morgan and Evan are coming in for Christmas." she began excitedly, "They want to have dinner with us this Friday."

"That's great. Where do you want to eat?"

"Morgan said she's never had Filipino food. I know a place on the North Side. It's a BYOB."

Sullivan picked up a six-pack on his way to Mama Pinoy's. The joint was so small, he almost missed it. He walked into a place the size of his kitchen. Morgan and Evan had already grabbed a table. They had brought a bottle of champagne. When Morgan saw him, she hugged him warmly. Morgan looked positively radiant. Her features were sun-kissed and her hair had natural highlights.

Evan greeted him with a steady handshake. He looked like a man who spent his days outdoors. They held off uncorking the champagne until Charly arrived. After Charly took her seat, they toasted with bubbly while Sullivan stuck to beer. Charly had grown up on Filipino food and did the ordering. Sullivan enjoyed the oxtail soup but picked at his chicken curry.

Morgan couldn't contain herself talking about their work in Australia. They were assigned to a station in the outback, where they took soil samples and analyzed minerals. Sullivan could see that Morgan had blossomed. She seemed so relaxed and full of life.

"I supposed you have a pet koala by now?" Sullivan mused.

Evan was a bit startled by the question. "Mr. Sullivan, it's against the law to keep a koala as a pet."

"He's *kidding*, Evan," Morgan said with emphasis.

"Sorry Mr. Sullivan, I'm still jetlagged."

"We do have a cattle dog," Morgan said brightly, "Her name is Tilly. We take her to this farm, where she herds cattle. You should see her work. Tilly is an athlete."

Charly had been quiet but finally talked about her agency. Evan was impressed by how many different kinds of cases she investigated. Charly came alive describing their trip to Euphoria. "It reminded me of so many adventures Mike and I have had."

The subject of Sullivan Investigations came up, but Sullivan was reluctant to talk about it. Morgan, though, mused about her time working there. "I sure learned my way around Chicago," she said proudly. The three of them fell into a warm reminiscence, while Evan listened quietly. When the bill came, Sullivan tried to grab it but Evan was too quick. Sullivan promised to buy him a beer, if he ever made it to Australia.

Sullivan felt recharged by the reunion and was in good spirits on Christmas morning. He sipped his coffee while Tara and Flynn tore open their presents. When the doorbell rang, the festivities came to a screeching halt. They weren't expecting anyone. Tara went to the door and returned with a bewildered look. "Uncle Pat is here," she announced uncertainly.

Sullivan's brother never came to family parties. They had long ago given up on inviting him. Patrick was waiting on the steps, when Sullivan opened the door. He was holding an unopened bottle of Jameson's. He hadn't been drinking but there was a haunted look in his eyes.

"Merry Christmas, little brother," Patrick said warmly, "I thought you might be thirsty. I know I am."

CHAPTER 20

G lad you're thirsty, Pat, you're just in time for our cocoa party." Sullivan said, inviting him in.

"Cocoa party? Who *are* you, Mr. Rogers?"

"No, it's this thing we do after we open presents. We have cocoa and cookies and listen to Christmas music."

Patrick set down the bottle of Jameson's to shrug off his coat. "Thanks, Pat," Sullivan said, grabbing the bottle, "We'll save this for a special occasion."

He was a bit puzzled about Sullivan taking his bottle, but the haunted look was gone. "Mike, are you sure I'm not – I mean I just had no place to go."

"I'm glad you came. We're having prime rib for dinner."

Ann came from the kitchen to give Pat a hug. She led him into the living room to greet Tara and Flynn. Their uncle's surprise visit had set them both on edge. Patrick had rarely seen his niece and nephew over the years and noted how much they had grown. Tara and Flynn were civil but not exactly friendly. They hurriedly left the living room to carry their presents upstairs.

"Mike, I know it's Christmas but I've got to talk to you."

Sullivan refused to allow Pat's troubles to disturb his family's Christmas. "We'll talk tomorrow, but first we're having cocoa and listening to Ella sing 'Jingle Bells.'" Patrick didn't protest. Sullivan was relieved when his brother didn't request anything stronger to drink.

During dinner, Flynn asked his uncle a flurry of questions, mostly centered on his high school basketball career. Pat was only too happy to brag. Then Uncle Pat politely asked Tara about school. She gave terse one word answers. Ann asked how Carolyn and the girls were doing and he claimed they were just fine. He explained they were celebrating Christmas with Carolyn's folks. One question was so obvious that no one asked it. Why wasn't Uncle Pat with his family?

Patrick lingered late into the evening hoping to be invited to stay the night. Sullivan and Ann would normally be imbibing Christmas cheer but Pat's presence stopped them. The last thing they wanted was to facilitate Pat getting drunk and causing a scene. They toasted with Bailey's, however, and politely offered a glass to Patrick. He shook his head. "Polite drinking" didn't interest him. He had often expressed contempt for the "lightweights" who engaged in it.

Ann made up a bed in their spare room and insisted Pat stay the night. He made a show of refusing their hospitality but quickly relented. It felt so odd to Sullivan to have his big brother back under the same roof, but he acted like it was perfectly natural.

When Sullivan and Ann climbed into bed, they had a whispered conversation about what had brought Pat to their door. Sullivan speculated that he had had a fight with Carolyn. He did not let on that he was in trouble at the Board.

The next morning, Patrick's tousled hair made him look like he hadn't slept. Sullivan pretended not to notice how his brother's hands shook. He took Pat to Louie's Diner for breakfast. Patrick surveyed the familiar surroundings and spoke of all the times they had eaten there with their dad.

"The last time dad and I had lunch here," Sullivan recalled, "We barely said a word the whole time. It was weird, because we used to talk constantly at the office. For some reason, we both felt like we had nothing left to say. He had his stroke a week later."

"Carolyn kicked me out," Pat interrupted bitterly.

"Before you tell me about it, I've got something you need to know. We're losing the house. We can put you up for a little while, but we've got to be out of there in three months."

Pat was shocked. He had no idea his brother was in trouble, not that he bothered to ask. "Jeez, Mike, where are you going to go?"

"My lawyer has a buddy in real estate but I don't have a plan beyond that. I'm just trying to get through the holidays."

Patrick then launched into a long litany about his own difficulties. Sullivan listened intently but was careful not to offer advice. Pat confided that he had an accomplice at his company, who knew how to manipulate numbers to hide the losses. Pat had compensated the bookkeeper for taking the risk.

"I couldn't tell Carolyn that I was losing her parent's money," he declared, "I had taken a position that would have paid off big if commodity prices fell. But damn if they didn't keep going up! I was sinking more and more money into the market. But I was still taking my usual draw. Carolyn was used to the country club life. My girls took riding lessons. I couldn't let on that we were broke."

"Besides that, Carolyn was always on me about drinking," Patrick added, "She even thought I was having an affair."

"Were you?" Sullivan asked directly.

Pat's long pause was practically an admission in itself.

"You know, Mike, when you spend a lot of time in bars, women start seeing you as available, whether you're married or not."

"Forget the question, it's none of my business."

"I had a few flings," Pat confessed, "But nothing serious. Well, sometimes *they* thought it was serious. Carolyn would come across strange charges on my credit card, but I always came up with an excuse. I kept hoping to replace the money I was losing at the Board."

"Patrick, this reminds me of the time you collected the money for mom and dad's anniversary present but spent the money on golf clubs instead," Sullivan stated straightforwardly, "Clare was so pissed."

"That was a couple of hundred bucks, Mike, I'm talking about six figures now. I went behind Carolyn's back and took out a second mortgage on the house. But that's not what got me in trouble."

"Let me guess, there was a surprise audit at your company? That's what happens in the movies," Sullivan said lightly.

"It was worse than that," he continued, "We took Carolyn's parents out for dinner. I gave the server my company credit card. It was declined. Carolyn was so embarrassed. My father-in-law had to pick up the tab. He was all of a sudden suspicious and had *his* accountant go over the books. He found the fudged numbers. The accountant told my father-in-law that the company was practically bankrupt."

"I'll never forget when Carolyn's dad confronted me. He was calm but I could tell I had let him down. That hurt the most. He said he wouldn't press charges but that I had to repay every penny. He put me on this strict payment plan his accountant came up with. After I signed the agreement, he hounded me if I was a day late. I was taking money out of the house to pay him back."

"Did Carolyn know anything about this?"

"No, her dad kept everything from her. She found out in a strange way that we were in trouble. One morning, Carolyn was going to take a shower but there was no hot water. I checked the gas meter and there was a big padlock on it. The gas company had shut us off because I didn't keep up with the payments. I called to find out how much we owed. I mailed a check that day but it took two weeks for them to turn the gas back on. Imagine telling your wife and three daughters they aren't going to have hot water for two weeks!"

"You mean, cold showers?" Sullivan asked in disbelief.

"No cooking. No dryer," Pat grumbled, "I used to microwave a bowl of water in the morning, so I could wash up. It reminded me of those Westerns when the cowboy splashes water on his face from a basin."

"No wonder those guys smelled bad," Sullivan said, attempting to lighten the mood.

Pat didn't even smile. "One morning, my mother-in-law came over and caught me carrying a bowl of hot water. She knew the score right away."

"Carolyn's parents decided their granddaughters couldn't live in a house without hot water, so the girls went to stay with them."

"Pat this is like a 'Lifetime' movie and you're the suburban dad who turns out to be a crook."

"It is like a bad movie," he agreed, "Especially when this bimbo from the bar texted me to meet her there and Carolyn found the message. That happened on Christmas Eve."

"It's time to get out of here," Sullivan announced abruptly, "Louie's looking at us like he needs this table."

They were walking back to the house, when Sullivan leveled with his brother. "You can stay until New Year's," Sullivan said firmly, "But, after that, you need to find your own place."

Patrick took the news in stride, "Any suggestions little brother?"

"Let's drop the little brother, OK?" Sullivan said, looking into Pat's anguished eyes. "Actually, I *do* have an idea. Do you remember Big Mike, that young guy dad helped out?"

Pat nodded. "After Big Mike got sober, he started this Welcome House for recovering drunks. It would be a good environment for you. They have meetings every night. They set you up with a job."

"Whoa, Mike, I already have a job. Who told you I needed to sober up, Carolyn?"

"I haven't talked to Carolyn in months," Sullivan insisted, "This is my idea. If you think you're going back to the Board, you're nuts."

Sullivan was keenly aware of Pat's disdain for Big Mike and their dad's other AA buddies. He considered them a bunch of miserable losers.

"We'll go for breakfast with Big Mike." Sullivan suggested, "We can at least talk to him about it."

Pat became sullen. Life without alcohol was unthinkable.

"Alright, if there's a free meal involved, I'll go," he said slowly, "But I'm not making any promises."

As they walked into the house, Tara and Flynn were glued to a Christmas movie. They barely looked up at their dad and uncle. Ann was back at work.

"I'll call Big Mike, maybe we can meet him at Louie's tomorrow?"

Pat barely nodded. "I'm going back to bed," he said wearily.

Sullivan first called DeSantis at his office. He knew from experience that Pete didn't slow down for the holidays. DeSantis gave him the phone number of his real estate buddy and wished him luck.

"Mike, I almost forgot. Trisa's sending you my final bill for your foreclosure case. Like I said, we're kicking your file into the bankruptcy pile."

DeSantis' friend ran a small company called Your Humble Abode. Sullivan called and made an appointment. Heavy snow began to fall. It piled up for hours. It was tough work to get Tara and Flynn off the couch but he finally persuaded them to help shovel. After they cleared the walkways, a snowball fight broke out.

They came inside to sip hot tea. It felt so good to be warm again, it was almost worth braving the winter chill. Sullivan texted Big Mike to see if he was up for breakfast the next morning. He texted back, "See you at 10:00." Big Mike was a daily fixture at the diner.

When Sullivan finally woke Patrick from his nap, he was reluctant to join them for dinner. Even when they were kids, Pat had little interest in food. He reminded Sullivan of the drunk gunslinger in "Blazing Saddles" who declares, "Food makes me sick!"

Patrick was quietly picking at his plate when Tara ventured a question.

"Uncle Pat, how come we don't see Carrie, or Jennifer and Kirsten anymore? They're our cousins. I miss them. Remember the time we all went to the beach?"

Pat smiled at the recollection. "Mike, I never saw you so sunburnt. You were painful to look at."

Reminiscing about summer during the grip of a Chicago winter was a good tonic for everyone.

"It was fun jumping off your shoulders, Uncle Pat," said Flynn, "Remember it was you and me against dad and Tara in the chicken fight?"

Patrick's eyes became misty. "Yeah, we kicked their butt," he said, with a catch in his throat. "Ann, this roast is perfect," he said collecting himself, "You should give Carolyn the recipe."

"You didn't answer my question, Uncle Pat," Tara persisted, "Maybe we can do something with them over Christmas break?" she asked hopefully.

Pat smiled. "You've got yourself a real sweetheart, Mike." He looked directly at Tara, "I'll try to make it happen."

The next morning, Sullivan roused his brother from a heavy sleep. He resorted to slapping the soles of his feet, like their dad used to do. "C'mon Pat, I told Big Mike we'd meet him at 10:00." Patrick looked pale and Sullivan noticed his t-shirt was soaked with sweat.

"You go ahead, Mike" he moaned, "I threw up last night. I'm too queasy to eat anything."

"You can just have coffee. Let's go, it'll do you good."

As they trudged through the snow to Louie's, Patrick was morose. "I never liked Big Mike. Remember the time we got into an argument? He wanted to take it outside."

"That was when he was drinking," Sullivan explained, "He's a different guy, now."

They found Big Mike in a booth poring over a newspaper. He was a barrel-chested ex-Marine with a bulldog tattoo on his left bicep. He greeted them with a booming voice that startled the other customers. Big Mike addressed the patrons, "Hey, I haven't seen these guys in years. Give me a break? Karen, bring two more coffees and some menus. You already know what I want."

When the waitress brought water and coffee, Big Mike complimented her hair and grabbed her playfully around the waist. Karen pulled away but loved his attention. Big Mike might be overbearing but he held a mysterious attraction to women.

Big Mike silently sipped his coffee as Patrick poured out his tale of woe. When he was finished, Big Mike finally spoke up.

"So, let me get this straight," he said summing up, "You want to go back to the Board but you can't because they know you're a thief?" Pat nodded glumly.

"So, what are you going to order?" Big Mike asked cheerfully, "I always get the mushroom omelet." In Big Mike's world, if you were powerless over a situation, there was no point in discussing it. After they were finished, Big Mike got serious.

"If it wasn't for your dad," Big Mike began solemnly, "I wouldn't take a chance on you, Pat. He helped me get sober in my 20s. Otherwise, I'd be dead."

Frank Sullivan didn't only give Big Mike advice, he hired him to serve a stack of summonses. Instead of handing them to the defendants, Big Mike slipped them under their doors. It was his first and last day at Sullivan Investigations. Big Mike, though, continued to hang out at the office soaking up Frank Sullivan's wisdom.

"I'm giving you the same chance your dad gave me," Big Mike promised, "It's not *much* of a chance. We don't have a good track record. About ten percent of us stay sober. But I'll put you up at Welcome House. I charge $130 a week to cover groceries."

Pat was desperate enough to accompany Big Mike to the halfway house. Sullivan begged off, explaining he had an appointment at Your Humble Abode. Sullivan was relieved to shift the responsibility of his brother to Big Mike for a while.

When Sullivan arrived at the realty office, only the owner was present. Gus Ferrara had made a special trip just to help out a friend of DeSantis. He was a short dapper man with dark features. He was one of the few Chicagoans walking around with a winter tan. He told Sullivan that he had grown up with DeSantis on Taylor Street. "Pete and I planned to be mobsters, or cops, it was almost the same thing," Ferrara recalled, "but the first time we got arrested for shoplifting we decided to take a different direction."

"Pete says you're looking for a place," Ferrara continued, "I have a couple of two-flats that are opening up in April. I can show you them right now, if you have time." Gus drove Sullivan to a brick two-flat where the tenants graciously allowed them to tour the place. Sullivan could picture himself living there. He didn't think Ann would object. She had grown up on the second floor of a two-flat. Sullivan didn't care for its location, though, on a busy street.

The second property they visited was on a quiet cul de sac. It had three bedrooms and a large yard. The rent was half what his mortgage payment had been. He told Gus that he liked it but his wife would have the final word. Sullivan assumed that Flynn and Tara would see it as a comedown from their five-bedroom house, but they had no idea how limited their options were. Renting from Ferrara had another perk. Because he was a friend of Pete's he wouldn't bother with a credit check.

Sullivan was anxious to hear how it had gone at Welcome House but when he got home, he could see Pat's mood hadn't improved a bit.

"Big Mike's a nice guy but that place he runs, it's like the army. We have to be up by 6:00. First thing in the morning, we have to clean our rooms and make our beds. Breakfast is at 7:00 and we have to be out the door by 8:00. Big Mike said he can set me up with a factory job in the suburbs. The owner is in the 'club.' Oh, and there's a mandatory meeting every night at 7:00."

"Sounds awful," Sullivan agreed, "But I think being around Big Mike and those guys will be good for you. It's not like you'll be staying there forever."

"That's for sure. He only lets guys live there for six months. Oh, I forgot, we have to help with the chores. He wants to start me out on kitchen duty."

"Before you make any commitments to Big Mike, you better talk it over with Carolyn," Sullivan suggested, "I can drive you up there."

Patrick allowed a weak smile. "I'd rather break open that bottle of Jameson's."

Sullivan wasn't expecting any work until after the holidays, but one of his long-time clients called with a rush assignment. He represented a daughter who was trying to declare her mother mentally incompetent. "You can pick up the court order from my office. She has to be served before the New Year."

Sullivan asked where the mother lived and it wasn't far from his brother's house. He approached Pat with the idea of giving him a ride to meet with Carolyn. Sullivan would drop him off, serve his paper and return to pick him up. Pat said he would have to check with Carolyn. She was agreeable to the meeting. The next day, the two brothers drove downtown to pick up the Order. Sullivan waited in the car, while Pat ran in. When they were on the expressway, Patrick said he was scared about what he was going to say to Carolyn.

"I would tell her everything," Sullivan suggested, "She's going to find out anyway."

"How can I tell her how sorry I am for everything I've done? I feel terrible about what I've done to my family."

"Feeling terrible isn't going to help, Pat. 'You're just setting yourself up for another drink to forget it," Sullivan warned, "You can't change what you did. You have to hope Carolyn can forgive you."

When they pulled into Pat's driveway, Sullivan stayed in the car. He and Carolyn had a frosty relationship. She saw Sullivan as another one of her husband's drinking buddies. After he wished his brother luck, Sullivan headed to the address listed on the Order. It was in an exclusive suburb that was dotted with horse farms. He turned into the driveway of a large mansion that was surrounded by extensive grounds.

The house was in obvious decay and reminded Sullivan of Norma Desmond's crumbling palace in "Sunset Boulevard." All it lacked was an empty swimming pool. Sullivan emerged from his car with a sense of dread. Crazy people were dangerous to serve. Handing her the Order might set her off. He might have a real Norma Desmond on his hands.

There was no answer at the front door. Sullivan also tried the back door and side door without success. The house felt empty. He walked a considerable distance in the snow to reach the nearest neighbor. When he rang the bell, elegant chimes sounded and a security light came on. A woman spoke cautiously on the intercom. People in horse country were not accustomed to strangers at their door.

Finally, a middle-aged woman came to the door and opened it a quarter way. Sullivan explained that he was trying to deliver a court document to her neighbor.

"Marilyn? Isn't she home?" Sullivan explained he didn't get an answer. Having sympathy for Sullivan standing in the cold, she invited him in.

"What is the document for may I ask?" Her gray hair was swept back from her lined face. Her outfit was impeccably put together. She looked positively regal.

Sullivan explained that the woman's daughter wanted to have control of her mother's finances and have her declared unfit.

"It's about time," the woman declared, "Marilyn's been losing it for years. She used to walk into my house unannounced. Once, when I wasn't home, my housekeeper let her in. Marilyn asked my housekeeper to make her a hamburger. Gretchen was scared half to death. So, she cooked her a cheeseburger. Marilyn sat in my kitchen and ate it. She kept saying how delicious the burger was. When she was finished, she took out her checkbook. She wrote Gretchen a check for a million dollars! She said it was to pay for the burger."

Sullivan was astonished by the story. "You don't still have that check, do you?"

"Of course I do," the woman snapped. "Anyway, when I got home, Marilyn was still in my kitchen. There was this wild look in her eyes but a big smile on her face. She gushed about how kind Gretchen had been and what a good cook she was. I took the check from her. For all I know she was good for it. I told Marilyn to call from now on, if she was coming over. I also told her she couldn't come over if I wasn't home. She acted like a kid I had just punished. Hold on a second, I'll find that check."

When she returned with it, Sullivan saw it had been filled out in a childish scrawl. It was properly signed and dated, though, and payable to Gretchen. Marilyn had written "Cheeseburger" in the memo. "Do you mind if I borrow this?" he asked the neighbor, "We might be able to use it in court."

"Do what you want with it," she replied imperiously, "Just don't try to cash it."

"I'll send the check back to you after the proceedings," Sullivan offered, "Do you have any idea where I can find Marilyn?"

"Let's see," the woman thought, "its Wednesday. She's probably getting her hair done at Romero's. He works out of his home. Let me look up his address."

Sullivan thanked the woman for everything. "Get Marilyn some help," she said gravely, "She shouldn't be all by herself in that big house."

It was a short drive to Romero's. He lived in a modest house and had his shop in the basement. When Sullivan descended the stairs, he found an elderly woman with jet black hair sitting in the chair. Sullivan confessed to Romero he wasn't a customer but had to hand Marilyn a court document.

The dark haired woman turned her head with a big smile, "You came to see *me*?" she asked with delight, "Do I know you?"

"I'm afraid not. I'm just here to give you this."

Marilyn took the Order and stared at it without any comprehension. The law required Sullivan to explain it. He said it was a court order about her finances. "It's from your daughter. She's worried about you. Do you have a lawyer you can show this to?"

The big smile was replaced by a worried look. Romero was stunned that his loyal customer was being served right in front of him.

"Marilyn, I'll have my lawyer look this over." he said gently, "Are you finished?" he coldly asked Sullivan. As Sullivan left the shop, he presumed Romero could be a witness to the service. He also thought of the neighbor testifying about the million-dollar burger.

Sullivan felt great. He could charge for the trip to Patrick's house.

When he was parked back in his brother's driveway, he texted that he was waiting outside. It was a long time before Patrick emerged from the house looking dejected.

CHAPTER 21

As Pat climbed into the car, Sullivan could see his eyes were red. He had never seen his brother cry, even at their parents' funerals. They drove in silence, while Pat stared straight ahead. Finally, he spoke, "Mike, I need a drink bad."

"I'm sure you do," Sullivan said evenly, "But it's not going to be with me."

Silence descended once again.

"Are you going to tell me what Carolyn had to say?" Sullivan demanded.

Patrick broke into sobs and Sullivan gingerly patted his shoulder. It was terribly awkward for siblings who had never been affectionate. Pat brushed his hand away, ashamed about crying in front of his brother. At last, he composed himself enough to speak in halting sentences.

"I could hardly look at her," he confessed, "I had never seen that kind of hurt in her eyes. I was expecting her to be furious but she never raised her voice. She handed me these letters the girls had written to me. I was scared to read them."

"Carrie wrote that I had broken her heart so many times, she stopped inviting me to her school plays or to watch her ride in competitions. She claimed I got drunk at her graduation party. Jennifer stopped inviting her friends over because she was afraid I'd embarrass her. It was Kirsten's letter that made me cry. She wrote about waiting for me to come home from work to start a fire. She had the newspapers all crumpled up in the fireplace, but by the time I got home, she'd already gone to bed."

"I told you that you missed out on the dad fun," Sullivan reminded him, "What did Carolyn say?"

"She just sat there while I read the letters. Then she read her own letter out loud. It was kind of cold and businesslike. She spelled out the conditions for me to move back home."

Carolyn's demands included Patrick quitting the Board, paying back her father, and staying at Welcome House for the full six months.

"She said if I took another drink I'd never see her or the girls again."

"Can she do that?" Sullivan wondered.

"I don't know, I don't want to find out, but what she's asking me to do is impossible."

"When do you move into Big Mike's place?"

"He said he'll have a room ready for me right after the first of the year."

"OK, in the meantime, try to cheer up. At least you're on speaking terms with Carolyn."

Pat gave a faint smile, "I liked how Kirsten signed her name with x's and o's."

After they returned home and explained the plan to Ann, she volunteered to take her brother-in-law shopping. "You're going to need some toiletries and maybe a couple of shirts and pants. Everything is on sale at my store, plus I get the employee discount."

Patrick was surprised by Ann's offer, but the prospect appealed to him. "Carolyn used to practically dress me. I haven't picked out my own clothes in years."

On the day of the shopping trip, Tara went along to add her fashion expertise. Sullivan was planning to go bowling with Flynn, when DeSantis called him about a prospective assignment.

"Mike, I'm handling a divorce for this couple. My client is a top executive, the kind they send a car for every morning. She works for an advertising agency downtown. She's real Type A and has this fear her husband is going to take their daughter back to Pakistan. She wants to pay you to monitor his weekly visitations. She thinks the guy is a flight risk. She'll pay your usual rate and write you a check on the spot."

Sullivan had never done what the FBI calls lockstep surveillance. They used it to harass mob figures. Agents would be open and obvious in following the subjects wherever they went. They used to walk beside the subjects at airports, golf courses and even on the public sidewalk. To say this provoked the mobsters is an understatement. This assignment sounded something like that, except it would be a dad and his four-year-old daughter.

Every Wednesday, Sullivan would meet up with Ali and his little girl, Alexa. The visits were prearranged and the father graciously accepted Sullivan's presence. He didn't even object to Sullivan videotaping the proceedings. He was a handsome man in his 40s and had a warm smile. He owned a very successful Indian restaurant, so Sullivan couldn't imagine him being a flight risk. Alexa was an exquisite little girl with a head of dark curls.

Sullivan's client, Jessica, by contrast, had an officious manner and expressed a cold distrust of her soon-to-be ex-husband. Sullivan gave her brief accounts of the four-hour visits, and she would then tear off his weekly check. Sullivan found it incongruous that he was getting paid to spend days at the Children's Museum, Chuck E. Cheese, and various playgrounds. It was easy and pleasant work, but he loathed invading Ali's private moments with his daughter. He also thought the whole thing was unnecessary.

One afternoon, it was too cold for an outing and they spent the visit confined to Ali's apartment. While Sullivan filmed, Ali was roughhousing with Alexa on the carpet. She was giggling helplessly when she suddenly tumbled off Ali's knee. She hit the floor with a thump and burst out crying. Ali was mortified, trying to comfort his daughter while glancing back at Sullivan's camera.

"You don't have to report this?" Ali asked in a panic. Sullivan shut off the camera.

"It was an accident, Ali," Sullivan assured him, "It used to happen to me all the time when my kids were little."

"I know, Mr. Sullivan," Ali said nervously, "But you don't know my ex-wife. She could use this to take away my visitation rights."

"Ali, you're a good dad." Sullivan assured him, "I've been filming you and Alexa for weeks. I'm going to erase that part and I'm not telling Jessica anything about it." Sullivan inwardly vowed this would be the last time he supervised one of Ali's visits. The money was good, but it was tearing him up inside. He would tell his cold-eyed client to find another investigator.

Ann wasn't surprised by his decision. "Spying on another dad. It sounds awful. You never did like surveillance."

Right away, Sullivan was offered another surveillance job. This time, Jake Houlihan hired him as extra manpower to stake out a North Side bar. Jake's buddy owned the touristy nightspot and suspected his bartenders were stealing some of the proceeds.

"I thought they had computers and cameras to catch bartenders," Sullivan surmised.

"They do but my guy wants eyewitnesses. You can meet me there tomorrow night," Jake suggested, "And bring Charlevoix along. It would look better if you were a couple."

"I'll ask her, Jake. Are we allowed to drink on the job?"

"Sure," Jake said, "As long as you don't go crazy."

The next morning, the Sullivan family was scheduled to meet Gus Ferrara to tour the two-flat he had for rent. Tara and Flynn were anxious to see it. Sullivan pulled up behind Ferrara's car on the dead end street. Tara looked doubtfully at the aged brick building.

"We're going to live on an alley?"

Ferrara was waiting inside the second floor apartment. He shook Sullivan's hand and flashed Ann a big smile, "This is it," he waved his hand to take in the living room, "I used to live here, myself, when I first got started in real estate. It's still the best place I ever lived."

Ann took in the plaster walls and dark woodwork, "This is just like the place I grew up," she said agreeably, "Mike, remember my folks' place?"

How could he forget? When they were dating, Ann's dad had made him very uncomfortable if he stayed past ten.

Ferrara turned to Tara, "What do you think?" She ignored him.

"Mom, which room is going to be mine?" Tara demanded.

"I don't know, let's see what they look like?"

They crowded into the front bedroom, which had a mirrored wall to make it look bigger. "Flynn can have this one," Tara said dismissively, "He's always checking himself out."

Sullivan didn't care for her tone but couldn't make a scene in front of Ferrara. He asked what Flynn thought of it.

"It's OK. Are you sure my bed is going to fit?"

They shuffled out of the room to check the kitchen. "It's so small," Tara complained.

Ferrara grinned, "Don't worry it's not going to get any smaller."

"What do you care?" Flynn sniped, "You don't do any cooking."

While they bickered, Ann was opening and closing drawers and cabinets. "Oh it has a pantry," she exclaimed, "I've always wanted one."

Tara flounced into the back bedroom. It was dark and had a low slanting ceiling. Sullivan saw the pained look on her face and feared she'd start crying. "It's for only a year or so," Ann said calmly, "You'll be moving into a dorm room."

After Tara had sufficiently lowered her standards, she admitted that she liked the spacious bathroom.

"This place will be so much easier to keep clean," Ann observed, "That house. Three floors. That was too much."

Sullivan found the rent reasonable, lower than other landlords in the neighborhood. He told Ferrara they'd take it and asked when he needed the security deposit. Being a friend of Pete's, Sullivan wouldn't need to pay one. "Just be on time with the rent. I'm going to have this place painted before you move in." Ann asked if he could paint the walls gray. Ferrara flashed his smile and asked her what shade.

Sullivan planned to move in on April 1st. Not that he had much choice in the matter. His lender had specified their house had to be "broom clean" by the end of March. Meanwhile, they would have to get through the doldrums of a Chicago winter.

Working the case for Jake turned out to be a bright spot. It offered another chance to hang out with Charly. They were assigned to the 8:00 pm to midnight shift. They met there on a frigid February evening. Sullivan had paid a fortune to park in this entertainment district and vowed to charge Jake.

The club called Celestial sported kind of an outer space theme. The lighting was supplied by "stars" twinkling on the dark ceiling. Charly was waiting inside the door wearing her puffy winter coat. The music was loud and the place was packed for a weeknight. Sullivan could see Jake at the bar flirting with the bartender.

When Sullivan and Charly walked up to him, Jake whispered, "My name is Brian and I'm in town for a sales meeting." He then introduced them to Karli, the bartender. She was a stunning Latino beauty, whose dazzling smile brought her sizable tips. It was easy to see why Jake had pulled her shift.

"Do you really know this guy?" Karli asked, placing drink napkins in front of them, "He tells the oldest bar jokes I've ever heard."

"Karli, did I tell you the one about the guy with amnesia?" The bartender gave him a resigned look, "No."

"He walks into a bar and asks this beautiful blonde, 'Do I come here often?'"

Karli laughed politely, while Jake cracked himself up.

"What do you folks want?" Karli asked politely. Sullivan ordered his usual Guinness, while Charly asked for a glass of white wine. When she brought the drinks, Karli asked if they could settle up right away, because she was cashing out. Sullivan reached for his credit card but Charly beat him to it. Jake excused himself to go to the washroom and Sullivan waited a beat before joining him.

Jake was washing his hands. "If somebody's stealing here," Jake declared, "It isn't Karli. She doesn't need to. She's making more in tips than I make in a week."

"Are you sure she isn't under-ringing?" Sullivan asked. It was a common practice for customers to make a deal with a bartender to undercharge on drinks in exchange for a large tip.

"Not that I can see and believe me I've watched her closely," Jake said with a smirk. "Anyway, I've been sipping a glass of straight tequila for the last hour. It tastes terrible. I'll leave Karli a nice tip."

As Jake was saying goodbye, he attempted to give Charly a hug. She expertly arched her back to minimize the contact. Charly was wearing a loose-fitting peasant blouse. It was conservative by most standards but the most daring top Sullivan had seen her wear. The new bartender coming on felt the need to introduce himself to Charly. His name was Lance.

He was about 6'3" with a carefully trimmed moustache and lightly-gelled brown hair. Lance was dashingly handsome and no one knew this better than him. Lance was also a busy man as customers flocked to the bar. Sullivan sized them up as the tourist crowd and could detect some twangy accents. Celestial charged sky high prices, and the tourists ordered fancy drinks. Sullivan chatted amiably with Charly but could tell she was preoccupied with Lance.

Sullivan watched as he slyly slipped tips into his pocket that customers had intended for Karli. He was just getting started. Sullivan saw a group of five order a tray full of drinks. The guy who was paying handed over a wad of cash, and Sullivan watched Lance ring up $14.00. The customer was oblivious and told Lance to keep the change.

Whenever Lance had a free moment, he parked himself in front of Charly. Sullivan guessed that the peasant blouse was working its magic.

Lance was very attentive, polishing the bar, while chatting with Charly. Her second glass of white wine was on him. Sullivan continued to watch Lance ring up ludicrous amounts for pricey drinks. He tried to be subtle about it, Sullivan could easily spot him slipping money from the cash register and placing it in his tip jar.

Charly pretended to find Lance fascinating. She was impressed he had an MBA and wondered why he was bartending. "I got downsized like a lot of guys I know," he complained, "This is easy money and I bring home cash every night. Besides," he said gazing into Charly's eyes, "I meet such interesting people."

After two hours of this, Sullivan was feeling bloated and bored. Charly was doing the heavy lifting, while he contented himself with a college basketball game. He noticed now that when customers paid with credit cards, Lance would undercharge and remove the excess cash from the register.

They were supposed to remain on duty until midnight but Sullivan had seen enough. As they got up to leave, Lance insisted on getting Charly's phone number. She smiled as she gave him the number for Streets and Sanitation.

When they were outside, they both felt relieved. "How do people hang out in places like that?" Charly wondered, "It's so boring, plus it's expensive."

"Make sure you charge Jake for our drinks," Sullivan reminded her.

"Oh, what they really cost, or what Lance was charging?" she said with a laugh. "Really Mike I don't see the point of going to bars."

"That explains why you don't have a love life," Sullivan teased.

"Really?" she retorted, "I was paying attention, too. I saw people come in with their family and friends and leave with them. They didn't leave with strangers they had just met. That only happens in movies. It crossed my mind to wait for Lance to get off work," her voice trailed off.

"You mean go out with the target of our investigation?" Sullivan teased, "I realize he's good looking but you can do much better than Lance."

One thing Sullivan knew for sure about Charly. She would never settle.

After Sullivan reported Lance's misdeeds to Jake, he seemed a bit disappointed. "I was planning to go back tonight to see Karli," he said wistfully, "Jeez Mike, don't you know how to milk a case?"

"Sure, remember the time we were supposed to be doing surveillance on that guy and we played golf for three days straight."

Jake smiled at the memory. "Yeah, but that last night we caught him arm wrestling with his 'bad' arm at the VFW. I'll make sure you and Charlevoix get paid right away. I don't think we'll need to go back."

With another case ready to be billed, Sullivan wondered how Patrick was making out at *his* job. Sullivan hadn't spoken with him since the day he left their house with the business casual outfits and a bag of essentials Ann had bought him. When Pat first arrived at Welcome House, he was forced to surrender his phone among other things. He was restricted to using Big Mike's landline. At last, Pat had a day pass and called his brother to say he was coming over.

When Sullivan first saw Patrick, he looked less haggard. He claimed he was sleeping well at Big Mike's place, despite an annoying roommate who needed late-night TV to get to sleep. Patrick was also eating well and had lost about twenty pounds.

"Look at these pants Ann bought me. I think I need to go down a size."

"How's your job going?"

"Big Mike got me a job in a candy factory," Pat said with some distaste, "I've never worked harder in my life."

"What's your job?"

"It changes every half hour," he explained, "They switch us to different work stations because it's so monotonous. They also don't want us to get what they call repetitive motion injuries. I start out in this room that's a hundred degrees. The candy is liquid. Mike you can't believe how intense the smell is. If I had brought the girls there when they were kids, they would never have eaten candy."

"Then they shift me down floor-by-floor, where I fill trays full of candy. We wear gloves and hairnets. No one talks to me, not that many of them speak English. Most of them have a look in their eyes like they'd rather be dead. Finally, I end up in shipping and have to pack boxes of candy into cartons. The boxes comes off the conveyor belt so fast. Remember that episode of 'I Love Lucy?' I feel like Ethel."

"How's the money?"

Patrick scoffed, "Compared to what I used to make at the Board? You know Mike, it's always the people who work the hardest who get paid the least. I used to put in six hours a day at the Board, now I'm one of the working poor."

"Aren't you in a union?"

"Sure, it's a, pardon the pun, sweetheart union that has never gone on strike," Pat grumbled.

"Patrick, I don't care how hard it gets, at least you're not drinking."

"Big Mike says that I'm still in the 'white knuckle' phase and it's going to get easier. I actually like the meetings. Guys are really honest about their problems. It's kind of like shooting the shit at a bar, except there's no booze. Before I forget, they're having a big Family Day in March. Carolyn and the girls are coming. I was hoping you and Ann can make it."

"Are you kidding? Tara and Flynn will come too. They haven't seen their cousins in a year."

CHAPTER 22

Sullivan got a call from his mortgage company, only it wasn't from the stern woman he had fought with for months. On the line was an easy-going guy named Randy, who said he was in charge of transferring the property from Sullivan to his company.

"Let me first congratulate you, Mr. Sullivan, on obtaining that loan modification," Randy began pleasantly, "Only twenty percent of homeowners have accomplished that." His words sounded hollow to Sullivan.

"Only, you modified it in the wrong direction. I asked for a payment reduction, not an increase."

"I'm sure that was disappointing, Mr. Sullivan, but we have to test the homeowner first to see if they can make a higher payment before we agree to reduce it. You know, like how the government tests financial institutions."

"I never understood that either," Sullivan muttered, "How are we going to work the transfer?"

"It will be very simple," Randy said brightly, "Just make sure the house is broom clean before the first of April. Are you still living in the house?"

Sullivan thought it was a stupid question, "Why?"

"Our company requires a family member to reside in the house until the property is transferred. We also need you to keep the utilities on. We don't want the pipes to freeze or the home to go dark. If the house looks empty, squatters might move in."

"I'm staying here until the end of the month," Sullivan assured him, "My wife and kids are moving into our new apartment."

"That's good to hear," Randy said, "I'll come for the final inspection. If the place is empty and reasonably clean, I'll give you a check for $3,000 to pay your moving expenses. It's called our 'cash for keys' program."

Sullivan liked the sound of that and couldn't wait to tell Ann.

"I'll simply have you sign a form relinquishing your ownership of the property. I'll then hand you the check and you give me the keys."

Sullivan was pleased by the arrangement. They could use the money to pay for the dumpster and moving truck, and there'd be enough left over for the first month's rent.

When he told Ann about the arrangement, she said it sounded like "pennies from heaven."

"Are you sure you'll be OK staying at the house by yourself?" she fretted, "It sounds depressing."

"I'll be fine," Sullivan assured her, "You guys are better off at the new place, until this is all over."

Sullivan was feeling better about their situation knowing their housing ordeal would soon be over. In the meantime, he looked forward to joining Jake for St. Patrick's Day. They always met up at an Irish pub that featured dancers all day and bands and bagpipes throughout the night. Just before the big day, Sullivan had suffered his mishap on the back stairs and torn his favorite green shirt.

When Sullivan found him in the crush at Molly Malone's, Jake's attention was drawn immediately to the bandage above Sullivan's right eye.

"What the hell happened to you?" Jake asked with concern.

"Fell down my backstairs," Sullivan replied with some embarrassment. Jake made the drinking gesture.

"No, it was the middle of the day. The stairs are so rickety I think everyone in the family has taken a tumble."

"It's good you're moving," Jake shouted above the clamor of the crowd, "Your house sounds dangerous."

The two friends found a narrow shelf where they could balance their drinks and watch young girls in Irish costumes and curly blonde wigs bounce up and down. Jake asked how Patrick was doing. Sullivan filled him in.

"A candy factory?" Jake marveled, "A guy like Pat. I can't picture it."

Sullivan recalled that Jake had known his brother in high school, though he was a few years behind.

"He's miserable there," Sullivan said sadly, "I don't suppose you could take him on?"

Jake laughed, "Pat was always a wild man. I can't trust him. He'd steal my clients."

"Yeah, but he'd be good at the work. You remember how smooth Pat can be. He can talk anyone into anything. Besides, if he doesn't get a better job, he'll have a perfect excuse to start drinking."

"I'll think about it," Jake exclaimed, "But hey it's St. Patrick's Day! Time to be irresponsible!"

Sullivan clinked his glass to irresponsibility, but promised to run the idea past Patrick when he saw him on Family Day.

In the meantime, he arranged for a dumpster to be delivered to their house and reserved a rental truck. They started the move on a Saturday morning. Tara and Flynn helped but Sullivan could tell their hearts weren't into it. Sullivan started with Ann on the basement. They worked tirelessly carrying junk to the dumpster. They came across a few sentimental items, like Tara's first swim suit with built-in floaties. They also found her beloved "blankie" with the silky border.

Tara was not interested in keeping either. Flynn was equally unsentimental about his sports trophies and his game balls. Neither wanted any reminder of the house. Sullivan was saddened by their reaction and kept a lookout for something they might want to keep.

"Are we going to throw away all your dolls?" he asked Tara, "Don't you even want this American Girl?"

Tara stared at him like the question wasn't worth answering. "Do whatever you want with them."

Ann suggested donating them to a daycare center and Tara dutifully boxed them up.

Sullivan carefully protected their stack of china dinner plates. Their red pattern reminded him of setting the table for family feasts. He caught Flynn carrying the stack to the dumpster and stopped him from tossing them in.

They received some unexpected help from a middle-aged Hispanic man, who pulled up in his pick-up truck and spotted some metal in the dumpster. Sullivan encouraged him to take the items. He also led the man upstairs to remove three air conditioners. Sullivan was astonished at the man's strength, as he hoisted the window units onto the bed of his pick-up. The ultimate challenge, though, was moving the gun metal desk that once belonged to Frank Sullivan. The entire family, plus the scrap metal collector, was needed to carry it down the stairs and lift it into the pick-up.

Sullivan later saw Flynn lugging a plastic tub to the dumpster. It was full of family photos that hadn't been looked at since the day they were developed. He stopped Flynn from emptying it into the dumpster and asked him to place it on the moving truck. Fitting furniture and belongings into the rental truck was like playing a game of Tetris.

At last, they were packed up and the dumpster was filled to its brim. All they left behind was a couch, a coffee table, and a TV. Sullivan assured Ann that he would be comfortable sleeping there. They drove to their new apartment. Ferrara met them there to hand over the keys. The place smelled like paint and there were still blue strips of masking tape on the wall.

Gradually, they set up their beds and moved the furniture into place. Sullivan carried the tub of photos into Tara's room. She was lying listlessly on her bed staring at her new surroundings. "Tara, you've got to take a look at these?" Sullivan said. He grabbed a handful of family pictures and started flipping through them.

There were class pictures, team pictures, and photos from dance recitals. There was a shot of Flynn as a toddler in front of the Christmas tree. Tara looked to be about six posing in her baseball uniform, wearing her impossibly large mitt. He also found photos of her wearing formal dresses. Tara couldn't contain her curiosity and started glancing over Sullivan's shoulder.

They both became so animated commenting on the pictures that Ann and Flynn came to see what they were doing. The four of them sat on the floor sorting through the shots. Most of them had been taken at their old house and it brought back warm memories of birthday parties and other happy gatherings. Tara held up a picture of her with Flynn. It was taken when they were toddlers against a fake forested backdrop.

"I can't believe how blonde we were," she said wistfully.

She was wearing a white party dress and Flynn wore a jumper with sailboats on it. The family became so engrossed with the photos, they didn't notice it was getting dark. Ann called for a pizza and had to ask Sullivan their new address.

That night, Sullivan returned to the house alone. He flipped on some lights along with the TV. He sat down to watch and drifted off to sleep. He was startled awake by some weird noises and tried to get comfortable again on the couch. The room that had once been so familiar seemed suddenly strange. Sullivan felt as empty as the house.

A week after the move, the Sullivan clan was on their way to Family Day. When they arrived at Welcome House, they were directed to the basement. The downstairs was filled with residents milling about with their families. Folding chairs were arranged in a circle. A large punchbowl was busy and there were stacks of ham sandwiches.

Sullivan saw Carolyn and Pat huddled with their daughters in a corner. It looked like a family pow-wow so Sullivan didn't intrude. Carolyn looked paler than he remembered. She was a willowy blonde with refined looks that couldn't hide her hurt. The girls looked a bit shell shocked. Patrick was doing his best to act normal.

Big Mike's voice suddenly filled the room. He welcomed the families and invited them to sit down. Then he picked up a guitar and started strumming. "I! Should have known better, with a group like you," he began in his deep baritone, "That I would love everything that you do." The crowd was startled at first but clapped along with Big Mike's made-up lyrics. Sullivan saw that the Beatles could heal anything.

When it was time to eat, they sat at a table with Pat and his family. Carrie entertained Tara with tales about college life. Flynn made awkward small talk with Jennifer about their completely different high schools. He went to a small private school while she strolled a sprawling suburban campus. Kristen looked like she'd prefer to be anywhere else.

Ann engaged Carolyn in an animated conversation about their kids. Pat looked sad sipping his punch. Sullivan asked him about work and he made a face, like he didn't want to talk about it.

"I was talking to Jake about possible taking you on," Sullivan said, "We think you'd make a good investigator."

Patrick, who had looked down on detective work in the past, was suddenly intrigued.

"You've got great people skills and a mind for detail," Sullivan continued, "That's all you need in this job."

"I'd have to check with Big Mike first," he said, "He thinks that working for his buddy at the factory is good for our character."

Big Mike was making the rounds visiting each table to meet the families of his residents. When he stopped at Sullivan's table, Carolyn thanked him for allowing her husband to stay and participate in the program.

"You should be thanking this guy," Big Mike said, grabbing Sullivan's shoulder, "If it wasn't for Mike, I wouldn't know Pat needed help." While Big Mike again told the story of how Frank Sullivan had saved his life, Carolyn was looking at Sullivan with appreciation. As soon as Big Mike moved on, Kristen bolted from the table and fled the room in tears. Carolyn started to go after her, but Sullivan volunteered to talk to her.

"I'm her godfather, remember?"

Sullivan found Kristen sobbing in the parlor. He sank down beside her on the sofa.

"Kristen, I have to apologize to you. I'm the worst godfather ever. I never give you anything for Christmas. I never remember your birthday."

"Not - even a phone call," she stammered between sobs.

"I know, but I can't make up for all the birthdays I missed. I can only be a better godfather from now on."

"I don't need a godfather," she wailed, "I need my dad!"

Sullivan tentatively put his arm around her but she pulled away.

"I need my dad back home with us," she said starting to calm herself, "I can't stand this weird place and these strange people. Some of these men look scary."

Many of the residents seemed dissipated. Some had hard looks in their eyes, or a vacant stare. It was obvious they had been fighting some kind of personal war they had lost.

"Your dad looks better, doesn't he?"

Kristen nodded.

"I know you want him home but this is where he needs to be right now. It won't be forever."

"Even when he did live with us, he was never home," Kristen complained, "I stopped waiting up for him."

"I understand, but that was because you're dad has a disease."

"That's just an excuse," Kristen snapped, "He could stop drinking if he wanted to. He's just selfish."

"Kristen you have to separate your dad from the disease. He's a good guy down deep. He didn't intentionally hurt you. It was the disease that kept him from coming home."

Kristen was completely composed now but wasn't buying a word of what Sullivan was saying.

"I don't expect you to forgive him right away," Sullivan said, "But I know *he* feels terrible."

"I can barely forgive you, Uncle Mike, this is the longest you've ever talked to me."

Sullivan smiled. "That's going to change. Tara and Flynn want us to get together with you guys like we used to. Maybe a state park, or just a picnic. They miss their cousins."

Kristen climbed off the couch, ready to face the strangers in the next room.

"That would be nice," Kristen said with a sigh, "By the way, my birthday is May 19th. I'm too old for video games but I wouldn't mind a card. It doesn't even have to have a check in it."

When they returned to the table, Jennifer asked Sullivan, "Remember how you used to tell us your detective stories, Uncle Mike?"

Sullivan felt like he was being put on the spot but rummaged through his memory to come up with one.

"OK, this is one I've never told anyone."

Sullivan gave a brief account of Tamika's accident and told her about the sad doll.

Jennifer looked underwhelmed by the story. "That's it? I thought you were going to tell me about terrorism or something."

"Have you ever seen a doll with a sad face?" he asked her.

"No, what's the big deal about that?"

"I don't know," Sullivan answered, "But I haven't seen one before or since."

He and Pat decided to approach Big Mike about working for Jake. Big Mike listened thoughtfully.

"I don't think it's a good idea. That wouldn't be a good environment for you, Pat. Besides, you committed to work at the factory for six months. It's important you keep your promises. After six months, I don't care where you work. But I would stay away from bartending."

Before the group broke up, they assembled back in the circle of folding chairs. Each family member in the circle was to express gratitude for the resident they had in treatment.

When it was Carolyn's turn, she spoke about bringing Patrick his old clothes and how they no longer fit, because he had lost so much weight from factory work and not drinking.

"I'm grateful my husband is finally in shape," she quipped.

Carrie was thankful that her dad was getting help and looked forward to Pat visiting her at college. Jennifer was glad her dad had kept his sense of humor and could still make her laugh. Kristen said she was proud her dad was fighting his "disease."

After they left Welcome House, Sullivan returned to the empty house. He was sitting there morosely when Ann walked in. She had brought over some clean clothes. She sat down on the couch next to him.

"I'm so glad I have you, Mike. I know this has been hard but it's almost over. Can you believe all we've been through and we're still together?"

"This calls for something special," he said getting off the couch and disappearing into the kitchen. He came back holding Patrick's bottle of Jamison's, and two plastic cups. In that quiet empty house they were abandoning, they toasted to a fresh start.

It was later that night, while Sullivan listlessly watched a Bulls game, that he received another visitor. It was Jake pounding at the door. As Jake came into the room, he announced that he had good news. "Get your coat," he commanded, "We're going to McGaffer's to celebrate."

"Celebrate what?"

Jake didn't answer until they were seated in the neighborhood joint. That's when Jake told Sullivan about his new "career."

"A friend of mine is in administration at this community college. He wanted to hire me to teach Criminology. Imagine that?" Jake laughed, "Putting the class clown in charge of a classroom. I told him I wasn't interested but I had a buddy who might be good at it."

"Really? A professor? I don't even have a teaching degree."

"He said your detective work is worth credit. He's anxious to meet you. They need someone for the spring semester."

When Sullivan met with the administrator and described his long career in investigation, the man was impressed. "Mr. Sullivan you could give our students some real world lessons. All we need now is your college transcripts."

Sullivan was suddenly bewildered and didn't know what to say.

"I didn't go," he admitted, "How about my high school transcripts?"

"Mr. Sullivan we have several instructors that lack the traditional credentials to teach. We have a newspaper reporter teaching journalism. We value practical experience over advanced degrees. Your high school transcripts will be sufficient."

When the administrator told Sullivan he would be paid $75 an hour, it sounded like a dream. He handed Sullivan a thick textbook on criminology. He emphasized, however, that Sullivan's personal stories might be more valuable than what the students would find in textbooks.

A month later, Sullivan found himself facing a sea of attentive faces. Not that they were all eager. The back row residents looked unimpressed. After finishing the preliminary announcements, Sullivan introduced himself and launched into a story.

"I'd like to tell you about a girl that was about your age. She got killed in a car accident. Her name was Tamika."

ABOUT THE AUTHOR

John Rice operated a private detective agency in Chicago for forty years. During this time, he has been a journalist for the "Wednesday Journal" newspaper and weekly columnist for the "Forest Park Review" newspaper. In 2019, he published his first novel, The Ghost of Cleopatra, which he co-wrote with Gail Tanzer. He also tutored Hispanic students in writing at St. Augustine College for five years and taught writing to French-speaking students for three of those years. He can be reached at jrice1038@aol.com or on his Facebook page.

Made in the USA
Columbia, SC
12 April 2022

58714509R00148